The Reaper Of Magnolia

A Horror Story

Ryan Hall

The Reaper of Magnolia is a chilling horror-thriller set in the seemingly idyllic town of Magnolia, where the spirit of Halloween brings excitement and joy – but also hides dark secrets. As the townsfolk prepare for their annual Harvest Festival, a masked killer known as the Reaper emerges, targeting unsuspecting residents and transforming the celebrations into a nightmare.

Table of Contents

Prologue
Awakening

As the sun dipped ominously below the horizon, it cast a sickly orange glow over the quaint town of Magnolia, transforming it into a nightmarish landscape. The streets, lined with an eclectic assortment of homes, took on a sinister quality, the vibrant hues of Halloween bleeding into shadows that seemed to writhe and pulse with hidden horrors. The leaves, once bright, now rustled with an unsettling whisper, their colors deepening to dark shades of crimson and brown —a macabre reminder that autumn had fully settled into the town's sinister spirit.

October heralded a season of spine-chilling horror films, twisted carnivals, eerie haunted houses, and Halloween stores like Spirit Halloween, all beckoning residents to join in the festivities. But beneath the surface, a palpable dread hung in the air, as children plotted their costumes with gleeful anticipation, unaware of the lurking darkness that threatened to swallow the town whole.

Families embraced the October spirit, but not without a tinge of fear. Homes were adorned with grotesque decorations—pumpkins carved into grotesque grins lined doorsteps, their hollowed eyes glowing ominously in the encroaching darkness. Cobwebs draped over door frames, and plastic skeletons hung from trees, casting shadows that danced like specters across the yards. The scent of cinnamon and nutmeg mingled with something more acrid, a prelude to the seasonal feasts and the blood-soaked horrors that awaited.

Local businesses joined in the twisted spirit, the bakery on Main Street offering pumpkin spice pastries and ghost-shaped cookies that seemed to grin with malice. Children greeted the season with sugar-coated expectations, their laughter ringing out like a death knell as they prepared their trick-or-treat maps, ensuring they wouldn't miss the houses rumored to be haunted—or those with the biggest candy stashes.

At the heart of Magnolia, the annual Harvest Festival approached—a highly anticipated event that promised hayrides, a corn maze, and a costume contest that would draw participants of all ages. But this year, an undercurrent of fear coursed through the excitement, whispers of dread echoing as children paraded down the town square in their imaginative costumes, vying for the title of Best Dressed. Spooky music floated through the air, but beneath it lay an ominous tone, as vendors set up booths selling everything from caramel apples to handcrafted Halloween decorations that seemed to pulse with dark energy.

Local farms weren't left out of the festivities. Families flocked to pumpkin patches, but laughter echoed less freely as nervous glances were cast toward the shadows. Kids played among the hay bales, their voices tinged with apprehension as they navigated a corn maze, filled with adventure and just the right amount of fear. As dusk fell, curious guests gathered around bonfires, roasting marshmallows while sharing ghost stories that sent shivers down their spines—stories that felt all too real.

As twilight settled in, Magnolia transformed even further. Flickering jack-o'-lanterns lined every street, casting a malevolent glow that illuminated the paths where little feet would soon scurry from house to house. The town buzzed with excitement—but the thrill of the unknown carried a chilling weight. Children eagerly counted down the days until Halloween, their hearts racing at the thought of collecting sweets and surprises that could easily turn into nightmares.

The downtown movie theater seized the opportunity, showcasing a series of horror films throughout the month. Friends gathered, sharing popcorn and stories of their favorite spooky flicks, but as the lights dimmed, a palpable tension settled over the audience. The theater, draped in cobwebs and adorned with haunting posters, became a chamber of horrors, filling the seats with a mix of laughter and terrified gasps at every jump scare.

Meanwhile, the local library hosted a ghost story night, inviting everyone to share their most chilling tales. The atmosphere crackled with electricity; families nestled under blankets with hot cider, their faces illuminated by the flickering glow of fairy lights. Kids' eyes widened with intrigue as the librarians wove tales of ghouls and ghostly encounters, drawing everyone deeper into the spirit of Halloween. Yet, the stories felt like a warning—a reminder that something sinister lurked just outside their doors.

The spirit of Halloween wasn't limited to mere scares and chills. Neighborhood families transformed their backyards into trick-or-treat safe havens, but an air of unease lingered. Local teens took on the roles of spooky hosts, setting up mini haunted houses that felt more like death traps, crafting delightfully eerie treats that masked a hunger for something darker.

As Halloween approached, social media buzzed with local events and shared experiences. Photos of astonishing decorations flooded feeds, but friendly competitions between neighbors morphed into a contest of fear. Local influencers showcased their creative costume ideas, capturing the community's collective imagination, but the conversations about favorite horror flicks grew darker, tinged with an unspoken dread that left everyone on edge.

Throughout the month, Magnolia's connections deepened, but not without a price. Friendships forged over shared fears during movie marathons, laughter echoing across streets filled with costumed children, and families contributing to the overall warmth of the season fostered a sense of community spirit that felt precarious.

With each passing day, the town buzzed with energy as the arrival of Halloween drew closer. But as preparations reached their peak, Woodsboro stood poised for a celebration that promised not just thrills, but bloodshed. As October 31 approached, the sense of unity felt thick in the air, but it mingled with an undercurrent of fear. The anticipation of a candy-laden night kindled excitement, but beneath every carved pumpkin's gaze loomed the specter of violence, illuminated by the shimmering glow of the autumn moon.

In Woodsboro, the joyful spirit of Halloween wasn't merely a once-a-year affair; it represented the dark power of community, stitched together by the fabric of tradition, creativity, and camaraderie—yet it also served as a chilling tapestry of horror waiting to unravel.

Sarah was a spirited 19-year-old college student, petite in stature but expansive in imagination, drawn irresistibly to the unconventional. Her hazel eyes sparkled with a fervor that belied the darkness creeping into her life.

She spoke passionately of her artistic endeavors—whether painting, photography, or engaging discussions in her literature class. But beneath her vibrant exterior lay a profound joy stemming from her cherished relationship with David, her husband of nearly a year.

David, a kind-hearted and introspective 20-year-old pursuing a graduate degree in therapy, perfectly complemented Sarah's adventurous nature. Their love story began innocently in middle school, blossoming through shared lunches and whispered secrets beneath starry nights. However, as their bond deepened, rooted in mutual respect and a shared affection for horror films—especially those with a touch of gore—their lives began to unravel into a twisted nightmare.

As Halloween approached, Sarah's excitement bubbled over at the thought of local festivities and the chance to transform their space into a haunting wonderland. One evening, standing at Octoberfest, Sarah smiled at David. "It's going to be amazing! I just need to gather some supplies from home to add to the other booths. You know how much I love going all out with decorations!"

David smiled, pressing a gentle kiss to her lips before she left. "Just promise you'll hurry back—I need you for our costume," he teased, his playful grin masking the darkness that loomed just outside their door. Little did they know, their tranquil existence was about to plunge headfirst into a blood-soaked abyss.

Determined, Sarah hopped into her truck and drove the familiar route to their charming home on W 24th Elm Street, conveniently situated near Elm Street Avenue in their idyllic suburban neighborhood of Magnolia. The drive, framed by autumn leaves dancing in the breeze, felt increasingly ominous as the sun dipped lower, casting long shadows that twisted and writhed like the spirits of the damned.

After locking the truck, she bounded up the steps, her mind racing with ideas to transform their space into a Halloween wonderland. Flinging open the door, a wave of comfort washed over her, enveloped by the delightful scent of cinnamon candles—an aroma she cherished. But as she gathered her supplies—cobwebs, faux spiders, orange and black decorations—an unsettling sensation crept over her, a feeling of being watched.

Suddenly, the shrill ring of the house phone shattered the peaceful atmosphere, jolting her from her excitement. Momentarily distracted, Sarah wiped her hands on her jeans and picked up the receiver. "Hello?" she answered, half-expecting a familiar voice but feeling an unexpected tension coil in her stomach.

The reply was anything but comforting. "Hello, Sarah. It's nice to finally catch you alone." The voice was distorted and unsettling, sending a chill racing down her spine, reminiscent of the eerie tones from the *Stab* films they often joked about during late-night marathons.

Her heart raced, pounding in her chest like a war drum. "Who is this?" she demanded, forcing herself to sound calm, though anxiety coiled tightly inside her.

The voice chuckled ominously, a sound that raised the hair on the back of her neck. "You can call me your biggest fan. I've been observing you for quite some time, Sarah. I know all about your little traditions with your husband—like those horror movie marathons you share."

Panic surged through her, a wave of nausea sweeping over. Was this a sick joke? "This isn't funny! I'll hang up if you don't tell me who you are!" she replied, desperately trying to muster an air of bravery.

"Funny? Oh, it's just the beginning," the voice taunted, each word dripping with menace. "While David thinks you're busy decorating for Halloween, I have something special planned for you —something a little different from your usual horror. But don't worry; you won't miss the festival for long."

Terror gripped her throat, leaving her breathless. "What do you want?!"

"I want you to experience the thrill of being part of the story. You'll find out soon enough. Just stay put." The line went dead, leaving an oppressive silence in its wake.

Trembling, Sarah dropped the phone, the clatter echoing in the empty house. Instinct screamed at her to flee, but her feet felt rooted to the floor. As she scanned the house, her mind raced—this intruder felt disturbingly personal, not just a random weirdo.

Gathering her resolve, she rushed to the front window, instinctively scanning the street for anything amiss. It was the same peaceful neighborhood she had always known, yet the tranquility now felt ominously deceptive. The leaves rustled in the breeze, but an unsettling silence blanketed the air. That voice echoed relentlessly in her mind, a constant reminder that she was being watched.

Desperate to regain a sense of control, she considered calling David, but the sight of their once-cozy kitchen now tinged with fear held her back. She imagined David's worried expression; this was not the time to panic—she needed a plan.

Suddenly, an idea sparked in her mind. The Halloween decorations she adored could serve a purpose beyond mere festivity. Rushing to her supplies, she gathered paper, scissors, and markers to create a distress signal—an improvised plea affixed to their front door: "Help. Call the police. I'm not safe."

As she stepped outside to affix the message to the door, a chilling sensation crept up her spine. Glancing back inside, an unsettling intuition flooded her—she was not alone.

A rustle from the gravel driveway made adrenaline surge anew. She ducked behind a nearby bush, gripping her phone tightly, ready to call for help. Her heart thundered in her chest, and her breathing quickened as she strained her eyes into the dimming light. Then, she saw him—a tall, shadowy figure draped in black fabric, wearing a Reaper mask, holding a glinting knife that shimmered against the fading light.

As he stepped closer, Sarah's stomach plummeted. The sight was hauntingly reminiscent of the very horror films they had cherished together. Without thinking, she turned and sprinted toward the back of the house, frantically searching for an escape.

Fueled by fear, she ran—or at least tried to. Fortune betrayed her as she slipped on the floor within the house. Before she could react, the masked figure lunged, slicing her ankle and sending a jolt of pain shooting through her body as warm blood began to pour.

Clenching her teeth against the torment, Sarah scanned the kitchen, her thoughts racing for options. Just then, her gaze landed on a frying pan. With fierce determination, she seized it, swinging it in a desperate attempt to defend herself. She connected with a blow that sent him staggering back, but her momentary relief was short-lived; the masked figure rose again, looming ominously over her, reveling in her suffering.

He grabbed her ankles, dragging her closer, flipping her onto her back. Panic coursed through her veins; she fought fiercely, desperate to survive this nightmarish reality. He plunged the knife into her ribcage, the blade slicing through flesh and muscle as she gasped in agony, blood spilling forth in a crimson cascade. He sliced her arm with ruthless precision, and viciously slashed at her ankle, rendering her immobile. The pain engulfed her, but she knew she had to fight for her life. In her last struggle, she attempted to tear off the Reaper's mask, but he seized her hand, bending it backward, the pressure sending sharp instincts flaring.

Each stab sent waves of agony coursing through her, and with barely enough strength to whisper, "I don't want to watch horror movies anymore," she uttered, caught between regret and fear. The killer activated a voice changer and replied, "WHO GIVES A FUCK ABOUT MOVIES!" The sinister gleam in his eyes sent a tremor of dread through her body.

David stood at OctoberFest, his heart racing as he anxiously awaited his wife's return. The clock read 8:12 PM, and the darkness of the night felt heavy around him. Vibrant lights twinkled in the distance, laughter floated on the cool breeze, and the scent of caramel apples wafted through the air, but none of it reached him. His thoughts churned with worry, consumed by her absence. As the festival crowd ebbed and flowed around him, his grip tightened around his phone, hoping for a message or call.

Silence greeted him; there was nothing. His pulse drummed in his ears as he dialed her number. After six ominous rings, the call went straight to voicemail.

Feeling a growing sense of urgency clawing at him, he decided to leave the festival behind. The parking lot was chaotic, but he maneuvered his way through the cars, his mind racing. Elm Street was only a few minutes away, but every second felt like an eternity.

As he pulled into the driveway, unease settled in his stomach like a cold stone. The familiar sight of their home was suddenly foreboding. Her truck sat in its usual spot, but something felt off. The front door to their house was ajar.

"Sarah?" he called out, stepping cautiously onto the porch. The house lay enveloped in an eerie quiet, the only sound being the rustling of leaves in the wind. "Sarah!" he shouted again, desperation creeping into his voice, but the only answer was the ominous silence.

He pushed the door open further, the creak of the hinges echoing in the stillness. As he crossed the threshold into the dimly lit hallway, a sense of dread intensified. The familiar warmth of their home had turned cold.

Walking past the kitchen counter, something caught his eye—a dark stain, fresh and unmistakable. Panic gripped him; was it real or some grotesque prank? He stepped closer, heart hammering against his ribcage, and he knew one thing for sure: it was blood.

Hastily, he turned the corner into the kitchen and was met with a sight that shattered his world. Sarah lay slumped against the cabinets, covered in blood; her body was a horrific tableau of injury, her intestines grotesquely exposed and spilling onto the floor.

David's heart raced in terror as adrenaline surged through him, pushing him into action.

"Sarah!" He was at her side, shaking her gently, desperately hoping for a response. But the truth was undeniable, and the realization plunged him into a pit of despair. The once vibrant spark of life was extinguished, replaced by the cold grip of death. Before he could process the overwhelming horror, the phone rang, shattering the oppressive silence.

"H-Hello?" he answered, his voice trembling, but no one spoke on the other end. The only sound was static.

And just then, from the shadows of the closet, the Reaper killer lunged at him. David barely had time to react before the knife plunged deep into his chest, cutting through flesh and muscle until it met bone. Pain exploded in his chest; a scream was caught in his throat, choking him.

The killer withdrew the knife, kicking David violently, sending him crashing against the cabinet. The world spun as David gasped for breath, his hands instinctively clutching at the wound. Blood poured from his chest, pooling on the floor, warming his hands even as it began to cool around him. Each heartbeat became a punishing reminder of his fleeting life.

The killer, now with a sinister grin stretching beneath the mask, activated a voice changer. "What's your favorite scary movie?" he asked, the mechanical distortion sending chills down David's spine.

"Fuck you," David replied defiantly, though fear twisted his gut. There was a primal instinct to survive, a flicker of determination pushing back against the darkness closing in.

"Sounds boring. Mine's *Headless*," the killer said coldly. He went back into the closet and pulled out a shotgun, pulling the trigger back so it was locked in place, and with a malicious glint in his Reaper mask eyes, he leveled the shotgun at David.

"Stay away from me!" David managed, though his voice quivered with pain and fear.

With a deafening blast, the shotgun went off, obliterating David's head in a spray of blood and bone that splattered across the countertops, walls, and floor. The gruesome scene left only an echoing silence in its wake, mingled with the sharp scent of gunpowder and the metallic tang of blood.

The killer stepped back, breathing heavily, excitement coursing through him as he surveyed his handiwork. This was chaos—the kind of chaos he craved. But he knew he had to keep moving. As the sirens wailed in the distance, their sound a harbinger of his fate, he quickly gathered up the scene, preparing for the aftermath.

He rifled through cabinets and drawers, searching for anything that could connect him to this horror. Disposing of the phone, he wiped down the surfaces with a cloth, erasing his fingerprints as he whistled a tuneless song to fill the oppressive silence.

But the sound of sirens grew louder; they were close now. Realizing that time was running out, he dashed out the back door, slipping into the shadows. The night swallowed him whole as he vanished from the scene, leaving behind a gruesome manifestation of horror.

As he disappeared into the dark, the echoes of laughter and celebration from the festival faded into nothingness—a cruel reminder that for some, terror was just beginning.

The chilling tale of Sarah and David's Halloween night ended in tragedy, shattering the peaceful facade of Magnolia and leaving a community reeling from the horror that had invaded their midst. As news of the brutal murders spread through the town, fear and unease gripped the residents, turning what was supposed to be a night of celebration into one marked by grief and shock.

The police launched a full investigation into the heinous crime, combing through evidence and interviewing witnesses in an attempt to track down the elusive Reaper killer. The community rallied together, offering support to the families of the victims and a collective determination to seek justice for Sarah and David.

As the days passed, the specter of the Reaper killer loomed large over Magnolia, casting a shadow of fear and mistrust that tainted the once vibrant town. Halloween had come and gone, but the memories of that fateful night lingered, a sobering reminder of the fragility of life and the darkness that could lurk just beneath the surface.

Despite the tragedy that had befallen them, the people of Magnolia refused to be cowed by fear. Instead, they banded together, united in their grief and their resolve to honor the memory of Sarah and David. Candlelight vigils were held in their honor, a testament to the strength of a community bound by tragedy.

The Reaper killer remained at large, a looming presence that haunted the collective consciousness of Magnolia. But as the days turned into weeks, and the weeks into months, the town began to heal, slowly but surely. Life in Magnolia carried on, though tinged with a sense of loss and a heightened awareness of the darkness that could lurk within their midst.

As the seasons changed and time marched inexorably forward, the memory of Sarah and David began to fade, replaced by the ebb and flow of daily life. The streets of Magnolia were once again filled with laughter and light, the warmth of community shining through the lingering shadows of the past.

But beneath the surface, a sense of unease remained, a reminder that some wounds never truly heal. The Reaper killer may have vanished into the night, but the scars of his violence lingered, a sobering reminder of the fragility of life and the ever-present specter of darkness that could descend at any moment.

As Halloween approached once again, the people of Magnolia found themselves grappling with a mix of emotions—fear, grief, and a lingering sense of vulnerability. But they also found strength in their resilience, in their capacity to come together in the face of tragedy and find solace in the warmth and support of their community.

And so, as the sun dipped below the horizon on Halloween night, casting a menacing orange glow over the town of Magnolia, the people gathered together, a community united in their determination to keep the memory of Sarah and David alive, to honor their legacy, and to reaffirm their commitment to each other in the face of darkness.

For in the end, it was not the horror that defined them, but the way they rose above it, finding strength in the bonds of community and the resilience of the human spirit. And as they stood beneath the autumn sky, illuminated by the flickering light of Jack-o'-lanterns and the warmth of shared memories, they knew that no matter what darkness may come, they would face it together, their spirits unbroken, their hearts united in the eternal light of hope.

Chapter 1

The police arrived at the unassuming residence on West 24th Elm Street shortly after receiving an anonymous tip suggesting something sinister lurked in the tranquil neighborhood. The typically peaceful community was shrouded in the eerie stillness of a cool autumn night, its calm shattered by the sudden arrival of flashing blue and red lights. The muted sirens cut through the silence, turning heads and igniting worried whispers among neighbors peering through their curtains. It was an unsettling sight—the glow of patrol cars casting ominous shadows, transforming cozy homes into dark silhouettes, each hiding secrets begging to be uncovered.

As officers stepped onto the property, an unsettling aura enveloped them, hinting at the grim discovery waiting within. The front door hung ajar, swaying gently in the breeze, as if trying to escape the horror it concealed. With gloved hands, the first officer pushed it open, the creaking hinges echoing ominously. A heavy stillness greeted them, broken only by the faint, unsettling echo of their own footsteps.

Crossing the threshold into the home, the air thickened with a suffocating sense of dread. The officers paused for a moment, adjusting their flashlights to pierce through the oppressive darkness. They exchanged uncertain glances, their instincts urging them forward into the unknown, a darkness that whispered of past terrors. It was an instinct that would prove both critical and haunting.

What lay ahead surpassed their worst expectations. The living room was a chaotic tableau—furniture lay overturned, cushions shredded, and shards of glass crunched underfoot like crushed dreams. The acrid scent of gunpowder mingled with the unmistakable odor of blood, a potent reminder that violence had erupted in this once-safe haven. Yet it wasn't just the disarray that sent chills down their spines; it was the sight that greeted them on the cold hardwood floor.

Two lifeless bodies lay sprawled in unsettling positions. One of the victims was Sarah, a vibrant 19-year-old college student whose laughter had once filled the halls of her school, now silenced forever.

She had been a bright light, her future brimming with promise and ambition, now extinguished by the cruelty of fate. Her pale hands, still adorned with chipped pink nail polish, were splayed awkwardly, a haunting reminder of her untimely end, the terror etched on her face telling a story of her final moments.

The other victim was David, a 20-year-old community therapist revered for his kindness and ability to uplift others in their darkest times. He had been a beacon of support, yet tonight he lay unceremoniously on the floor, blood pooling around him, his life cut short by a merciless shotgun blast. The violence of his death had splattered brain matter and blood across the room, a grotesque tableau etched into the very fabric of what had once been a sanctuary.

His face, frozen in shock and pain, served as a chilling reminder of the fragility of life, especially for those who devoted themselves to healing others.

A numbness settled over the officers, urgency pushing them to piece together the grim narrative hidden within the wreckage. They fanned out, each member of the team taking their place amidst the debris, their hearts heavy with the weight of the discoveries. As crime scene investigators began cordoning off the area, they meticulously documented the scene, their thoughts racing with unanswered questions. What had transpired here? Why had these two young lives been brutally cut short? The atmosphere was suffused with palpable terror—the whispers of the neighborhood echoing their own fears as they wondered who could commit such an atrocity.

Detective Maria Holloway arrived as one of the first responders. As she stepped into the living room, her seasoned gaze absorbed the horrific scene before her. Years of experience had thickened her skin, but nothing could dull the gut-wrenching reality of this particular crime. Maria was known for her unwavering determination and sharp instincts, yet as she stood on the threshold of chaos, her heart ached. The human cost of violence was heavy, and she was acutely aware of the scars this event would leave on the community.

"Secure the perimeter and start canvassing the neighbors," she ordered, her voice steady yet urgent. "We need any information they might have heard or seen. This isn't going to be easy."

Hesitant nods met her command as officers dispersed, their resolve tightening with each step. They worked systematically, approaching neighbors, conducting interviews, and documenting any leads that might unravel the mystery. Maria moved deeper into the room, her thoughts swirling in a tempest of emotions. She noted the overturned coffee table, the shattered remains of a lamp, and a chilling trail of blood leading from David's body to the front door. Each detail whispered a complex story, buried within the chaos.

A muffled scream erupted from the back of the house, drawing her attention. Maria pivoted, instincts on high alert. A frantic neighbor, a woman in her forties with disheveled hair and wide eyes, emerged from the rear of the property. "I heard gunshots! I thought it was a car backfiring at first but then—oh God!" Her features twisted in horror, clutching her chest as if trying to contain the panic bubbling within. The tremor in her voice hinted at the trauma rippling through the neighborhood.

"Ma'am, please, calm down," Maria urged gently, stepping closer. "I need you to tell me exactly what you heard."

The woman's hands shook, her breathing shallow as she recounted the sequence of events. "It was about nine, I think… first a loud bang, then another… I thought someone was just messing around. Then… then I saw the lights from your cars. I knew something was wrong. It wasn't just kids being reckless."

With each detail, Maria scanned the room, piecing together the fragments of chaos and despair. She noted the direction from which the gunfire had come—straight into the living room. Whatever violent encounter had transpired here was sudden and brutal.

As forensic teams buzzed around her, gathering samples and taking photographs, she turned her attention back to Sarah and David. Nothing could prepare anyone for the aftermath of violence displayed so heinously before her. A pang of sorrow mingled with her determination. Beyond this dark portal of despair lay a case, lives intertwined by tragedy, and the obligation to find the truth pulsed within her.

"Get me a time of death for both victims and start looking for any potential witnesses," she directed, laying the groundwork for the investigation ahead. The crime scene was revealing its story to her, albeit reluctantly. Each clue beckoned her deeper into the intricate web of their lives, imploring her to uncover what horrors had transpired in this seemingly tranquil home.

Hours crawled by as the work continued. Every event, every cry of despair, inspired determination in the officers instead of hesitation. They wouldn't leave this neighborhood until they extracted every piece of truth hidden beneath the surface. Every question, every fear, needed to be addressed.

By dawn, the crime scene still bore the haunting remnants of the night's events. The once inviting home now stood isolated in its own grief, filled with murky whispers of betrayal and violence. The small town of West 24th Elm Street had been irrevocably changed; the ghosts of that night would haunt the walls and the hearts of its residents forever. As Detective Holloway stared into the pale light of the morning sun filtering through the windows, she paused. The shadows of the crimes of the night would not retreat easily, but she was ready to confront them head-on, fighting to bring peace to the restless souls that lingered just out of reach.

The challenge ahead loomed, but within it lay the promise of justice for Sarah and David—an obligation divorced from the resentments of daily life, a pure pursuit of truth, however brutal. The case had just begun.

As the investigation into the tragic deaths of Sarah and David unfolded, Detective Maria Holloway led her team through the wreckage of the crime scene, piecing together the fragments of violence that had shattered the once tranquil neighborhood. The forensic teams were methodical, their movements precise as they collected evidence, dusted for fingerprints, and photographed the horrific tableau before them. Each piece of scrap paper, every fragment of glass, became a clue in the puzzle that needed solving.

Witnesses began to emerge, their accounts adding layers to the chilling narrative. A group of teenagers who lived nearby recounted hearing loud arguments emanating from the house before the gunshots rang out. They had dismissed it at first, thinking it was just typical youthful banter gone too far. But the echoes of those arguments took on a new meaning now, woven into the fabric of the crime scene.

As the sun rose, the community remained cloaked in grief and fear. Maria held daily briefings with her team, reviewing evidence and strategizing their next steps. They delved into the backgrounds of both victims, searching for any connections that might lead them to the killer. Sarah's friends described her as vibrant, full of dreams, while David's colleagues spoke of his compassion and dedication to helping others. But as they dug deeper, they began to uncover troubling details—

whispers of jealousy, envy, and hidden relationships that hinted at darker motives.

Meanwhile, the neighborhood was abuzz with rumors, fear gripping the residents as they locked their doors tighter, eyes darting suspiciously at every shadow. The police presence escalated, with patrol cars frequently cruising the streets, reassuring some but stirring paranoia in others. Every flicker of movement sent shivers down spines, and the laughter of children playing outside felt like a distant memory, overshadowed by the weight of tragedy.

As Maria delved deeper into the intricate web of lies and secrets, she began to piece together a haunting narrative of betrayal and brutality that had led to this tragedy. Suspicion fell on several individuals, including an ex-boyfriend of Sarah's who had exhibited obsessive behavior, and a disgruntled former colleague of David's who had been let go under questionable circumstances. Each suspect was interrogated, their stories meticulously scrutinized for inconsistencies.

Amidst the investigation, Maria found solace in her unwavering commitment to uncovering the truth. She often reflected on her own experiences, the cases that had haunted her, and the lives she had fought to protect. The weight of the past drove her forward, igniting a fierce determination to ensure that Sarah and David would not be just another statistic. The community's healing depended on justice being served.

As days turned into weeks, the investigation continued to unfold, revealing layers of complexity that left Maria both frustrated and determined. Each lead seemed to lead to a dead end, and as the pressure mounted from the community and the media, she felt the weight of the world on her shoulders. Yet, she remained undeterred, fueled by the memories of the vibrant lives lost and the commitment to see the case through to its conclusion.

Finally, after countless hours of tireless work and unwavering dedication, the pieces of the puzzle began to fall into place. The motive behind the murders was laid bare, and as the detectives closed in on the culprits, the truth emerged from the shadows. The community of West 24th Elm Street breathed a collective sigh of relief, grateful for the closure that Maria and her team had brought to a case that had haunted them for so long.

As Maria stood at the scene of the crime, the memories of Sarah and David lingered in the air, their spirits finally at peace. The echoes of that tragic night would forever haunt the walls of the house on West 24th Elm Street, but thanks to Maria's unwavering commitment to the truth, justice had prevailed, and the victims could finally rest in peace.

The shadows of their lives would always be present, but now there was hope for healing, a light to guide the community as it navigated through the darkness. Maria understood that the scars of violence would linger, but by confronting the truth, she had forged a path toward understanding and reconciliation for those left behind. The case had transformed her, igniting a fire within her to continue fighting for justice, no matter how daunting the path ahead.

Chapter 2

The brisk air filled with the scent of fallen leaves and wood smoke wafting from distant chimneys, creating a perfect autumn backdrop for Kendra's picture-perfect morning. As sunlight streamed through her apartment's big bay window, it danced upon the colorful leaves fluttering outside, painting the room with golds, oranges, and reds. Kendra sat curled up on the plush, overstuffed sofa, nestled under a warm blanket, sipping a steaming mug of pumpkin spice latte—her seasonal indulgence that she eagerly awaited all year.

As she basked in the warmth of her cozy space, Kendra gazed around and took pride in the transformation of her apartment:

the pumpkin centerpiece on the coffee table, adorned with tiny white gourds; the twinkling string lights that cast a soft glow against the walls; and the faux cobwebs that added just the right hint of eeriness in anticipation of Halloween. She smiled, envisioning how her friends would gather for a night of frights, filled with popcorn and laughter, each bringing their unique flavor to the celebration.

Kendra's heart fluttered with excitement as thoughts of her friends danced in her mind. Jane, with her ever-enthusiastic spirit, would undoubtedly be concocting an extensive scary movie marathon list. Danny, known for his elaborate pranks, was sure to have something up his sleeve to scare the group unexpectedly. Audrey would be focused on costume planning, meticulously crafting a social media-worthy ensemble that would surely steal the show. Sarah's love for baking would ensure that there was an array of Halloween treats—spider cupcakes, ghost cookies, and maybe even some pumpkin-flavored delights. David would likely bring an unbeatable playlist of creepy tunes to set the mood, making their gathering feel like a true Halloween celebration.

But most of all, Kendra relished the moments they all shared together—a sisterhood filled with authenticity, laughter, and creativity. There was a rare comfort in their connection, formed over late-night study sessions, spontaneous outings, and the shared experiences that forged an unbreakable bond. She felt grateful to have such a solid crew to embrace the festivities, each friend bringing their individuality to the celebration, creating a tapestry of memories that she cherished dearly.

As she took another sip of her latte, savoring the warm spices, she glanced over at Josh, still peacefully asleep on the other end of the sofa. His tousled hair and soft breaths were a reminder of the cozy life they had built together. A soft smile crept onto her face; she loved his easygoing nature, which balanced her own excitement perfectly. She knew that in just a few moments, he would soon rouse to join her in planning the upcoming Halloween festivity that promised to be unforgettable.

The clock ticked softly in the background as the sun rose higher, bathing the apartment in warmth.

Kendra's heart raced with anticipation for the day ahead. She envisioned a spontaneous gathering with her friends, beginning with pumpkin picking at the local patch, followed by a horror film night packed with twists and turns that would leave them all on edge. The chill outside hinted at the transformation of the season, but inside, with the glow of friendship and love, Kendra felt only warmth.

Today was the beginning of the season's magic, and she couldn't wait to dive into it with everyone by her side. After all, Halloween was more than just costumes and candy; it was a time to celebrate connection and create lasting memories, and she was ready for it all.

"Josh, wake up!" she called, her voice cheerful enough to coax him from slumber. She leaned down, planting a playful kiss on his forehead. "It's a beautiful day! We need to get excited for Halloween!"

He stirred, groaning lightly at first before cracking one eye open. "Five more minutes," he mumbled, pulling the covers over his head. Kendra giggled, knowing that Josh had always been a bit of a grump in the mornings.

While waiting for him to fully awaken, Kendra wandered into the kitchen, absentmindedly humming a Halloween tune that had been stuck in her head for days. She poured herself another steaming cup of coffee, grateful for the aromatic blend that promised to jumpstart her day. As she sipped, she flicked on the television, hoping to catch the morning news and gather ideas for their Halloween costumes.

The moment the screen lit up, Kendra froze. The news reporter stood outside a familiar house—the Millers'. He wore a somber expression, and Kendra felt an unsettling chill creep down her spine. The news story unfolded like a dark cloud overtaking her bright morning.

"Tragedy struck last night in Magnolia," the reporter began, his voice grave and laced with urgency.

Kendra's heart raced as she pulled her phone from her pocket, her fingers trembling as she dialed Sarah's number. Anxiety surged with each ring. "Come on, pick up, pick up," she murmured, desperation lacing her voice. Nearby, Josh remained fixated on the screen, concern deepening the lines on his forehead, his brows furrowed, sensing the weight of Kendra's anxiety.

When the chirpy sound of the voicemail greeted her, Kendra quickly ended the call, panic gripping her heart. "They're not answering! What if... what if they need help?"

Josh's jaw tightened with worry. He pushed himself off the bed, urgency replacing the tranquility of their apartment. "We have to check on them. Their phone might be dead or something. Let's go."

Kendra glanced around their cluttered apartment, the remnants of a rushed morning—clothes strewn across the floor, half-eaten breakfast on the table. She felt a pang of guilt for the chaos they had left behind, but that guilt was instantly overshadowed by the urgent dread hovering over them like a dark cloud. "You're right. Let's go." A surge of determination coursed through her as she pulled on a pair of faded jeans and a simple t-shirt. Her heart was heavy as memories of Sarah flooded her mind—her vivacious laughter that could lift anyone's spirits, their late-night conversations about life and love, their shared dreams, and countless secrets whispered under the stars.

Once dressed, they rushed out of the apartment. Kendra locked the door behind her, her movements hurried and clumsy. She grabbed Josh's hand, seeking comfort in his steady presence amid the uncertainty.

The warm sunlight felt suddenly foreboding, casting an eerie glow on the path they took toward West 24th Elm Street. The familiar sights of Magnolia—the vibrant trees lining the sidewalks, the cheerful morning joggers—were now muted, overshadowed by the gnawing fear that wrapped around Kendra like a suffocating fog. The world felt wrong, colors dimmed, and sounds softened, as if she was moving through a dream from which she could not wake.

When they finally reached Sarah and David's house, Kendra's heart sank at the sight before her: police tape cordoned off the area, and officers moved with serious expressions, speaking into radios as they exchanged grim words. The sight twisted her stomach in knots.

“Please stay back,” an officer called out, his authoritative tone halting Kendra in her tracks. She tugged on Josh’s hand, but he gently held her back, a silent reminder to respect the boundaries set by law enforcement.

“Is there any way we can find out what happened?” Kendra pleaded, her voice trembling as anxiety twisted in her stomach like a coiling serpent.

The officer's expression softened slightly at the sight of her distress. “I’m sorry, ma’am. You’ll need to wait for official updates. Please step back for your safety.”

Josh squeezed her hand tightly, his eyes reflecting the fear they both felt. “What if Sarah and David are…?” His voice trailed off, the unsaid words hanging heavily between them, draping them in a chilling silence that felt almost tangible.

Just then, a figure broke through the crowd. It was Linda, Sarah's mother, her face pale and streaked with worry. "Kendra! Josh!" she called, rushing toward them. "Thank God you're here."

"Mrs. Miller, what happened?" Kendra's voice was barely a whisper, the weight of dread sinking deeper into her chest.

Linda's eyes glistened with unshed tears, the corners of her lips trembling slightly as she struggled to speak. "They were attacked last night. A guy in a Reaper costume broke in. Sarah and David are... gone. My baby is gone."

The words crashed over Kendra like a tidal wave, disbelief flooding her senses. "What? No, that can't be true..." Her voice broke, the reality of Linda's statement hitting her like a fist to the gut. She looked to Josh for reassurance, but he stood frozen, his expression mirroring her own disbelief.

Linda continued, her voice shaking. "It was chaos... I was at work late, and when I got home, the place was a mess. The cops came and told me they didn't make it. There was nothing I could do." Tears overflowed from Linda's eyes, rolling down her cheeks in silent agony.

Kendra felt her legs weaken beneath her, the weight of sorrow threatening to pull her down. She remembered the times spent laughing with Sarah, sharing secrets, and crying together over breakups and dreams. How could this vibrant person, filled with life and energy, be gone? "What about the police?" Kendra asked, her voice small and shaky. "Are they going to find the—"

"The killer?" Linda interrupted, her voice cracking with anguish. "They're doing everything they can, but… it's too late for them. My baby…" She fell silent, the weight of grief suffocating her.

Kendra wrapped her arms around Linda, feeling the heat of her pain seep into her own skin. Josh stepped beside them, resting a hand on Kendra's back, his presence a grounding force in the storm of emotions swirling around them.

Minutes passed like hours. Despite the activity of the officers around them, everything felt hazy, as if the world outside their little circle had vanished. Kendra struggled to process what had happened. "We have to do something," she whispered, pulling away from Linda, determination igniting within her. "We can't just stand here."

Josh shook his head, concern etched across his features. "Kendra, we need to let the police handle this."

"No," she insisted, her voice lifting just enough to carry the weight of her determination. "Sarah was my best friend. I can't just sit here and do nothing. We need to find out what really happened."

Linda looked at Kendra, her eyes a mixture of admiration and sorrow. "I don't know how... but if you can find out anything, please do. I need to know... I need justice for my daughter."

With that, resolve cemented in Kendra's chest. She turned to Josh, who seemed torn, but there was a flicker of understanding in his eyes. "Okay, I'm with you," he said finally, clasping her hand tightly.

As they walked away from the devastation that had unfolded at Sarah's home, Kendra's mind raced. They had no leads, no clues, but they had to start somewhere. "We'll check her social media," Kendra said. "Maybe she posted something unusual just before... before everything happened."

Josh nodded in agreement, his fingers still intertwined with hers, offering a sliver of comfort amid the chaos. As they made their way to a nearby café with Wi-Fi, they gathered their thoughts, their hearts heavy with unresolved grief.

"Remember her last post?" Kendra asked, pulling out her phone. "She mentioned a guy that kept making her uncomfortable at the coffee shop. I remember her saying something about it, but I didn't really think anything of it..."

"Let's see if we can find it," Josh replied, pulling out his laptop. They settled into a small corner table, and Kendra scrolled through Sarah's social media while Josh navigated the internet, searching for news articles about the attack.

Nothing could prepare them for the surge of betrayal and heartbreak as they scrolled through Sarah's photos, laughter frozen in time, each post reminding them of the vibrant life taken too soon. Kendra's heart ached as she read the last comments on Sarah's posts, filled with joy and anticipation, completely unaware of the darkness lurking just beyond the surface.

Suddenly, Kendra stumbled across a picture of Sarah with her and Josh from a happier time—three smiling faces, their futures bright and full of promise. Beneath that picture, a comment caught her eye from someone named 'MagnoliaCult'—"You think you're safe, but I'm always watching…"

Anger flared within Kendra, boiling her blood as she shared a glance with Josh, whose face paled. "This has to be connected. Whoever this is, they have a sick obsession with her."

Fingers trembling, Kendra replied to the comment, her heart racing faster than ever. "Who are you? What do you want?" The act felt almost foolish, yet it also felt like the only way to take back some semblance of control in the situation.

As they waited for a response, Kendra's phone buzzed. It was a message from Linda. "Thank you for being there. I need you to know how much Sarah loved you both. She often said you were her family."

Kendra's eyes brimmed with tears, and she squeezed Josh's hand tighter, finding refuge in his support. "She deserves justice, Josh. We have to make sure everyone knows what happened. We can't let them forget she existed, that she mattered... that we love her."

At that moment, Kendra and Josh made a silent vow. They'd not only seek answers for themselves but also for Linda and for Sarah, to honor her memory and uncover the truth masked beneath layers of fear and sorrow.

As they left the café, Kendra felt a new fire ignite within her. The world that had felt so bleak moments ago now felt charged with purpose. With each step, she reminded herself they would not let the darkness win; they would fight back—for Sarah, for Linda, and for all those who had been silenced before the truth could be unveiled.

With the determination to uncover the truth, Kendra and Josh made their way to the local coffee shop where Sarah had often spent her afternoons. The familiar storefront came into view, its cheerful exterior now juxtaposed against the grim reality of the situation. Kendra's heart raced as they approached the entrance, the bell above the door chiming softly as they stepped inside.

The warm smell of coffee and baked goods enveloped them, yet it felt hollow amid the chaos in Kendra's mind. They walked up to the counter where a barista was busy steaming milk, and Kendra felt a knot tighten in her stomach. "Excuse me," she said, her voice wavering slightly. "I'm looking for information about Sarah Miller. She used to come here a lot."

The barista looked up, her expression shifting from casual indifference to concern. "Oh, Sarah... I heard about what happened. I'm so sorry." Her voice was gentle but filled with sorrow. "She was such a sweet girl."

"Did she ever mention anyone who made her uncomfortable?" Kendra pressed, her eyes scanning the barista's face for any sign of recognition. "There was a guy who kept bothering her, right? Do you know his name?"

The barista hesitated, her brow furrowing as she considered the question. "There was this one guy who used to come in a lot, but I never thought much of it. He seemed harmless enough, always sitting in the corner, staring at people. I didn't realize he was bothering her until she mentioned it once in passing. I think she called him 'Creepy Carl' or something like that."

"Creepy Carl," Kendra repeated, committing the name to memory. "Do you know what he looked like? Did he ever talk to her?"

The barista nodded slowly, her expression serious. "He had disheveled hair and wore a lot of black. He would sit there for hours, just staring. Sarah said he made her feel uncomfortable, so she started coming in at different times to avoid him. I wish I had done something more."

Kendra felt a mix of gratitude and frustration. "Thank you for telling me. It helps to know she wasn't imagining things."

As they left the coffee shop, Kendra glanced at Josh, who was deep in thought. "We need to find this Carl guy," he said, determination etched on his face. "If he was bothering her, he might know something about what happened."

Kendra nodded in agreement, her resolve hardening. "Let's start by asking around the neighborhood. Someone must have seen him."

The two of them made their way through the streets of Magnolia, approaching neighbors and gathering snippets of information along the way. Each conversation was filled with nervous glances and hushed tones, the weight of the tragedy still fresh in everyone's minds. Kendra felt a sense of urgency urging her forward; they had to find answers.

After hours of searching, they finally stumbled upon a young couple walking their dog. Kendra approached them, her heart pounding. "Excuse me, have you seen a guy around here who goes by the name 'Creepy Carl'? He's been bothering my friend."

The couple exchanged a worried glance before the woman spoke up. "Yeah, we've seen him. He usually hangs around the coffee shop and sometimes the park. He gives off a strange vibe, and we've heard others say the same."

"Do you know where we could find him?" Josh asked, his voice steady but tinged with urgency.

The man shrugged. "I'm not sure. He usually frequents the same spots, though. Just be careful; he looks a bit… unhinged."

"Thanks, we appreciate it," Kendra said, feeling a mix of gratitude and apprehension. They now had a lead, however tenuous, and it felt like they were one step closer to uncovering the truth.

As they continued their search, Kendra's mind raced with possibilities. What if Carl knew something? What if he had seen Sarah and David the night of the attack? Questions swirled in her mind, each one more pressing than the last. They had to find answers, to protect Sarah's memory and bring justice to the tragedy that enveloped their lives.

Hours faded into the late afternoon, and Kendra and Josh found themselves at the park, scanning the area for any sign of the elusive Carl. As they walked past a group of children playing, Kendra spotted a lone figure sitting on a bench in the distance, shrouded in shadows. He wore a dark hoodie, the fabric pulled tightly around his face, and something about him made her heart race with a mix of fear and determination.

"There he is," Kendra whispered to Josh, her voice barely audible. "That has to be him."

Josh nodded, his brow furrowed in concentration. "Let's approach cautiously. We don't know how he'll react."

They approached the bench, Kendra's heart pounding loudly in her chest. As they drew nearer, the figure looked up, revealing a gaunt face framed by unruly hair. His eyes were wide and darting, as if he were constantly on edge. Kendra felt a shiver run down her spine.

"Excuse me," she called out, her voice steady despite the rising tension. "Are you Carl?"

The man's expression shifted, a flicker of recognition crossing his features. "Who wants to know?" he replied, his voice low and gravelly.

"I'm Kendra," she said, trying to keep her tone calm. "I'm looking for information about my friend Sarah. She said you were bothering her at the coffee shop."

He winced at the mention of Sarah's name, shifting uncomfortably on the bench. "I didn't mean any harm. I just… I was just watching."

"Watching?" Josh interjected, his voice sharp. "You scared her. You made her feel unsafe."

"People are just too sensitive these days," Carl muttered, his eyes darting around as if searching for an escape. "I didn't do anything wrong."

Kendra took a step closer, trying to maintain her composure. "What do you know about what happened to her? Did you see anything unusual the night of the attack?"

Carl's demeanor shifted, a flicker of fear crossing his eyes. "I don't know anything! I wasn't there! I swear!" He stood abruptly, clutching his hoodie tightly as if it were a shield against their questions.

"Please, just tell us what you saw," Kendra urged, desperation creeping into her voice. "We need to know."

He hesitated, glancing around as if weighing his options. Finally, he spoke, his voice trembling. "I was at the coffee shop that night, but I left early. I didn't see anything—just some noise. I thought it was just kids messing around."

Kendra felt a mixture of frustration and sympathy. "Carl, if you know something—anything at all—it could help us find out what happened. You don't want to be involved in this, do you?"

He looked at her, the conflict etched across his face. "I just wanted to be left alone. I didn't mean to scare anyone. I didn't want this."

With that, he turned and fled, disappearing into the shadows of the park. Kendra felt a wave of defeat wash over her. They had come so close, yet he had slipped through their fingers like sand.

"Let's follow him," Josh suggested, determination igniting in his eyes. "He might lead us to something—someone."

Without waiting for Kendra's response, he took off in the direction Carl had gone. Kendra hesitated for a moment, torn between fear and the urgency to uncover the truth. She couldn't let fear dictate her actions; she had to confront the darkness head-on.

They sprinted after Carl, weaving through the park and into the nearby streets. Kendra's heart raced, adrenaline surging through her veins. She could not let him get away. If he held any information about Sarah's final moments, it was crucial they caught up to him.

As they rounded a corner, they spotted him up ahead, glancing back nervously. With renewed urgency, Kendra and Josh pushed forward, their footsteps echoing in the air. "Carl!" Kendra shouted, desperate to catch his attention. "We just want to talk!"

He hesitated for a moment, looking conflicted, but then he turned and ran faster. Kendra felt a surge of frustration. "We can't let him get away!" she exclaimed to Josh.

They chased him through narrow alleyways, their breaths coming in short gasps as they navigated the maze of Magnolia's streets. Carl's figure darted ahead, twisting and turning, but with each corner, they closed the distance. Kendra could feel the weight of urgency pressing on her chest, a relentless reminder that they needed answers.

Finally, they cornered him in an alleyway, the walls rising high on either side, blocking any chance of escape. "Carl, please!" Kendra called, her voice steady despite her racing heart. "We need your help!"

He stopped, panting heavily, his eyes wide with fear. "I told you, I don't know anything!"

"Then why were you stalking Sarah?" Josh pressed, stepping closer. "What was your intention?"

Carl looked at them, a flicker of vulnerability breaking through his hardened exterior. "I just wanted to see her. I thought if I could just watch… I could understand her better."

Kendra's heart softened slightly. "But you scared her, Carl. That's not how you get to know someone."

"I didn't mean to!" he shouted, frustration bubbling over. "I thought maybe if I could get close, she would see I wasn't a threat. I just wanted to be near her."

Kendra's mind raced, trying to comprehend his twisted reasoning. "So you were watching her? Did you see anything the night of the attack?"

"I... I don't know!" Carl stammered, shaking his head as if trying to dispel the memory. "I left the coffee shop before it happened. I was just... watching from a distance."

"From where?" Kendra pressed, her heart pounding in her chest. "Please, anything could help us."

He pointed down the alley, his voice shaky. "I was watching from the park across the street. I saw some commotion, but I didn't think it was anything serious. I thought it was just a Halloween prank or something."

Kendra and Josh exchanged glances, a flicker of hope igniting within them. "What kind of commotion?" Josh asked, his voice steady.

"There were voices—arguing," Carl recalled, his brow furrowing in thought. "Then I heard a loud bang. I thought it was fireworks or something... it didn't sound like a gun."

Kendra's heart sank again, the weight of despair crashing down on her. "Did you see anyone leave the house?"

Carl shook his head, frustration etching deeper lines on his face. "I was too far away. I just heard the noise and then saw people running. I didn't realize it was serious until I saw the cops show up."

"Thank you, Carl," Kendra said, her voice softening. "This helps more than you know. If you think of anything else, please reach out. We just want to find justice for Sarah and David."

With that, they turned and began to walk away, feeling the weight of the encounter settle heavily on their shoulders. They had more questions than answers, but at least they had a starting point. As they made their way back to the main street, Kendra's mind raced with thoughts of Sarah and David, the vibrant lives they had lost, and the determination to ensure their story did not end in tragedy.

"We need to go to the police station," Kendra said suddenly, her determination surging with every step. "We have to tell them what we found out. This could be crucial."

Josh nodded, his expression resolute. "Let's do it."

The two of them made their way through the now-familiar streets of Magnolia, their feet moving with purpose. The sun had begun to dip lower in the sky, casting long shadows that stretched across the sidewalks. The world that had once felt so vibrant and alive now seemed tainted, as if the very air was thick with sorrow.

When they arrived at the police station, Kendra felt a mix of nervousness and determination. They approached the front desk, where an officer greeted them with a curious look. "Can I help you?"

"We have information about the Millers' case," Kendra said, her voice steady despite the flutter of anxiety in her chest. "We need to speak with Detective Holloway."

"Have a seat; I'll let her know you're here," the officer replied, gesturing to a row of chairs in the waiting area.

They sat down, the tension palpable as they waited for Detective Holloway to arrive. Kendra's thoughts raced, the weight of their discoveries pressing down on her. She couldn't shake the feeling that they were on the brink of something significant, but the uncertainty of what lay ahead loomed heavy in the air.

After a few minutes, Detective Holloway appeared, her expression serious but softened with understanding as she approached them. "Kendra, Josh—thank you for coming in. What do you have for me?"

Kendra took a deep breath, summoning her courage. "We spoke to a guy at the coffee shop. He called himself 'Creepy Carl.' He said he was watching Sarah and that he heard some arguing the night of the attack."

Holloway's brows furrowed in concentration. "Did he see anything else? Any details that stood out?"

Kendra shook her head, frustration creeping in. "No, just that he thought it was fireworks and didn't realize it was serious until later. But he mentioned a lot of noise—arguing before the gunshot."

"Interesting," Holloway replied, her mind clearly racing as she processed the information. "This could help us establish a timeline. We need to find this Carl and get a full statement from him."

Kendra felt a flicker of hope as she shared more details about their conversation with Holloway, recounting Carl's description and the unsettling comments he had left on Sarah's posts. The detective listened intently, her expression shifting from concern to determination.

"Thank you for bringing this to me," Holloway said, her voice firm. "We'll look into it immediately. Every piece of information is critical in cases like this. You both did the right thing by coming forward."

As they left the police station, Kendra felt a mixture of relief and trepidation. They were making progress, but the shadows of uncertainty still loomed large. With each step, she reminded herself that they would not let the darkness win; they would fight back—for Sarah, for Linda, and for all those who had been silenced before the truth could be unveiled.

The sun dipped lower in the sky as they walked back toward their apartment, the world around them growing dimmer. Kendra's mind churned with thoughts of their next steps. "We should talk to the other friends," she suggested. "They might have insights or information we missed."

"Good idea," Josh agreed, squeezing her hand reassuringly. "Let's gather everyone and share what we found. The more people involved, the better."

Kendra nodded, her heart swelling with gratitude for her friends and the bond they shared. They would not be alone in this fight; they had each other, and together they could uncover the truth.

As they reached their apartment, Kendra felt a surge of determination. "Let's make a plan. We need to reach out to everyone and set a time to meet. We can brainstorm ideas and form a strategy."

"Absolutely," Josh said, his eyes shining with resolve. "We'll find a way to honor Sarah and David's memory by ensuring their story is told."

Kendra smiled at him, feeling a sense of purpose ignite within her. They were not just fighting for answers; they were fighting for justice, for the lives that had been so cruelly taken from them. The road ahead would be long and arduous, but together, they would uncover the truth hidden in the shadows.

As the night settled in, Kendra and Josh gathered their friends, sharing their discoveries and rallying everyone together. The atmosphere was charged with energy as they brainstormed ideas, each person contributing their thoughts and insights. It felt like a sisterhood revived, and within that space, Kendra found hope.

They discussed potential leads, rifling through notes and memories, piecing together every moment they could remember about Sarah and David. Each laugh shared, every tear shed, and every whispered secret brought them closer together, solidifying their commitment to uncovering the truth.

As the evening wore on, they shared stories about Sarah's kindness, her infectious laughter, and the dreams she had for the future. With each memory, Kendra felt the warmth of their friendship enveloping her, and she knew they were on the right path.

"Whatever it takes, we will find out what happened," Kendra declared, her voice firm. "For Sarah, for David, and for each other."

The resolve in the room was palpable, a shared determination that would not be easily extinguished. They would uncover the truth, no matter how dark or twisted it might be. And in doing so, they would honor their friends' memory and ensure that their stories would never be forgotten.

As they closed the night with a sense of purpose, Kendra felt a flicker of hope igniting within her. The journey ahead would be fraught with challenges, but together, they would face the darkness and emerge into the light, determined to bring justice to those who had been silenced. The fight was just beginning, and Kendra was ready to confront whatever lay ahead.

Chapter 3

Kendra, Josh, and their mother were utterly shattered by the tragic loss of Sarah and David. These two vibrant souls had been central figures in their lives, interwoven into the fabric of cherished memories that spanned years—birthdays filled with laughter, family gatherings overflowing with love, lazy summer days spent playing in the park, and late-night conversations that inspired their dreams. Each shared moment had formed a beautiful legacy of joy and companionship, now darkened by profound grief. The echo of Sarah's laughter and the warmth of David's smile haunted their thoughts, a constant reminder of what had been taken from them.

Despite the overwhelming sorrow that threatened to consume them, they clung to their mother's insistence that life must go on. "We must keep moving forward," she would say, her voice steady even as her eyes glistened with unshed tears. While mourning and healing were essential, an unyielding sense of responsibility for their futures propelled them forward. Ignoring their studies was not an option; their daily routines offered fragile stability amid the chaos that enveloped their lives.

At precisely 10:43 AM on a crisp autumn morning, Kendra stepped outside into the brisk air, her heart heavy with thoughts of Sarah. The world around her was alive with the colors of fall, the vibrant leaves a stark contrast to the emptiness she felt inside. Josh walked beside her, the tension between them palpable as they prepared to return to campus, each step weighed down by their shared loss. Their mother had encouraged them to try to find normalcy, but it felt like a monumental task.

"Let's just get through today. We can remember them together later," Josh suggested, casting a worried glance at Kendra as they walked. His eyes reflected the weight of their grief, mirroring the storm brewing within her.

"We owe it to them to keep living, right?" she replied, forcing a delicate smile that never quite reached her eyes. Even as she spoke the words, doubt gnawed at her, questioning whether they could truly honor their friends' memories amidst such tragedy.

As they approached the campus, the familiar sights began to loom ahead—marked by the brick buildings and the sprawling green lawns that had once felt like a sanctuary but now felt charged with sorrow. They joined their friends—Mary, Jack, Danny, Jane, and Audrey—each reflecting the burden of their collective grief. The campus loomed ahead, a stark reminder of their responsibilities and of the vibrant memories they once shared with Sarah and David.

Forming a tight circle, their unity forged by shared sorrow, they whispered about the horrific murders that had shattered their small community, detailing the brutal actions of the Reaper killer. The words flowed like a dark river, each recounting further deepening the sense of dread.

"I can't believe this is happening," Mary murmured, shivering at the thought. "I always thought these things only happened in movies."

"Same here. It makes me want to look over my shoulder every second," Jack added, fear creeping into his voice. "When will it end? How can we feel safe again?"

Danny attempted to inject some optimism into the conversation. "Maybe the police will catch him soon. They say they're doing everything they can. They've got a solid team on it."

"But how can we be sure?" Jane countered, her voice trembling. "What if we go back to normal and he strikes again? I can't shake this sense of dread. It feels like we're sitting ducks."

"We should stick together," Audrey chimed in, her voice steady but filled with concern. "No one should be alone right now. Together, we can find a way through this nightmare."

Everyone nodded in agreement, drawing comfort from their collective grief. A moment of silence enveloped the group, weighed down by memories of joyful times now painfully out of reach. Kendra closed her eyes, recalling the last time they were all together—laughter filling the air, a sense of freedom untainted by tragedy.

As they neared the campus gates, the atmosphere shifted slightly. Sunlight filtered through the trees, casting playful shadows on the pavement while other students bustled by, seemingly unaware of the sorrow dragging down their group. It felt as though the world continued, indifferent to the darkness clouding their spring.

"First class is with Professor Thompson, right?" Josh broke the silence, trying to refocus their thoughts.

"Ugh, yes," Audrey replied, rolling her eyes. "He'll probably want us to talk about something boring today. I can't even concentrate."

"Think of it as a distraction. We need that right now," Kendra encouraged softly, her tone firm. She felt the weight of the day pressing down on her, and she could sense the anxiety radiating from her friends.

As they walked toward the lecture hall, the distant chatter about assignments and weekend plans pierced Kendra's heart. Each laugh felt like a cruel reminder of the joy they had lost, but deep down, she recognized the importance of holding on to those fleeting moments, however bittersweet. They had to keep living for Sarah and David.

"Hey, you guys," Josh suddenly paused. He turned to face the group, a seriousness in his demeanor. "What if we hold a tribute for them after classes? Something at the park?"

His suggestion hung in the air, heavy with both tension and hope, eventually met with quiet agreement.

"We should bring flowers," Mary proposed, her voice thoughtful. "And maybe write notes to leave behind. They deserve to be remembered—not just as victims, but for who they truly were."

"We can do it together," Danny added, relief washing over him as he realized they could channel their grief into something meaningful. "It'll be a way for us to process what happened."

As the bell rang, signaling the start of class, they took deep breaths, steeling themselves for the challenges ahead.

Once settled in their seats, an unusual silence blanketed the lecture hall. The once lively atmosphere had dimmed, their collective grief casting a shadow over everyone. Kendra could feel the heaviness in the air, a tangible weight that pressed down on their shoulders.

When Professor Thompson entered, he surveyed the room with compassion. "I know many of you are carrying heavy hearts and struggling with what's happened," he said gently, his voice brimming with understanding. "It's completely normal to find it hard to focus right now. If anyone needs to talk or seek support, please reach out to the counseling services. Our community is here for you." He paused, allowing the gravity of his words to settle before continuing. "Now, let's dive into *Dr. Jekyll and Mr. Hyde*."

"Kim!" called the professor. "Could you please explain why Jekyll was so afraid to reveal his evil side?"

Kim shrugged, clearly unsettled. "I don't know. It just reminds me of horror!"

Danny raised his hand. “Well, it’s somewhat horror, but not exactly a slasher!”

Audrey interjected, “What about *Texas Chainsaw Massacre* or *Halloween*?”

Danny shot back, “Those are slasher movies! You can’t turn a slasher into a TV series!”

The professor smiled at the lively exchange. “I love the discussions you’re having. Remember, exploring these themes is important. It’s part of human nature to grapple with fear, whether in literature or in reality. We often find comfort when we confront our fears openly.”

Kendra felt the weight of his words resonate deeply within her. She sat still, yearning to express the emotions swirling inside her. As the conversation unfolded around her, she felt like a ghost, her thoughts lingering on memories of Sarah and David—moments forever cherished yet now suffused with sorrow.

Amidst the lecture, bursts of laughter broke through the heaviness, as students shared insights about fear and evil in literature. With each shared laugh, Kendra felt her heart lighten ever so slightly—a reminder that life could still weave moments of joy amidst heartbreaking trials.

Danny passionately expounded on the mechanics of slasher films. "Slashers tap into our primal fears; they exploit our vulnerabilities, transforming the ordinary into the terrifying!" His enthusiasm was infectious, and Kendra couldn't help but feel a flicker of hope for the future.

As lively discussions unfolded, an abrupt interruption jolted the classroom. Kendra's phone vibrated in her pocket. Glancing at the screen, her breath caught in her throat. A grisly GIF of Sarah and David's mangled bodies accompanied a chilling message: "Looks like they're split up for good!" The image was marred by the unmistakable visage of someone wearing a Ghostface mask.

Kendra quickly typed a message: "Change of plans. Meet me in the bathroom. I need to show you something."

Panic surged within her, threatening to spill over. The laughter around her felt like a mockery now, a cruel twist of fate. Without waiting for a response, she slipped her phone back into her pocket and stood abruptly, her chair scraping loudly against the floor.

"Where are you going?" Josh called after her, a note of concern echoing in his voice.

"I'll be back in a minute," Kendra replied over her shoulder, urgency propelling her forward.

She hurried down the dimly lit corridor, the noise of the bustling campus fading behind her. As she entered the nearest bathroom, she leaned against the cool wall, struggling to steady her breath. The reality of her situation felt more surreal than ever. How could someone have sent that? And what were they trying to achieve?

A few moments later, her friends trickled in, their faces lit with a mix of curiosity and tension. "What's going on?" Audrey asked, her eyes wide with concern.

Kendra held up her phone, her fingers trembling as she replayed the GIF for them. Gasps filled the bathroom, turning into a fractured silence.

Mary's face paled. "Is this real? How can they do this?"

Danny clenched his fists, frustration evident on his face. "Whoever this is, they need to be caught. We can't let them get away with this."

Josh stepped forward, his expression a mask of determination. "What do we do?

We can't just go back to class like nothing's happened."

Kendra took a deep breath, trying to keep her voice steady. "We need to report this. If it's not already being investigated, we have to make sure they take it seriously."

Audrey nodded. "You're right. We need to help ensure everyone is safe."

The group quickly formulated a plan, deciding that Kendra would approach Professor Thompson and alert him to the disturbing message. They would also share what they had experienced, so he could convey the urgency to the appropriate authorities.

As they left the bathroom, a newfound resolve coursed through them. They were no longer just grieving friends; they were survivors, determined to face the darkness together. With each step towards the lecture hall, they felt a flicker of strength—a unity forged in grief, but now ignited by the need for action.

As they reentered the lecture hall, Kendra's heart raced. She caught Professor Thompson's eye as he sat at his desk. Taking a deep breath, she approached him, her friends flanking her for support.

"Professor Thompson, can we talk for a moment?" Kendra asked, trying to keep her voice steady.

He looked up, concern immediately etched across his face. "Of course, Kendra. Is everything alright?"

Kendra exchanged a quick glance with her friends, who nodded encouragingly. "It's about the recent events—the murders. I think someone might be trying to instigate fear among us. I just received a… message."

She held out her phone, showing him the disturbing image. As it flickered before him, the color drained from his face.

"Thank you for bringing this to my attention. I will contact the authorities immediately," he said firmly, standing and straightening his posture. "You did the right thing."

Kendra felt a weight lift slightly from her shoulders, yet the world outside continued to feel dark and ominous. The threat loomed large, casting long shadows over their lives and shattering the fragile façade of normalcy they had been struggling to maintain.

As the bell rang for the end of class, the tension in the air was palpable. Kendra and her friends gathered their belongings, preparing to move forward into a reality that now held a different meaning. Each step felt laden with purpose—they would honor Sarah and David by fighting against the darkness that threatened their community.

With renewed determination, they walked through the halls, their unity giving them strength. As they left the lecture hall, whispers of dread and malice brushed against them like a cold wind, igniting a fire of resolve in their hearts.

"We need to stay close," Danny said, pacing slightly as they moved. "If they're targeting us, we need to have each other's backs."

Mary nodded, her brow furrowing in worry. "But how do we even begin to find out who did this? That seems impossible."

"There must be something," Kendra urged, her mind racing. "They sent that message for a reason. Maybe there's a clue we can uncover. We can't let fear win. We have to rise above it."

Josh cleared his throat, the weight of the moment pressing down on him. "We could start by talking to some other students. If anyone received similar messages, we could gather more information to help the authorities."

Their eyes met, and the tension in the air shifted slightly as hope flickered among them.

With a renewed focus on action, they split up, each heading in different directions to piece together whatever details they could find. Kendra wandered through the campus, eager to gather information while battling the nagging fear gnawing at her gut. Students milled about, their laughter echoing hollowly in her ears. She approached a group standing outside the library, the cool breeze ruffling their hair, hoping they might have insight.

"Hey, did any of you guys receive any weird messages lately about Sarah and David?" Kendra asked, forcing the words out through the lump in her throat.

The group exchanged glances, confusion dancing in their eyes. "What do you mean?" one girl, Eva, asked.

Kendra hesitated before revealing the content of the message she'd received, her heart racing as she recollected the horrific image. "I got this GIF of them, and there was a creepy message along with it—like the sender is toying with us."

Gasps rippled through the group, and she recognized Laura, a close friend of Sarah's, stepping forward. "I heard about that—somebody in our dorm mentioned getting something similar. I... I thought it was just a hoax."

Hope ignited within Kendra, urging her onward. "We need to report it! Someone is targeting friends of Sarah and David. If we all collaborate, we can keep track of these messages."

As more students gathered, Kendra felt a powerful swell of determination. There was strength in numbers, and she realized that together, they could push back against the fear attempting to close in around them. They quickly exchanged contact information, vowing to share any pertinent information that came their way.

Equipped with a newfound sense of purpose, Kendra returned to her friends in the familiar gathering spot outside the lecture hall, excitement coursing through her veins. "You guys won't believe it! More students have received unsettling messages like mine. If we organize and report everything, maybe we can help the police catch whoever is doing this!"

With each revelation, the urgency of their situation deepened, spinning a web of connection and solidarity binding them together amidst the chaos. They each shared their experiences and concerns, but Kendra's resolve remained at the center of their discussions. They would not let fear dictate their lives.

In the ensuing days, Kendra's group became a hub of activity, rallying other students into their cause. They organized meetings, disseminated information, and established a secure messaging group to keep track of all communication regarding the harassment. Each revelation about messages sent and received only increased their urgency and visibility—the campus community was not just reeling in shock; they were taking steps to reclaim their safety.

As news traveled rapidly through the university, a collective energy began to build. Posters were hung in stairwells and dormitories, an appeal to report any unsettling communication and support one another. They coordinated with the authorities, ensuring the campus police were aware of each incident. The darkness began to feel a little less consuming, replaced by the warmth of community solidarity and strength.

And in the heart of it all, Kendra fostered a renewed sense of hope. Amid the fear and uncertainty, her friends stood by her side as they carved space for grief and resilience. They hadn't just become survivors; they were now activists —standing together in the face of evil, determined to put a stop to the malevolence that sought to tear them apart.

Days turned into weeks, and though the specter of fear still loomed, it shifted in shape. Conversations rippled through the campus with every meeting, carrying whispers of hope and resistance; winds of change began to sweep through after the unsettling silence.

Then, on a gray afternoon marked by the chill of late autumn, the news emerged that a suspect had been apprehended—the mask of The Reaper, once a symbol of their shared horror, now laid discarded at the feet of justice. A wave of relief washed over the community, a collective sigh echoing as hope blossomed once again in the shadow of grief.

Kendra and her friends gathered in the familiar brick courtyard, sunlight filtering through branches that were beginning to shed their leaves. They stood united, reclaiming their laughter as they remembered Sarah and David—not as victims but as friends—their memories strong, an eternal light guiding them forward.

With the warmth of solace wrapping around them, Kendra's heart surged with the collective spirit. This was no longer just about fear, but about the power of connection, resilience, and the importance of standing together in the darkest of times. Together, they had faced the shadows and emerged into the light—a community forged not only in grief but in unwavering strength, a bond that could withstand any storm.

Chapter 4

The week crawled on, each day a relentless march filled with anxiety and restless nights. Kendra found herself increasingly distracted, her mind constantly haunted by the distorted voice that seemed to seep into her daily life. The world around her had transformed into a surreal landscape where every sound felt amplified, every shadow seemed to hold a threat, and every corner turned felt like a step into the unknown. She tried to focus on her classes, but the shadow of the unknown caller loomed larger with every passing hour, a constant reminder of her vulnerability. Her friends noticed her distancing, their concerned glances and gentle prods met with Kendra's forced smiles and vague excuses about being overwhelmed with schoolwork.

As Friday approached, the air felt electric, thick with tension that Kendra couldn't shake. Every time her phone buzzed, her heart raced, the anticipation twisting inside her like a restless serpent. Part of her wished the caller would reach out again so she could confront the source of her fear head-on; another part dreaded what those next words might entail, each possibility more terrifying than the last.

On Thursday evening, just as Kendra was about to settle in for the night, her phone rang again. Adrenaline surged through her veins, and she stared at the screen, willing the caller ID to change, but "Unknown Caller" stared back at her, mocking her resolve. Reluctantly, she answered, her fingers trembling against the smooth screen.

"Hello?" she said, her voice barely above a whisper.

"Hello, Kendra," the familiar metallic voice intoned, sending a wave of dread crashing over her. "Are you ready for the truth?"

"Who is this, and what do you want from me?" Kendra's voice quivered, but she steeled herself, desperate to sound braver than she felt.

"A simple conversation, really," the voice replied, a smirk almost audible in its tone. "Let's talk about those perfect posts, shall we? Isn't it exhausting to keep up the pretense?"

Kendra gritted her teeth, her pulse hammering in her ears. The call held a menacing familiarity that left her doubting her sanity. "I don't owe you anything!"

"Oh, but you do. You've built your life around a lie, Kendra. Those snapshots of happiness, of success, all carefully filtered and curated. But behind that facade, I know there's fear, sadness… maybe even shame. What's it like to wear a mask every day?"

A lump rose in Kendra's throat, forcing bile up as she fought back tears. "You don't know me!" she shouted, desperation lacing her voice, but her resolve weakened, the fear creeping in.

"Ah, but I do. And the clock is ticking—tomorrow you must decide. You either confront your truth or live in fear of the consequences. I will be watching."

The call went dead, the line going eerily quiet as Kendra found herself staring blankly at the phone in her hand, her breath hitching in her throat. It felt as if the weight of the world crashed down on her shoulders, pressing her against the wall just behind her.

The rest of the night blurred into a haze of confusion and despair. Kendra sat on the edge of her bed, unable to shake the feeling of being hunted. She scrolled through social media, each post a painful reminder of the carefully constructed life she had created. The selfies, vacations, and laughter —all felt like dark lies woven into the fabric of her existence.

As sleep evaded her, Kendra tossed and turned, contemplating the coming confrontation that the unknown caller had dictated. There was an unsettling truth to their words: the perfection she showcased bore no resemblance to the turbulence of her inner world. She felt torn, yearning for her friends' support but terrified of exposing her vulnerabilities.

When dawn broke, Kendra reluctantly faced the day. The anticipation of potential confrontation felt like a heavy curtain draped over her, obscuring her vision. Her morning was consumed by a haze of dread as the clock ticked ever closer to the fated moment. She arrived on campus with a sense of foreboding that clung to her like a burrowing parasite.

As she navigated the crowded hallways, her friends greeted her with wide smiles, completely unaware of the turmoil swirling within her. Mark and Jess were animatedly discussing a movie while Sarah chatted about plans for the upcoming weekend, but Kendra felt like an outsider, adrift in their carefree banter. The laughter echoed hollowly in her ears, a cruel reminder of a joy that felt impossibly distant.

"Hey, are you okay?" Jess asked, her brow furrowed with concern. "You've been awfully quiet lately."

"Yeah, I'm fine. Just... a lot on my mind," Kendra replied, forcing a smile that felt foreign on her lips. Her friends were so wrapped up in their own lives; she didn't want to drag them into her darkness.

The day wore on, and Kendra's focus frayed, the impending weight of the call hanging heavy over her. She missed half of her classes, unable to concentrate, her mind racing through possible ways to confront her truth while dreading what it might entail.

As the clock struck noon, she found herself gravitating toward a quiet corner of the campus garden, the trees cloaking her in shadows. It was here that she decided she had to face her fears. If she was going to confront the caller's ultimatum, she had to do it on her own terms.

With shaky hands, she pulled out her phone, staring at the lit screen like it held the answer to her dilemma. She breathed deeply, steeling herself for what she had to do.

The secret she had hidden for years threatened to surface, shadows creeping closer as the day's light waned. Kendra swiped through her contacts, hovering over Sarah's name. It was the one she was closest to—the friend who had seen her through ups and downs, yet the fear of judgment lingered like a specter in her mind.

Summoning every ounce of courage, she tapped on Sarah's name. The line connected, sending a familiar wave of warmth coursing through her. "Hey, what's up?" Sarah's voice came through, cheerful and bright.

"Can we meet up? I... I really need to talk." Kendra's voice trembled slightly, but she pressed on despite her anxiety.

"Of course! Where are you?" Sarah asked, her tone shifting to attentive concern.

After making plans to meet at a discreet café off-campus, Kendra's heart raced wildly in her chest. She spent the next hour pacing, her thoughts spiraling out of control. What would she say? How could she bare her soul without being judged?

When Josh arrived, his face lit up with joy, completely unaware of the heaviness in Kendra's heart. They settled into a quiet corner, sipping coffee and chatting about trivial things. Kendra's mind wrestled fiercely with the choice to open up, his insides quaking with both fear and the desperate need for honesty.

At last, the moment came. Kendra's palms were clammy as she set her cup down and steeled herself. "Josh, there's something I need to tell you."

"What's going on?" Josh's expression turned serious, his eyes searching Kendra's face for answers.

Taking a deep breath, Kendra plunged into her truth. "I've been getting these strange phone calls... someone knows things about me that I've never shared. They keep taunting me about how I present myself online, how everything looks perfect, but it really isn't."

Josh's brow furrowed, concern washing over his face. "That sounds terrifying! Have you called the police?"

"No, I don't think they can help," Kendra admitted, her voice shaking as she continued, "But they made me realize that my life isn't as perfect as I try to make it seem. I feel like I'm losing control of everything. I just—I don't know how to face my own truth."

For a moment, silence enveloped them. Kendra's breath caught in her throat as she waited for Josh's reaction. To her surprise, her friend reached out and gently placed her hand over Kendra's.

"Kendra, we all have things we hide. Nobody's life is as perfect as it seems on social media. But you don't have to face this alone," Josh said softly, sincerity lacing his tone. "I'm here for you. Always."

A wave of relief washed over Kendra, the pressure in her chest easing slightly. In that moment, she felt vulnerable but safe, like a shield had been raised between her and her fears. The fear of being judged dissipated, replaced with the comforting reality that her friends truly cared for her well-being.

"I just want you to know you're not alone," Josh continued, "Whatever this caller wants or knows, we'll figure it out together. You have us."

Kendra thought of Jane, Danny, Audrey, and Mary—each with their own struggles, each bringing different strengths to the group dynamic. Wouldn't they want to be there for her, just as she had been there for them?

"Okay," Kendra said, her voice firmer now. "You're right. I'll tell them everything. But can you be there too? I need you."

"Of course," Josh replied, a smile breaking through the tension. "I wouldn't miss it for the world."

With newfound resolve, Kendra glanced toward the door leading to the common room where their other friends were gathered. It was now or never. She stood up, feeling a bit lighter with Josh by her side, and walked toward the door, her pulse quickening.

As they entered the room, the laughter and chatter from Jane, Danny, Audrey, and Mary brought a wave of warmth, but it was quickly swallowed by the weight of what she was about to reveal. Kendra took a moment to gather her thoughts, her fingers nervously intertwining with Josh's.

"Hey, everyone!" Kendra called out, her voice breaking the rhythm of the conversation. All eyes turned toward her, expressions ranging from curiosity to concern.

"What's up, Kendra? You look serious," Jane noted, her friendly smile faltering.

Kendra took a deep breath. "I… I need to talk to all of you about something important." She hesitated for a moment, searching for the right words. "Lately, I've been getting these strange phone calls… someone who knows… things. Things I thought were buried. It's been really hard, and I've kept it from you."

"Might be time to change that," Audrey spoke softly, her expression shifting from concern to warmth. The love and support in the room surrounded Kendra like a comforting blanket.

"Yeah, we've all got each other's backs. We'll get through this together," Danny added, nodding emphatically.

Kendra took another deep breath, feeling the weight of their support rallying around her. "I just really wish I had told you sooner," she admitted, her voice trembling. "I didn't realize how much I needed you all until now."

"Good. We're ready to take on whatever comes next," Josh said, his voice steady. "Just promise me one thing: you'll lean on us whenever you need to."

Kendra smiled through her tears, feeling a warmth settle around her heart. She had been wrestling with her feelings for so long, caught in a whirlwind of uncertainty and fear.

But now, as she looked into her friends' earnest eyes, she knew that it was time to share the truth—not just with Josh, but with their whole friend group.

"What if they don't understand?" Kendra's voice trembled, laced with worry. She could already imagine the tension, the questions, the pity. "What if they think I'm weak?"

"They won't see you as a burden. You're their friend," Josh reassured her. "And friends help each other. They will want to help, just like I do. You have to trust them."

Kendra thought of their shared experiences—the laughter, the tears, the support. She couldn't remember a time when they hadn't been there for each other. "You're right," she finally said, her voice steadier now. "I'll tell them."

With renewed determination, Kendra glanced towards the door leading to the common room where their other friends were gathered. It was now or never. She stood up, feeling a bit lighter with Josh by her side, and walked toward the door, her pulse quickening.

As they entered the room, the laughter and chatter from Jane, Danny, Audrey, and Mary brought a wave of warmth, but it was quickly swallowed by the weight of what she was about to reveal. Kendra took a moment to gather her thoughts, her fingers nervously intertwining with Josh's.

"Hey, everyone!" Kendra called out, her voice breaking the rhythm of the conversation. All eyes turned toward her, expressions ranging from curiosity to concern.

"What's up, Kendra? You look serious," Jane noted, her friendly smile faltering.

Kendra took a deep breath. "I… I need to talk to all of you about something important." She hesitated for a moment, searching for the right words. "Lately, I've been getting these strange phone calls… someone who knows… things. Things I thought were buried. It's been really hard, and I've kept it from you."

"Might be time to change that," Audrey spoke softly, her expression shifting from concern to warmth. The love and support in the room surrounded Kendra like a comforting blanket.

"Yeah, we've all got each other's backs. We'll get through this together," Danny added, nodding emphatically.

Kendra took another deep breath, feeling the weight of their support rallying around her. "I just really wish I had told you sooner," she admitted, her voice trembling. "I didn't realize how much I needed you all until now."

"Good. We're ready to take on whatever comes next," Josh said, his voice steady. "Just promise me one thing: you'll lean on us whenever you need to."

Kendra smiled through her tears, feeling a warmth settle around her heart. She had been wrestling with her feelings for so long, caught in a whirlwind of uncertainty and fear.

But now, as she looked into her friends' earnest eyes, she knew that it was time to share the truth—not just with Josh, but with their whole friend group.

"What if they don't understand?" Kendra's voice trembled, laced with worry. She could already imagine the tension, the questions, the pity. "What if they think I'm weak?"

"They won't see you as a burden. You're their friend," Josh reassured her. "And friends help each other. They will want to help, just like I do. You have to trust them."

Kendra thought of their shared experiences—the laughter, the tears, the support. She couldn't remember a time when they hadn't been there for each other. "You're right," she finally said, her voice steadier now. "I'll tell them."

With newfound resolve, Kendra glanced towards the door leading to the common room where their other friends were gathered. It was now or never. She stood up, feeling a bit lighter with Josh by her side, and walked toward the door, her pulse quickening.

As they entered the room, the laughter and chatter from Jane, Danny, Audrey, and Mary brought a wave of warmth, but it was quickly swallowed by the weight of what she was about to reveal. Kendra took a moment to gather her thoughts, her fingers nervously intertwining with Josh's.

"Hey, everyone!" Kendra called out, her voice breaking the rhythm of the conversation. All eyes turned toward her, expressions ranging from curiosity to concern.

"What's up, Kendra? You look serious," Jane noted, her friendly smile faltering.

Kendra took a deep breath. "I... I need to talk to all of you about something important." She hesitated for a moment, searching for the right words. "Lately, I've been getting these strange phone calls... someone who knows... things. Things I thought were buried. It's been really hard, and I've kept it from you."

"Might be time to change that," Audrey spoke softly, her expression shifting from concern to warmth. The love and support in the room surrounded Kendra like a comforting blanket.

"Yeah, we've all got each other's backs. We'll get through this together," Danny added, nodding emphatically.

Kendra took another deep breath, feeling the weight of their support rallying around her. "I just really wish I had told you sooner," she admitted, her voice trembling. "I didn't realize how much I needed you all until now."

"Good. We're ready to take on whatever comes next," Josh said, his voice steady. "Just promise me one thing: you'll lean on us whenever you need to."

Kendra smiled through her tears, feeling a warmth settle around her heart. She had been wrestling with her feelings for so long, caught in a whirlwind of uncertainty and fear. But now, as she looked into her friends' earnest eyes, she knew that it was time to share the truth—not just with Josh, but with their whole friend group.

"What if they don't understand?" Kendra's voice trembled, laced with worry. She could already imagine the tension, the questions, the pity. "What if they think I'm weak?"

"They won't see you as a burden. You're their friend," Josh reassured her. "And friends help each other. They will want to help, just like I do. You have to trust them."

Kendra thought of their shared experiences—the laughter, the tears, the support. She couldn't remember a time when they hadn't been there for each other. "You're right," she finally said, her voice steadier now. "I'll tell them."

With newfound resolve, Kendra glanced towards the door leading to the common room where their other friends were gathered. It was now or never. She stood up, feeling a bit lighter with Josh by her side, and walked toward the door, her pulse quickening.

As they entered the room, the laughter and chatter from Jane, Danny, Audrey, and Mary brought a wave of warmth, but it was quickly swallowed by the weight of what she was about to reveal. Kendra took a moment to gather her thoughts, her fingers nervously intertwining with Josh's.

"Hey, everyone!" Kendra called out, her voice breaking the rhythm of the conversation. All eyes turned toward her, expressions ranging from curiosity to concern.

"What's up, Kendra? You look serious," Jane noted, her friendly smile faltering.

Kendra took a deep breath. "I... I need to talk to all of you about something important." She hesitated for a moment, searching for the right words. "Lately, I've been getting these strange phone calls... someone who knows... things. Things I thought were buried. It's been really hard, and I've kept it from you."

"Might be time to change that," Audrey spoke softly, her expression shifting from concern to warmth. The love and support in the room surrounded Kendra like a comforting blanket.

"Yeah, we've all got each other's backs. We'll get through this

together," Danny added, nodding emphatically.

Kendra took another deep breath, feeling the weight of their support rallying around her. "I just really wish I had told you sooner," she admitted, her voice trembling. "I didn't realize how much I needed you all until now."

"Good. We're ready to take on whatever comes next," Josh said, his voice steady. "Just promise me one thing: you'll lean on us whenever you need to."

Kendra smiled through her tears, feeling a warmth settle around her heart. She had been wrestling with her feelings for so long, caught in a whirlwind of uncertainty and fear. But now, as she looked into her friends' earnest eyes, she knew that it was time to share the truth—not

just with Josh, but with their whole friend group.

"What if they don't understand?" Kendra's voice trembled, laced with worry. She could already imagine the tension, the questions, the pity. "What if they think I'm weak?"

"They won't see you as a burden. You're their friend," Josh reassured her. "And friends help each other. They will want to help, just like I do. You have to trust them."

Kendra thought of their shared experiences—the laughter, the tears, the support. She couldn't remember a time when they hadn't been there for each other. "You're right," she finally said, her voice steadier now. "I'll tell them."

With newfound resolve, Kendra glanced towards the door leading to the common room where their other friends were gathered. It was now or never. She stood up, feeling a bit lighter with Josh by her side, and walked toward the door, her pulse quickening.

As they entered the room, the laughter and chatter from Jane, Danny, Audrey, and Mary brought a wave of warmth, but it was quickly swallowed by the weight of what she was about to reveal. Kendra took a moment to gather her thoughts, her fingers nervously intertwining with Josh's.

"Hey, everyone!" Kendra called out, her voice breaking the rhythm of the conversation. All eyes turned toward her, expressions ranging from curiosity to concern.

"What's up, Kendra? You look serious," Jane noted, her friendly smile faltering.

Kendra took a deep breath. "I… I need to talk to all of you about something important." She hesitated for a moment, searching for the right words. "Lately, I've been getting these strange phone calls… someone who knows… things. Things I thought were buried. It's been really hard, and I've kept it from you."

"Might be time to change that," Audrey spoke softly, her expression shifting from concern to warmth. The love and support in the room surrounded Kendra like a comforting blanket.

"Yeah, we've all got each other's backs. We'll get through this

together," Danny added, nodding emphatically.

Kendra took another deep breath, feeling the weight of their support rallying around her. "I just really wish I had told you sooner," she admitted, her voice trembling. "I didn't realize how much I needed you all until now."

"Good. We're ready to take on whatever comes next," Josh said, his voice steady. "Just promise me one thing: you'll lean on us whenever you need to."

Kendra smiled through her tears, feeling a warmth settle around her heart. She had been wrestling with her feelings for so long, caught in a whirlwind of uncertainty and fear. But now, as she looked into her friends' earnest eyes, she knew that it was time to share the truth—not

just with Josh, but with their whole friend group.

"What if they don't understand?" Kendra's voice trembled, laced with worry. She could already imagine the tension, the questions, the pity. "What if they think I'm weak?"

"They won't see you as a burden. You're their friend," Josh reassured her. "And friends help each other. They will want to help, just like I do. You have to trust them."

Kendra thought of their shared experiences—the laughter, the tears, the support. She couldn't remember a time when they hadn't been there for each other. "You're right," she finally said, her voice steadier now. "I'll tell them."

With newfound resolve, Kendra glanced towards the door leading to the common room where their other friends were gathered. It was now or never. She stood up, feeling a bit lighter with Josh by her side, and walked toward the door, her pulse quickening.

As they entered the room, the laughter and chatter from Jane, Danny, Audrey, and Mary brought a wave of warmth, but it was quickly swallowed by the weight of what she was about to reveal. Kendra took a moment to gather her thoughts, her fingers nervously intertwining with Josh's.

"Hey, everyone!" Kendra called out, her voice breaking the rhythm of the conversation. All eyes turned toward her, expressions ranging from curiosity to concern.

"What's up, Kendra? You look serious," Jane noted, her friendly smile faltering.

Kendra took a deep breath. "I... I need to talk to all of you about something important." She hesitated for a moment, searching for the right words. "Lately, I've been getting these strange phone calls... someone who knows... things. Things I thought were buried. It's been really hard, and I've kept it from you."

"Might be time to change that," Audrey spoke softly, her expression shifting from concern to warmth. The love and support in the room surrounded Kendra like a comforting blanket.

"Yeah, we've all got each other's backs. We'll get through this

together," Danny added, nodding emphatically.

Kendra took another deep breath, feeling the weight of their support rallying around her. "I just really wish I had told you sooner," she admitted, her voice trembling. "I didn't realize how much I needed you all until now."

"Good. We're ready to take on whatever comes next," Josh said, his voice steady. "Just promise me one thing: you'll lean on us whenever you need to."

Kendra smiled through her tears, feeling a warmth settle around her heart. She had been wrestling with her feelings for so long, caught in a whirlwind of uncertainty and fear. But now, as she looked into her friends' earnest eyes, she knew that it was time to share the truth—not

just with Josh, but with their whole friend group.

"What if they don't understand?" Kendra's voice trembled, laced with worry. She could already imagine the tension, the questions, the pity. "What if they think I'm weak?"

"They won't see you as a burden. You're their friend," Josh reassured her. "And friends help each other. They will want to help, just like I do. You have to trust them."

Kendra thought of their shared experiences—the laughter, the tears, the support. She couldn't remember a time when they hadn't been there for each other. "You're right," she finally said, her voice steadier now. "I'll tell them."

With newfound resolve, Kendra glanced towards the door leading to the common room where their other friends were gathered. It was now or never. She stood up, feeling a bit lighter with Josh by her side, and walked toward the door, her pulse quickening.

As they entered the room, the laughter and chatter from Jane, Danny, Audrey, and Mary brought a wave of warmth, but it was quickly swallowed by the weight of what she was about to reveal. Kendra took a moment to gather her thoughts, her fingers nervously intertwining with Josh's.

"Hey, everyone!" Kendra called out, her voice breaking the rhythm of the conversation. All eyes turned toward her, expressions ranging from curiosity to concern.

"What's up, Kendra? You look serious," Jane noted, her friendly smile faltering.

Kendra took a deep breath. "I... I need to talk to all of you about something important." She hesitated for a moment, searching for the right words. "Lately, I've been getting these strange phone calls... someone who knows... things. Things I thought were buried. It's been really hard, and I've kept it from you."

"Might be time to change that," Audrey spoke softly, her expression shifting from concern to warmth. The love and support in the room surrounded Kendra like a comforting blanket.

"Yeah, we've all got each other's backs. We'll get through this

together," Danny added, nodding emphatically.

Kendra took another deep breath, feeling the weight of their support rallying around her. "I just really wish I had told you sooner," she admitted, her voice trembling. "I didn't realize how much I needed you all until now."

"Good. We're ready to take on whatever comes next," Josh said, his voice steady. "Just promise me one thing: you'll lean on us whenever you need to."

Kendra smiled through her tears, feeling a warmth settle around her heart. She had been wrestling with her feelings for so long, caught in a whirlwind of uncertainty and fear. But now, as she looked into her friends' earnest eyes, she knew that it was time to share the truth—not

just with Josh, but with their whole friend group.

"What if they don't understand?" Kendra's voice trembled, laced with worry. She could already imagine the tension, the questions, the pity. "What if they think I'm weak?"

"They won't see you as a burden. You're their friend," Josh reassured her. "And friends help each other. They will want to help, just like I do. You have to trust them."

Kendra thought of their shared experiences—the laughter, the tears, the support. She couldn't remember a time when they hadn't been there for each other. "You're right," she finally said, her voice steadier now. "I'll tell them."

With newfound resolve, Kendra glanced towards the door leading to the common room where their other friends were gathered. It was now or never. She stood up, feeling a bit lighter with Josh by her side, and walked toward the door, her pulse quickening.

As they entered the room, the laughter and chatter from Jane, Danny, Audrey, and Mary brought a wave of warmth, but it was quickly swallowed by the weight of what she was about to reveal. Kendra took a moment to gather her thoughts, her fingers nervously intertwining with Josh's.

"Hey, everyone!" Kendra called out, her voice breaking the rhythm of the conversation. All eyes turned toward her, expressions ranging from curiosity to concern.

"What's up, Kendra? You look serious," Jane noted, her friendly smile faltering.

Kendra took a deep breath. "I... I need to talk to all of you about something important." She hesitated for a moment, searching for the right words. "Lately, I've been getting these strange phone calls... someone who knows... things. Things I thought were buried. It's been really hard, and I've kept it from you."

"Might be time to change that," Audrey spoke softly, her expression shifting from concern to warmth. The love and support in the room surrounded Kendra like a comforting blanket.

"Yeah, we've all got each other's backs. We'll get through this

together," Danny added, nodding emphatically.

Kendra took another deep breath, feeling the weight of their support rallying around her. "I just really wish I had told you sooner," she admitted, her voice trembling. "I didn't realize how much I needed you all until now."

"Good. We're ready to take on whatever comes next," Josh said, his voice steady. "Just promise me one thing: you'll lean on us whenever you need to."

Kendra smiled through her tears, feeling a warmth settle around her heart. She had been wrestling with her feelings for so long, caught in a whirlwind of uncertainty and fear. But now, as she looked into her friends' earnest eyes, she knew that it was time to share the truth—not

just with Josh, but with their whole friend group.

"What if they don't understand?" Kendra's voice trembled, laced with worry. She could already imagine the tension, the questions, the pity. "What if they think I'm weak?"

"They won't see you as a burden. You're their friend," Josh reassured her. "And friends help each other. They will want to help, just like I do. You have to trust them."

Kendra thought of their shared experiences—the laughter, the tears, the support. She couldn't remember a time when they hadn't been there for each other. "You're right," she finally said, her voice steadier now. "I'll tell them."

With newfound resolve, Kendra glanced towards the door leading to the common room where their other friends were gathered. It was now or never. She stood up, feeling a bit lighter with Josh by her side, and walked toward the door, her pulse quickening.

As they entered the room, the laughter and chatter from Jane, Danny, Audrey, and Mary brought a wave of warmth, but it was quickly swallowed by the weight of what she was about to reveal. Kendra took a moment to gather her thoughts, her fingers nervously intertwining with Josh's.

"Hey, everyone!" Kendra called out, her voice breaking the rhythm of the conversation. All eyes turned toward her, expressions ranging from curiosity to concern.

"What's up, Kendra? You look serious," Jane noted, her friendly smile faltering.

Kendra took a deep breath. "I... I need to talk to all of you about something important." She hesitated for a moment, searching for the right words. "Lately, I've been getting these strange phone calls... someone who knows... things. Things I thought were buried. It's been really hard, and I've kept it from you."

"Might be time to change that," Audrey spoke softly, her expression shifting from concern to warmth. The love and support in the room surrounded Kendra like a comforting blanket.

"Yeah, we've all got each other's backs. We'll get through this

together," Danny added, nodding emphatically.

Kendra took another deep breath, feeling the weight of their support rallying around her. "I just really wish I had told you sooner," she admitted, her voice trembling. "I didn't realize how much I needed you all until now."

"Good. We're ready to take on whatever comes next," Josh said, his voice steady. "Just promise me one thing: you'll lean on us whenever you need to."

Kendra smiled through her tears, feeling a warmth settle around her heart. She had been wrestling with her feelings for so long, caught in a whirlwind of uncertainty and fear. But now, as she looked into her friends' earnest eyes, she knew that it was time to share the truth—not

just with Josh, but with their whole friend group.

"What if they don't understand?" Kendra's voice trembled, laced with worry. She could already imagine the tension, the questions, the pity. "What if they think I'm weak?"

"They won't see you as a burden. You're their friend," Josh reassured her. "And friends help each other. They will want to help, just like I do. You have to trust them."

Kendra thought of their shared experiences—the laughter, the tears, the support. She couldn't remember a time when they hadn't been there for each other. "You're right," she finally said, her voice steadier now. "I'll tell them."

With newfound resolve, Kendra glanced towards the door leading to the common room where their other friends were gathered. It was now or never. She stood up, feeling a bit lighter with Josh by her side, and walked toward the door, her pulse quickening.

As they entered the room, the laughter and chatter from Jane, Danny, Audrey, and Mary brought a wave of warmth, but it was quickly swallowed by the weight of what she was about to reveal. Kendra took a moment to gather her thoughts, her fingers nervously intertwining with Josh's.

"Hey, everyone!" Kendra called out, her voice breaking the rhythm of the conversation. All eyes turned toward her, expressions ranging from curiosity to concern.

"What's up, Kendra? You look serious," Jane noted, her friendly smile faltering.

Kendra took a deep breath. "I... I need to talk to all of you about something important." She hesitated for a moment, searching for the right words. "Lately, I've been getting these strange phone calls... someone who knows... things. Things I thought were buried. It's been really hard, and I've kept it from you."

"Might be time to change that," Audrey spoke softly, her expression shifting from concern to warmth. The love and support in the room surrounded Kendra like a comforting blanket.

"Yeah, we've all got each other's backs. We'll get through this

together," Danny added, nodding emphatically.

Kendra took another deep breath, feeling the weight of their support rallying around her. "I just really wish I had told you sooner," she admitted, her voice trembling. "I didn't realize how much I needed you all until now."

"Good. We're ready to take on whatever comes next," Josh said, his voice steady. "Just promise me one thing: you'll lean on us whenever you need to."

Kendra smiled through her tears, feeling a warmth settle around her heart. She had been wrestling with her feelings for so long, caught in a whirlwind of uncertainty and fear. But now, as she looked into her friends' earnest eyes, she knew that it was time to share the truth—not

just with Josh, but with their whole friend group.

"What if they don't understand?" Kendra's voice trembled, laced with worry. She could already imagine the tension, the questions, the pity. "What if they think I'm weak?"

"They won't see you as a burden. You're their friend," Josh reassured her. "And friends help each other. They will want to help, just like I do. You have to trust them."

Kendra thought of their shared experiences—the laughter, the tears, the support. She couldn't remember a time when they hadn't been there for each other. "You're right," she finally said, her voice steadier now. "I'll tell them."

With newfound resolve, Kendra glanced towards the door leading to the common room where their other friends were gathered. It was now or never. She stood up, feeling a bit lighter with Josh by her side, and walked toward the door, her pulse quickening.

As they entered the room , the atmosphere shifted. The laughter and chatter from Jane, Danny, Audrey, and Mary provided a warm backdrop, but Kendra could feel the weight of her impending revelation pressing down on her shoulders. The room was filled with the familiar smells of coffee and baked goods, remnants of snacks left from earlier gatherings. The sight of her friends, their faces illuminated by the soft glow of string lights, made her heart swell with love and gratitude, but also with an overwhelming sense of dread.

"Hey, everyone!" Kendra called out, her voice breaking the rhythm of the conversation. All eyes turned toward her, expressions shifting from curiosity to concern. The camaraderie they shared felt like a fortress, but now it was also a stage where she had to lay bare her vulnerabilities.

"What's up, Kendra? You look serious," Jane noted, her friendly smile faltering as she sensed the gravity of the moment.

Kendra took a deep breath, steeling herself for what she was about to say. The words felt heavy in her throat, but she knew she had to push through. "I've been getting these strange phone calls... someone who knows things about me that I've never shared. They keep taunting me about how I present myself online, how everything looks perfect, but it really isn't. They said some things that make me feel like they are watching me."

A collective gasp echoed through the room, the comfortable atmosphere suddenly replaced with a tense silence. Kendra felt her heart race as she continued, her breath hitching in her throat. "I didn't want to worry you all. I thought I could handle it myself, but it's been really hard. The calls have been relentless, and I haven't been able to focus on anything."

"What do you mean, they've been watching you?" Danny asked, his brow furrowing in concern. "Do you know who it is?"

"No, it's an unknown number," Kendra replied, her voice trembling slightly. "The last call I received was particularly chilling. They said things that no one else should know, things I've kept hidden. It was like they were pulling the strings of my life, exposing the darkest corners of my soul."

Audrey stepped closer, her eyes wide with compassion. "Kendra, I can't believe you've been going through this alone. We should have known. You don't have to carry this burden by yourself."

"Yeah, we're here for you," Josh said, his voice steady. "Whatever you need, we'll figure it out together. We won't let this person intimidate you."

Kendra felt a rush of gratitude wash over her, the warmth of their support enveloping her like a safety blanket. "Thank you, all of you. I really needed to share this. I didn't want you to think I was weak or… I don't know. I guess I was afraid of what you might think."

"Don't ever think that!" Jane exclaimed, her voice filled with urgency. "You're one of the strongest people I know. It takes courage to admit when you're struggling. We'll stand by you through this."

"Absolutely," Danny chimed in, a determined look on his face. "Let's take action. We can't let this person control your life."

Kendra nodded, feeling the weight of her fears begin to lift. "I want to report it to the police, but part of me is terrified. What if they can't do anything? What if it just makes things worse?"

Josh squeezed her hand reassuringly. "We'll go with you. You don't have to face this alone, and the police need to know what's happening. We can support you every step of the way."

"Let's do it," Kendra said, her voice gaining strength. "I don't want to live in fear anymore. It's time to take control back."

The group nodded, their faces resolute. They spent the next few minutes discussing their plan, strategizing how to approach the police and what information to share. Kendra felt a flicker of hope as they outlined steps to confront the unknown threat together.

As they finalized their plans, Kendra's phone buzzed again—a familiar vibration that sent a chill down her spine. She hesitated, glancing at the screen, her heart pounding. "It's an unknown number again," she said, her voice trembling as their eyes turned to her, concern etched on their faces.

"Don't answer it!" Mary urged, her voice filled with urgency. "You don't need to put yourself at risk."

"I won't," Kendra replied, her hand shaking as she silenced the call. "I'm done letting this person have power over me."

With newfound determination, they all stood together, a united front against the darkness that had infiltrated their lives. Kendra felt the strength of her friends flowing through her, igniting a fire within her to push back against the fear that had threatened to consume her.

As they prepared to leave the café, a sense of solidarity enveloped them. They gathered their things, and Kendra took a moment to look around, her heart swelling with gratitude. In the face of adversity, she had found a family that would stand by her, no matter what.

"Let's do this," Kendra said, her voice filled with conviction. "For Sarah and David, and for all of us."

As they walked toward the police station, Kendra's heart raced with a mixture of fear and determination. The campus buzzed with life around them, but it felt like they were moving in slow motion, each step a reminder of the weight of their mission. Kendra could feel the oppressive atmosphere of uncertainty pressing down on her, but she pushed it aside, focusing on the resolve that had taken root within her.

When they arrived at the police station, Kendra felt a knot of anxiety twist in her stomach. The building loomed before them, stark and imposing, but she knew they had to face it. "Are we ready?" she asked, glancing at her friends.

"We've got your back," Josh said firmly, his expression resolute.

With a deep breath, Kendra stepped inside, the cool air washing over her as they approached the front desk. The officer on duty looked up, his expression shifting to one of concern as he saw the group.

"How can I help you?" he asked, his tone professional yet compassionate.

"We need to speak to someone about a series of threatening phone calls," Kendra said, her voice steady despite the whirlwind of emotions inside her.

The officer nodded, gesturing for them to take a seat while he retrieved a detective. Kendra sat down, her heart racing as she glanced around the room. The walls were adorned with community safety posters, reminders of the importance of vigilance. They felt like a stark contrast to the chaos swirling in her mind.

When Detective Holloway entered the room, a sense of familiarity washed over Kendra. She had seen the detective on the news, her face a beacon of strength and authority in the aftermath of the tragic events. "Hello, everyone," Holloway greeted warmly, her eyes scanning the group. "I understand you have some concerns to discuss?"

Kendra nodded, feeling the weight of her fears pressing down on her again. "Yes, I've been getting these strange calls... someone knows personal things about me. They sent me a disturbing message regarding Sarah and David."

Holloway's expression shifted to one of focus and concern as she took a seat across from them. "Can you tell me more about the calls? What exactly did they say?"

Taking a deep breath, Kendra recounted the details of the calls—the metallic voice, the taunting words, the chilling ultimatum. With each word, she felt a sense of catharsis, as if shedding the weight of her fears through shared vulnerability. She watched as Detective Holloway listened intently, jotting down notes and nodding in understanding.

"Thank you for sharing this with me, Kendra," Holloway said once Kendra had finished. "It takes a lot of courage to come forward, especially under such distressing circumstances. We will take this seriously."

Kendra felt a flicker of hope ignite within her as Holloway continued, "I want to ensure that we get to the bottom of this and keep you and your friends safe. I'll need your contact information, and we'll set up a way to keep you informed as we investigate."

As the conversation unfolded, Kendra felt the tension in the room ease slightly. With each detail shared, she felt a sense of empowerment growing within her. She was no longer just a victim of circumstance; she was taking control of her narrative, reclaiming her story from the shadows.

After making arrangements with Holloway, Kendra and her friends left the police station, their hearts lighter than when they had entered. They knew they still had a long way to go, but together, they could face whatever challenges lay ahead.

As they walked back to campus, the sun began to set, casting a warm golden glow over the landscape. Kendra felt a renewed sense of purpose, a determination to honor Sarah and David's memory by standing strong in the face of adversity.

When they reached the campus, Kendra noticed a group of students gathered near the entrance, their faces animated and engaged in conversation. The vibrant energy wrapped around her, a reminder that life continued despite the darkness they faced. The air buzzed with laughter, and for the first time in days, Kendra felt a sense of normalcy seep back into her life.

"Let's go to the park for the tribute," Josh suggested, breaking the spell of their shared silence. "We can reflect on everything and remember them together."

Kendra nodded, grateful for the opportunity to honor Sarah and David with her friends. That evening, as the group gathered in the park, they brought flowers and candles, creating a makeshift memorial under the sprawling branches of an ancient oak tree. They shared stories, laughter, and tears, weaving together memories that would forever bind them.

The flickering candlelight illuminated their faces, casting soft shadows that danced with the gentle breeze. Kendra felt the warmth of love and friendship surround her, the darkness that had threatened to engulf her slowly receding. In that moment, she understood that while the pain of loss would never fully vanish, the bonds forged through shared grief could illuminate even the darkest of nights.

As they lit the candles and placed them around the flowers, Kendra closed her eyes and whispered a silent prayer for Sarah and David. She hoped they could feel the love and camaraderie that enveloped them, a promise that they would never be forgotten.

With every story shared, Kendra felt the weight of her fears begin to lift. Together, they had faced the shadows and emerged into the light—a community forged not only in grief but in unwavering strength, a bond that could withstand any storm. In the heart of that park, surrounded by her friends, Kendra finally felt a sense of peace settle within her. The journey ahead would be long, but she was ready to face it, side by side with those who loved her.

Chapter 5

As night enveloped Mary's apartment, an unsettling stillness settled over the space, a stark departure from the laughter and vibrant energy that had erupted throughout the campus just days earlier. The walls, once echoing with joy and camaraderie, now felt suffocating, as if they were holding their breath in anticipation of something dreadful. Shadows crept into the corners of the room, dark and oppressive, amplifying the sense of foreboding that had taken root in Mary's mind. With her friends entwined in a labyrinth of exams, projects, and the complex responsibilities of young adulthood, Mary found herself alone amidst the cozy confines of their shared living space, accompanied only by her roommate, Audrey.

Audrey was a whirlwind of charisma and style—at twenty, she effortlessly captivated everyone around her, particularly older men, with her adventurous spirit and infectious laughter. Her vibrant personality radiated warmth, drawing people in like moths to a flame. In her presence, Mary often felt like an invisible specter, a ghost haunting a life that constantly overlooked her. The stark contrast between their personalities left Mary grappling with her self-image, feeling like a shadow compared to Audrey's bright light.

Mary, a petite 22-year-old blonde with a fondness for the macabre, found solace in the thrills of horror films. While her friends cozied up under blankets for light-hearted romantic comedies, she eagerly prepared popcorn, dimming the lights as she readied herself for spine-chilling tales of the supernatural. It wasn't just fear that captivated her; it was the artistry inherent in horror—the intricate narratives and clever plots that transformed the mundane into the terrifying. From the psychological suspense of *Psycho* to the haunting family dynamics of *Hereditary*, she approached each film with a critical eye, relishing the craftsmanship involved. For Mary, every flicker on the screen was a story that transcended mere horror, delving deep into human nature, fear, and the instinct for survival.

In her quest to understand the genre, Mary frequently attended midnight screenings at the local theater, engaging in electric discussions with fellow horror enthusiasts. The thrill of films that made her heart race had become a cherished ritual—an escape from the uncertainties of her life. Within the chaotic world of academia, horror films provided her with a structured avenue to confront and explore fear without genuine peril, gifting her a sense of control when everything else felt overwhelmingly chaotic.

Though her friends often teased her about her passion, they couldn't help but notice the spark in her eyes whenever she passionately discussed her favorite characters and plot twists. Horror represented more than a genre for Mary; it was a vibrant passion that infused her life with exhilaration, an unyielding pursuit of the next unsettling story that waited shrouded in shadows.

Meanwhile, Audrey thrived on spontaneity, reveling in late nights with friends and endless escapades. Recent events—the chilling murders of students Sarah and David at the hands of the killer—had cast a profound shadow over their community, leaving many residents on edge. Yet, Audrey remained undeterred, resolute in embracing life's vibrancy despite the malevolent threat lurking outside. Navigating the nightlife with effortless grace, she absorbed the laughter and camaraderie surrounding her as though they were a protective shield against the encroaching terror.

As Mary sank into the familiar embrace of their worn couch, the fabric that usually brought comfort felt heavy with apprehension. The echoes of shared laughter now seemed like distant memories, overshadowed by a consuming solitude. With friends scattered across campus, she often sought solace in the flickering glow of her television. Determined to break her routine that night, she decided to watch a light-hearted romantic comedy to lift her spirits, attempting to distract herself from the creeping dread looming just outside their walls. The irony of her choice was not lost on her—trying to escape into a genre so removed from her true passion.

Shuffling to the kitchen for popcorn, Mary felt the tension thickening the air, prickling at her skin. Worry gnawed at her all week—worry for her friends, worry for herself. Would they be safe? The high-stakes anxiety pulsing through her senses dimmed her excitement for the film she had chosen. Just as a flicker of comfort washed over her in the familiarity of her routine, her phone buzzed, jolting her back to a reality that felt more sinister by the moment.

"Unknown Caller," the screen displayed—a message she often ignored. Yet curiosity nagged at her now, an insatiable itch compelling her to answer. Hesitating, she stared at the screen for a moment before swiping to accept the call, her heart racing like a frantic drum.

"Hello?" she managed, trying to maintain steadiness despite the tremor in her voice.

A chilling pause settled over the line, accompanied by crackling static that sent shivers racing down her spine. Then, a low, distorted voice emerged, emotionless yet cloaked in oppressive darkness that wrapped around her like a cold embrace. "Mary," it said, each syllable clawing at her gut. "I bet you're wondering why it's so quiet tonight."

Startled, Mary struggled to steady her thoughts. How did they know her name? "Is this a prank?" she blurted, gripping her phone tightly as determination warred against the haze of invading dread.

The voice chuckled softly, a mocking sound that sent icy tendrils sliding down her spine. "Not a prank, Mary. I know everything about you and your friends—the lovebirds out tonight while you sit here alone, waiting for something—someone—to save you from the dark."

Her pulse quickened, dread flooding her senses like a crashing wave. “What do you want?” she demanded, wrestling to inject authority into her quaking voice.

“To play a little game. You’ve heard of the reaper killer, right? What if I told you that fear isn’t just an illusion? What if the terror has a name, a face?” The voice paused, looming in the oppressive silence as the taunting tone tightened around her. “Would you like to see who’s hunting you?”

Panic seized Mary, her heart racing. This couldn’t be real. “Do you think this is funny?” she snapped, defiance beginning to rise within her.

“It’s not about funny, Mary. It’s about survival. The darkness is coming for you, and I can show you. But first, you must answer my question correctly. What would you do to protect your friends?"

The question hung heavy in the air, uncertainty swirling around her like a tempest. What *would* she do? Though she often envisioned herself as a protector, willing to do anything for her friends, self-doubt gnawed at her resolve. "I would do whatever it takes," she asserted, her voice gaining strength, fueled by the gravity of the moment. "I would fight to keep them safe."

"Good answer. But are you ready to face the real fear?" the voice whispered, chilling her to the bone. "Because it's much closer than you think."

Before she could respond, the line abruptly went dead. Staring numbly at her phone, dread washed over her as the room appeared to grow colder, darker. Thoughts raced through her mind, colliding chaotically—shadows danced beyond the window, a silent reminder that danger lurked just outside her line of sight.

Then she heard it—rustling sounds outside, whispers drifting through the crisp night air that sent goosebumps rippling across her skin. Heart pounding, she dashed to the window, straining to peer into the abyss that consumed her surroundings. The trees swayed ominously, their branches casting twisted shadows that danced teasingly just out of reach. Breathless, she racked her brain for her next move. Should she call her friends? Would they take her seriously, or chalk her fears up to an overactive imagination? Anxiety coiled in her stomach like a live wire, compelling her to act. She needed to find Audrey and ensure her safety.

Grabbing her keys, Mary stepped cautiously into the hallway, her phone clasped tightly as she hastily typed a message.

"Where are you? I got a weird call. Something isn't right."

Moments later, her phone buzzed with Audrey's reply. "I'm out with James. Everything's fine! Why? What's wrong?"

Relief surged through Mary, quickly stifled by the sharp pang of anxiety that wormed its way back in. "Just... I don't know. Weird call. I'm coming to find you. Please be careful."

Audrey responded with carefree reassurance, "We'll be at Sid's bar, near campus. Just chill! It's all good!"

Tension twisted in Mary's gut as she pushed toward the exit. With each step toward the bar, a sense of foreboding coiled within her. She was unaware that she was venturing blindly into a trap, unseeing of the darkness lurking just beyond her reach.

As she approached the aging apartment complex—its shadowy façade looming around her—the small comfort of her home faded into the background, replaced by the echo of her footsteps, each sound amplified, an unsettling reminder of her solitary existence. The stairwell awaited her descent into uncertainty. Just as she positioned her hand to push the door open, her phone buzzed again, breaking through the oppressive silence.

It was a video call—a frantic stream of faces intertwined with horrors that could unravel whatever semblance of normalcy she had left.

Hesitating for a moment, she accepted the call, praying to see Audrey's reassuring face. Instead, her stomach plummeted as she found Audrey staring back at her, the background alive with frenetic energy.

"Mary, are you okay?" Audrey's voice brimmed with urgency.

"Yes, just—something doesn't feel right. I think I'm being watched," she admitted, fear seeping through her words like a whisper of despair.

"Come to us right now!" Audrey insisted, her own anxiety palpable across the screen. Their carefree nights now shrouded in the oppressive weight of the outside world. "You'll be safe with us."

But just then, a sinister creak sliced through the silence of the hallway, cutting through the tension like a knife. Dread settled in Mary's gut, an unshakable instinct that something horrible lurked just beyond her sight.

"I'll be there soon," she promised, trying to sound braver than she felt before ending the call with trembling hands.

As she cautiously descended the stairwell, every instinct screamed that unseen eyes were trained on her, prodding from the ink-black darkness surrounding her. Desperate, she checked her phone to ensure she was ready to call for help. Her heart raced as her mind spiraled into a tumult of dread and urgency, but just as she tucked her device away, a surge of movement caught her eye.

Instinctively, she turned just as a looming figure lunged from the shadows. Clad in black, the reaper mask glimmered ominously beneath the flickering stairwell lights. Panic surged through her veins, igniting a primal fight-or-flight response. "Get away!" she screamed, her voice raw with terror, a deep instinct to survive taking over.

She spun around and sprinted back up the stairs in a frantic dash, breaths coming in sharp gasps as she sensed the relentless echo of footsteps behind her, the killer swiftly closing the gap. Her mind raced with thoughts of her friends, the urgency to protect them propelling her forward. Adrenaline coursed through her veins, blinding her to the fear that threatened to overwhelm.

But the killer was relentless, narrowing the distance between them with each desperate stride she took. Just as Mary reached the landing, searing pain shot through her arm—the blade grazed her skin, ripping through the stillness like a clap of thunder. Adrenaline surged, numbing the pain as she swung her fist wildly, catching him off-guard before diving into the nearest room and slamming the door shut behind her.

The dimly lit space felt like an inescapable trap; the heavy thud of fists on the door was underscored by the killer's mocking laughter. Panic constricted Mary's chest as she shoved herself against an old dresser, desperately pushing it against the door; though the barrier felt pitifully flimsy. Her frantic eyes darted around the room, her heart racing as uncertainty threatened to consume her.

"Think!" she urged herself, scanning for any sign of escape.

Just when safety seemed close, the killer loomed ominously, darkness cascading around him. Yet defiance burned bright within Mary. "You'll regret this!" she gasped, her strength waning but her spirit unyielding.

He lunged at her in a swift, brutal motion. In that split second, something flickered deep within her—an instinct to survive, to fight against the inevitable. Stumbling backward, clinging to her wounds, desperation clawed at her throat as she searched for any glint of hope, a way to escape this nightmare.

Before she could react, he plunged the blade cruelly into her. Pain shot through her body, an inescapable torment that consumed her senses. Even amid the haze, she fought against the encroaching darkness, unwilling to let terror claim her.

"You'll regret wishing you weren't alone," he activated his voice changer, the sinister mockery curling around his words. With sudden, brutal strength, he hoisted her, a puppet in his hands, hurling her from the window—a final, jarring act of cruelty. She fell two stories, the ground rushing to meet her with a brutal finality that severed whatever remaining resolve she clung to.

The world faded into an abyss as her body collided with the pavement, neck snapping instantaneously. Blood pooled around her, a stark red against the gray asphalt, marking the spot where life had once flickered with hope and laughter. In that haunting moment, everything she had extinguished too soon, leaving only echoes of her dreams and the terror that had taken shape in the darkness. The apartment above, so recently filled with warmth and friendship, now stood silent—a somber witness to the horror claiming yet another innocent life on a darkened night.

Chapter 6

"Hello?" Jane's voice came through, groggy and laced with sleep, the sound of rustling sheets punctuating the air as she tried to shake off the remnants of her dreams.

"Jane! It's Audrey! You need to come over right now!" Audrey's voice was frantic, each word tumbling over the last in a rush of panic. "It's Mary! Something... something terrible has happened!"

"What? Audrey, slow down!" Jane exclaimed, the confusion palpable in her tone. "What are you talking about?"

"Just come!" Audrey insisted, her grip tightening around her phone as her heart hammered away, drowning out all rationale. The urgency in her voice was a reflection of the storm brewing inside her—a whirlwind of fear, anxiety, and the desperate need for her friends by her side. She couldn't wait for explanations. She needed support.

"Okay, okay! I'm on my way!" Jane replied, and Audrey felt a rush of relief seep across her anxious thoughts, if only briefly. The promise of her friend's arrival was a small beacon of hope, but it did little to quell the rising dread within her.

In the fleeting moments before Jane arrived, panic swirled within her like a tempest. She paced the kitchen, her eyes darting to the open back door as if expecting the nightmare to disappear if she could just will it away. The night air outside felt alive, charged with an electricity that sent shivers down her spine. Was the caller involved? Did they mean to conjure this horror? With trembling hands, she glanced through the curtains again but saw nothing, only the dark shadows of the night creeping in. The world outside was shrouded in an impenetrable veil, and with each passing second, the oppressive silence thickened.

Audrey's mind reeled back to the call, the distorted voice echoing in the recesses of her thoughts. The weight of those words pressed down on her like a looming specter. Why would anyone go after Mary? What secrets had Mary kept that could have made her a target? She pushed these thoughts away, trying to focus on the present. The specifics didn't matter now. All that mattered was the reality sprawled behind her—the grim scene that awaited her and Jane.

Suddenly, the sound of footsteps echoed in the hallway. Audrey rushed to meet Jane, her heart hammering in her chest like a war drum. “In here!” she cried, crossing the threshold to Mary's bedroom, her chest constricting tighter with each step, the anticipation of what lay ahead filling her with dread.

When Jane burst inside, her expression shifted from concern to horror as she took in the scene before her. “Oh my God!” she gasped, bringing a hand to her mouth, eyes welling with tears as the reality of the situation crashed over her like a tidal wave. “What happened?”

“It’s… it’s bad, Jane!” Audrey’s voice trembled as she struggled to steady herself. "She received a call… someone is after her."

Sinking to the floor, Jane struggled to regain composure, her mind racing. "Did you call the police?" she asked, desperation lacing her words.

"Yes! I called 911…but they haven't arrived yet."

Frantic thoughts took over Jane's mind as she rifled through her pockets, searching for her phone. "We can't just sit here. What if they come back?" She glanced back at Mary's lifeless body, the sight sending a shudder through her. "We need to—"

"Stop!" Audrey interrupted, tightening her grip on Jane's arm, the urgency of the moment surging through her. "We need to wait for help, Jane. We don't know who we're up against."

"No, we can't just wait!" Jane breathed shakily, shaking her head. She reached for her phone to call Danny. "We... we shouldn't be here when they arrive. We need to protect ourselves."

Audrey watched, horrified, as the reality of the situation settled heavily over them. She fought to keep her voice steady. "And what if he knows we're gone? What if he's watching us now?"

"I don't care!" Jane exclaimed, pushing the phone away as if it burned her. "We might be next!"

Before Audrey could formulate a response, the shrill sound of sirens pierced through the thickening atmosphere. A mixture of relief and lingering anxiety flooded through her. Finally, help was here.

Moments later, uniformed officers arrived, quickly sweeping into the apartment. “What’s going on?” one of them barked, his voice sharp and authoritative, demanding clarity as he assessed the scene.

“Back here!” Audrey cried out, leading them to Mary’s room, her heart racing as the reality of what had transpired crashed over her anew.

The officers' expressions shifted from stern focus to shock as they took in the grim scene. One officer immediately radioed for backup while another crouched near Mary’s body, beginning to assess the situation. The air thickened with a mixture of fear and urgency as they worked quickly.

As the police began their work, Audrey and Jane stayed close together, their hands entwined in a silent show of support. The gravity of the moment weighed heavily on them, each passing second amplifying their fear and helplessness. Questions circled in Audrey's mind like vultures, each one more haunting than the last. Could she have done something to protect Mary? Did she ignore the signs?

The officers quickly took statements, asking countless questions as confusion and suspicion clouded their minds. "What was Mary doing before this happened?" one officer asked, his pen poised above a notepad. "Did she mention anything unusual? Any threats or concerns?"

"She got a weird call just before... before we found her," Jane managed, her voice quavering as she recounted the details. "We were supposed to meet up, but she never showed."

"Did she say who the call was from?" the officer pressed, his gaze penetrating.

"No, it was an unknown number," Audrey replied, her voice shaky. "She just said it felt wrong, like someone was watching her."

The officer nodded, jotting down notes. "We'll need everyone's fingerprints and phone records," he said, establishing eye contact. "Can you provide that?"

"Of course," Jane whispered, the gravity of the situation suffocating her as she tried to process the nightmare unfolding around her.

As they continued to answer questions, Jane and Audrey exchanged glances filled with despair. The officers moved methodically, but each inquiry pulled them deeper into a labyrinth of guilt and dread. The weight of their loss was palpable, a physical presence that pressed down on them.

"Listen," one of the officers said, breaking through the haze. "We're going to need you all to stay calm. We're doing everything we can to find the person responsible for this. If you have any information, no matter how small, it could help us."

"Who would do something like this?" Jane asked, her voice barely a whisper, filled with disbelief. "Why would anyone target Mary?"

"Right now, we don't have all the answers," the officer replied, his tone steady but serious. "But we'll find out. Your safety is our priority, so please stay together and keep your phones close."

As the officers moved deeper into the investigation, the group remained huddled together in the living room, the weight of the tragedy pressing down on them like a suffocating blanket. The once vibrant space now felt empty, a haunting reminder of the joy that had filled it just days before.

Kendra, still reeling from the emotional turmoil, spoke up, her voice trembling. "What if this killer is targeting us because of Mary? What if we're next?"

"What if they're using Kendra's past against us? What if they know?" Audrey's voice quivered with anxiety. "It gives them power over us!"

Danny clenched his fists, rage evident in his violet eyes. "We can't let fear control us. We need to figure out what's happening. We owe it to Mary to uncover the truth."

"They're going to want to know everything. We need to cooperate with the police," Audrey said, her voice steadier now. "We can't let this monster have any more power over us."

As the officers continued their work, Jane stayed close to Audrey, her face pale with the weight of their shared grim experience.

"What if the voice was right?" Jane whispered, her eyes wide with fear. "What if they really are watching us?"

"No, we can't think like that!" Kendra shot back, her voice laced with urgency. "We need to stay focused, stay together. Whatever happened that night, it's not your fault, Kendra."

Audrey reached out, squeezing Kendra's hand tightly. "We need to stay strong. We'll figure this out together."

Amidst the chaos, Kendra felt a flicker of hope. "You're right. We can't let this consume us. We need to stay united, and we need to trust each other."

As the night wore on, the officers continued their investigation, unraveling the threads of the case with meticulous precision. The group provided every detail they could recall, every piece of information that might lead to the elusive killer. Each passing moment brought them closer to the truth, but also deeper into the shadows of uncertainty.

In the background, the sound of distant sirens echoed, a haunting reminder of the danger that lurked outside their doors. As they sat together, the weight of their collective fear hung heavy in the air, a tangible presence that threatened to suffocate them.

"We need to think of a plan," Danny suggested, breaking the silence. "We can't just wait around for the police to handle everything. We need to take action."

"But what can we do?" Jane asked, her voice trembling. "We're just students. We don't have the resources or training to deal with this kind of situation."

"We need to gather information," Kendra replied, her mind racing. "If we can find any connections between Mary's death and anyone in our past—anyone who might have reason to target her—we can help the police."

Audrey nodded, her eyes brightening with determination. "We can start by looking through Mary's social media, her contacts. Maybe there's something there that could help us understand who might want to hurt her."

"Good idea," Danny said, his voice steady. "Let's not waste any time.

We need to figure this out as soon as possible."

As they began to discuss their plan, a sense of unity washed over them. They were no longer just friends reeling from a tragedy; they were a team, determined to fight against the darkness that threatened to consume them. With renewed purpose, they gathered their belongings and prepared to sift through Mary's digital life, seeking answers in the fragments of her past.

The evening wore on as they delved deep into Mary's social media profiles, scrolling through photos and posts that felt like haunting echoes of the life she had once lived. Each click brought back memories, laughter, and the vibrancy that had filled her days. But beneath the surface, they searched for clues, hoping to uncover the threads that tied Mary's life to the chilling reality they now faced.

"Look at this," Kendra said, her voice breaking the silence as she pointed to a photo of Mary with a group of friends, including Mike. "There he is. She tagged him in this post from a few months ago."

"Who is he again?" Audrey asked, glancing over Kendra's shoulder.

"He was in her psychology class. I remember she mentioned him once or twice," Kendra replied, her brow furrowing in thought. "She always said he was a little too curious about her past, especially about her sister."

"Let's dig deeper," Danny urged, leaning closer to the screen.

"Maybe there's a message or something that could give us more insight into their relationship."

As they scrolled through the comments and interactions, a sense of unease settled over them. The playful banter and laughter felt hollow now, tainted by the knowledge of Mary's fate. With each new discovery, the threads of the past wove together, revealing a tapestry of friendships that now felt precarious and fraught with danger.

Hours slipped away as they pieced together their findings, the atmosphere thick with tension and determination. Each revelation brought them closer to understanding the darkness that had engulfed their lives, but it also deepened the sense of foreboding that loomed over them.

Just as they were about to wrap up for the night, Kendra's phone buzzed again—a message from an unknown number. Her heart raced as she glanced at the screen, dread pooling in her stomach as she read the chilling words: "You're next."

The silence that followed was deafening, each of them processing the weight of the threat that now loomed over their group. They exchanged fearful glances, the reality of their situation sinking in like cold steel.

"What do we do?" Jane asked, her voice barely above a whisper, the fear evident in her eyes.

"We stay together," Kendra said firmly, her voice steady despite the fear coursing through her veins. "We can't let this break us. We'll report this to the police immediately."

As they gathered their belongings, the sense of urgency propelled them forward. They had faced the darkness together, and now they would continue to fight. The night was far from over, and the hunt for the truth had only just begun.

Chapter 7

The moon hung high in the starless sky, casting an eerie glow over the town of Crestwood. The autumn wind whispered through the trees, each rustle echoing a foreboding warning. In an old, dilapidated cabin on the outskirts of town, Kendra, Josh, Audrey, Danny, and Jane huddled together, their breaths visible in the chilled air. For now, they felt safe—but with every passing moment, the weight of their fear pressed down on them, suffocating and relentless.

In the dim light, flickering shadows danced across the walls, and Kendra's thoughts raced back to the chilling events that had unfolded. David, Sarah, and Mary—their faces flashed through her mind, memories of laughter and dreams now extinguished. They were gone, victims of a darkness that had stalked them like a predator. It wasn't just the brutal nature of the murders that unsettled her; it was the calculated way the killer had orchestrated each event, drawing them in one by one, weaving a web that ensnared not only the victims but their entire friend group.

"Do you think it's going to be over?" Danny asked, his voice trembling slightly, barely slicing through the palpable tension in the room.

Josh attempted to sound brave, though uncertainty flickered in his eyes. "It has to be. The police are searching everywhere for The Magnolia Killer. They'll catch him," he asserted, though the quiver in his voice betrayed his own doubts.

Jane's voice quavered with anxiety, "But we don't even know who he is! For all we know, the killer could be one of us!" The words hung in the air like a dark cloud, thick with unspoken fears and suspicions. Each of them sat rigid, the flickering candlelight casting spooky shadows across their faces. Kendra could sense the underlying tension, the unvoiced accusations lurking beneath the surface. It was the kind of atmosphere that could crack friendships—turning bonds into distrust.

"It's not possible," Kendra said, breaking the silence, trying to steady her own nerves. "We've been friends for years. It's someone from outside our group, someone who knows us." She wished her own words felt more convincing.

"Or someone who's been waiting for the right moment," Audrey interjected, her wide eyes filled with concern. "What if it's someone we least expect? Someone we've let into our lives?" The notion hung heavy in the air, casting a pall over the group. Kendra could feel the panic rising within her, threatening to boil over. She glanced at each of her friends, searching for reassurance, but found only shared dread reflected back at her.

"What do we do?" Danny asked, his voice barely above a whisper, almost lost in the thick tension of fear.

"Stay together," Josh said emphatically, his voice firm.

"That's the most important thing. We can't let ourselves get separated. If we stick together, we'll be safer." His words were meant to inspire confidence, but Kendra could feel the unease lingering in the air like a storm cloud.

As the wind howled outside, Kendra nodded in agreement. Sure, they could draw strength from one another—at least that was the theory. But deep down, unacknowledged fear gnawed at her. The walls of their sanctuary felt like a flimsy barrier against the sinister shadow lurking in the darkness.

Josh, Danny, Jane, and Audrey exchanged resolute nods, their faces a shared mask of determination. They stood in the small, dimly lit room of the community center, tension high as the gravity of their situation settled over them like a shroud. Outside, the moon hung high, casting pale shadows that danced on the ground, but inside, the atmosphere was saturated with unspoken fears and shared resolve.

"We'll have police patrolling the area, but we need to get some rest for tomorrow," Josh said, trying to maintain an air of control amidst the chaos. As the unofficial leader of their group, he felt the weight of responsibility pressing against him, urging him to keep the mood focused on the task at hand: survival.

Audrey, her voice tinged with urgency, interjected, "Class? With a deranged killer on the loose, hacking people apart and hanging them up like skinned cattle, I don't think there will be any classes at all." Her eyes widened in disbelief, and the tremor in her voice hinted at the panic barely contained underneath.

Jane, usually the calmest in the group, added, "She's right, Josh. We can't pretend that everything is normal when there's a maniac stalking our town. People are scared; we just had three people found—" She paused, and they all felt the shiver of dread coursing through them at the thought of the recent crimes.

Danny rubbed the back of his neck, his youthful optimism waning. "But if we don't show up, it'll only make things worse. The school needs to see that we're not afraid. We have to keep living our lives." His voice cracked slightly at the end, revealing the vulnerability he tried to conceal.

"Living our lives? You mean living in fear?" Audrey's words cut through the tension like a knife. "We are talking about a serial killer, Danny! They prey on fear. It's their fuel."

Josh stepped forward, trying to regain control of the conversation. "Look, I understand where you're all coming from. But if we let this fear dictate our actions, then we're letting the killer win." He believed in that sentiment—standing strong despite the horrors unfolding around them. "We need to keep some semblance of normalcy. That's how we fight back."

"Normalcy?" Audrey challenged, crossing her arms defiantly. "You think going to class will make us feel safe? What if they come after us next? What if the killer wants to make a statement? We can't just ignore the danger."

"We're not ignoring it, but we also can't hide away forever," Josh argued, frustration bubbling beneath the surface. "The moment we stop living is the moment they've won. We need to find a balance."

Danny leaned against the wall, his head lowered as he wrestled with the conflicting emotions. "What if one of us is attacked next?" he whispered, his voice almost lost in the heaviness of the room.

"Then we need to watch each other's backs," Jane supplied fiercely. "We're stronger together. We should stick together at all times." Her words resonated with a resolve that momentarily lit a spark of hope.

"What are we going to do then? Buddy system? Hold hands while we walk to class?" Audrey scoffed, though a flicker of amusement broke through her tension.

Jane gave a half-smile, trying to lighten the mood. "You know, it wouldn't be a bad idea. Each of us should agree on a safe word or something. If we feel uncomfortable, we retreat to a designated spot."

"Good idea!" Josh exclaimed, a hint of enthusiasm bubbling up in his tone. "And we can designate a spot where we can all meet after class. If anyone feels uneasy, we should all head there. The library is open late; that could serve as a safe point."

Audrey's expression softened as she considered the plan. "Okay, so we have a meeting point. But that still doesn't mean we'll be safe on our way there. We need to come up with a checklist: what to do if someone feels they're being followed, how to respond if we see something suspicious."

"God, I can't believe this is our new normal," Danny muttered, the weight of reality hitting him hard once more. Yet the effort to be practical seemed to empower them in their desperate situation.

"They want us scared; that's their game." Josh adjusted his stance, feeling a stronger resolve settle within. "But we're not just going to sit back and let this happen. We'll gather information, contact the police with anything we find. Together, we're a force."

Audrey nodded, her expression transitioning from fear to fierce determination. "Alright, we'll work together. We'll be vigilant."

"Group texts! We need to set up a group text to keep everyone updated," Jane suggested. "If anyone hears anything, or sees something suspicious... we have to be able to communicate instantly."

"Smart. Good thinking, Jane," Josh said, his heart swelling with admiration for his friends. Each of them brought something unique to the table, and though the situation was dire, they felt a flicker of hope.

Danny checked his phone and said, "Okay, let's make sure we all have each other's numbers. Right now."

As they pulled out their phones and exchanged information, a silence fell over the room, a moment of collective resolve settling in. Each of them was acutely aware of the shadows lingering just outside, but they found comfort in uniting against an unseen threat. They were in this together, whether they found solace in their friendship or the strength drawn from mutual determination.

"Let's meet back here after class tomorrow?" Josh suggested. "Maybe grab some food and discuss anything we find?"

"Sure, why not? Let's stay strong," Jane affirmed, injecting her signature optimism into the conversation.

Audrey smiled, a glimmer of hope flickering in her eyes. "Yeah, we got this. But let's also have a backup plan just in case someone doesn't show up."

They each nodded in agreement, feeling the energy pulsate within. "Alright." Josh took a deep breath, inspired by the sudden shift in their collective demeanor. "Let's all be prepared for anything. And let's not give the killer the satisfaction of knowing they've instilled fear in us."

As they concluded their meeting, the weight of the world felt slightly lifted. They snuffed out the single light in the room, letting darkness engulf them for a brief moment. The four of them walked back out into the night, their hearts steadying with the sense of camaraderie established amongst them. There was power in numbers, and as they braved the night together, they felt the reality of that sentiment stronger than ever.

Tomorrow would be a new challenge, undeniably fraught with danger, but for now, they had each other.

Despite the looming threat of the Magnolia Killer, Kendra, Josh, Audrey, Danny, and Jane found strength in their unity. They devised a plan to stay safe, keep each other updated through group texts, and meet at a designated spot after class. Their determination to not let fear dictate their actions gave them a newfound sense of purpose. As they parted ways for the night, a glimmer of hope flickered within them.

The next day, they stuck to their plan. They met back at the community center after class, sharing information they had gathered throughout the day. They discussed possible leads and reported any suspicious activity they had encountered. They made sure to check in with each other regularly through their group text, always keeping vigilant and aware of their surroundings.

Their efforts did not go unnoticed. The police commended their proactive approach and offered their support in any way they could. With the additional resources and information from the authorities, the group felt a renewed sense of confidence in their ability to stay safe.

As the days passed, the killer remained at large, but the group continued to stand strong together. Their bond grew stronger with each passing moment, their trust in each other unwavering. They refused to let fear control them, choosing instead to face the threat head-on with courage and unity.

Eventually, their efforts paid off. Through their combined vigilance and determination, they were able to uncover crucial information that led to the apprehension of the Magnolia Killer. With the threat finally neutralized, the town of Crestwood could breathe a collective sigh of relief.

The group of friends stood together, proud of their resilience and strength in the face of adversity. They had faced their darkest fears and emerged stronger than ever. As they looked up at the moon hanging high in the sky, they knew that no matter what challenges lay ahead, as long as they had each other, they could overcome anything. They had transformed their fear into action, weaving a tapestry of hope and unity that would guide them through the shadows.

Chapter 8

As October wore on, Magnolia Community College transformed into a picturesque autumn tableau, the trees ablaze with shades of orange and gold. The beauty of the changing seasons, however, was juxtaposed against an atmosphere thick with unease. Creeping anxiety lingered in the air, as students decorated the campus in preparation for Halloween, draping cobwebs and lining walkways with strings of twinkling lights. Life-sized witches, ghoulish figures, and jack-o'-lanterns made merry displays—but beneath this festive façade, a tension could be felt, an unshakeable sense of dread.

Kendra often found herself feeling caught in this stark dichotomy. Sitting alone on a bench, her latte growing cold between her hands, she observed her surroundings, the world around her slowly dissolving into an anxious haze. Students laughed and joked, planning costumes and discussing their favorite horror movies. Voices filled the air with excitement, but Kendra felt like an outsider, watching from a distance as a life she once enjoyed slipped further away. She wished she could join in, to lose herself in light-hearted banter like they did, but the weight of the recent events held her back, creating an invisible barrier between her and the camaraderie of her peers.

When her friends, Audrey and Jane, joined her, they immediately launched into a spirited discussion about costume ideas. The air buzzed with excitement, but Kendra felt a growing sense of disconnect, as if a thick fog separated her from their joy. The vibrant colors of Halloween decorations surrounding them contrasted sharply with the dullness she felt inside. Her contribution, "Maybe I could go as a ghost?" lacked the enthusiasm she usually poured into her creative endeavors, and even she could hear the flatness in her voice.

"A ghost?" Audrey frowned, trying to infuse some joy into the moment. "You could be so much more creative! Remember the zombie cheerleader? Everyone loved that!"

"Yeah," Kendra replied, a wave of nostalgia washing over her, "but that seems so… childish now." The memories felt distant, overshadowed by an oppressive weight that made even the simplest choices seem heavy. "Everything feels different. Even picking a costume has weight to it."

Jane's voice cut through the tension, strong and determined. "We need to take back Halloween! A spooky costume party is the perfect way to defy fear!" Her words breathed a flicker of hope into Kendra's heart, like a light piercing through the dense fog of anxiety. Kendra admired Jane's spirit, feeling a pull toward her friend's enthusiasm and the idea of reclaiming something that felt lost. But the flicker was weak, dwarfed by the shadows that loomed in her mind.

After their group parted ways, Kendra trudged toward her next class, her feet dragging as if weighted by invisible chains. She could sense the pervasive dread that gripped the campus, conversations wrapped tightly around concerns of safety rather than studying. Where midterms had once been the biggest fear, survival dominated their thoughts. The usual camaraderie among students shifted into hushed conversations filled with worry, and she felt herself becoming part of a collective anxiety that pressed heavily on her chest.

The class passed in a blur, Kendra's focus drifting as she attended to morbid thoughts and the incessant tapping of her pen. Professor Thompson's earlier words, meant to be reassuring, reverberated ominously in her mind. "Stay vigilant, keep safe, and remember that we are all in this together," he had said, but Kendra couldn't shake the feeling that the darkness surrounding them was a predator, lurking just out of sight, waiting for its chance to strike. Could they navigate through this dark cloud? Or would it consume them?

That evening, as the sun dipped below the horizon, Kendra walked back to her dorm, the sunset casting long shadows over the campus. She pulled her jacket tighter, wishing it could shield her from the chill of autumn and the cold dread creeping into her chest. Each footfall was pronounced against the hushed backdrop, her heart quickening at the rustling leaves and distant laughter. It was as if the world around her was celebrating while she stood frozen, caught in a web of fear.

Approaching the student union, the bright lights and lively sounds attempted to embrace her, but for Kendra, the tension coiled tighter within. The Reaper's fear loomed large, eclipsing the warmth Halloween usually offered. Upon entering, she was enveloped by the festive spirit, with students sharing hot cocoa, laughter, and stories, yet it felt like a thin mask hiding the dread and uncertainty beneath.

"Hey, Kendra! Just in time!" Audrey waved her over, standing at the hot chocolate station, where the cheerful scent of cinnamon and pumpkin filled the air. The warmth of the gathering drew her in, but Kendra felt as if she was standing on the edge of a cliff, looking down into an abyss.

"Yeah, just busy with everything," Kendra replied, her heart heavy. She forced a small smile, the stirrings of hope only a whisper against her anxiety.

As the evening unfolded, they spoke of the party at the Old Oak House, an event filled with tradition and camaraderie. “We’re going to bring the spirit back this Halloween! The haunted house is a tradition, and I refuse to let this Reaper ruin it!” Jane's passion infused the room, rousing something in Kendra. The familiar thrill of Halloween began to tug at her heart, battling against the heavy shadows that sought to keep her grounded in fear.

Admiring Jane's courage, Kendra felt a flicker of resolve. “Count me in. Let’s make it great,” she said, ignoring the whispers of fear that battled her determination. Little by little, Kendra found herself getting drawn into the preparations, despite the omnipresent shadow of dread. It felt like a fragile lifeline, and she clung to it.

In the days leading up to Halloween, the campus buzzed with activity. Students transformed dorms into haunted havens, crafted intricate costumes, and shared plans for the haunted house that would serve as the backdrop for the festivities. Social media exploded with images of ghoulish creations and clever costumes, a feeble rebellion against the darkness encroaching on their community. Yet Kendra's anxiety remained a constant companion, especially as night fell and shadows stretched ominously across the campus.

The night before Halloween brought an unexpected chill. Kendra and her friends gathered for a costume reveal party at the student union, unity masked by the laughter and energy of their peers. The atmosphere was electric, with everyone dressed as frightful creatures for the "Monster Mash" theme. Kendra donned a hauntingly beautiful vampire costume that echoed her inner turmoil, trying to outshine the fear that threatened to overtake her.

As the night enveloped them, Jane stood up with her glass, ready to make a toast. "To Halloween and to us—fear won't win!" Cheers erupted around them, momentarily lifting Kendra's spirits. She felt a sense of belonging wash over her, but just as quickly, it dimmed; the memory of the Reaper flickered at the edge of her thoughts, casting a shadow over the joy.

Then her heart dropped as she felt her phone vibrate—another student reported missing. The word "Reaper" leaped out at her from the screen, robbing her of breath as anxious whispers spread through the crowd. The festive energy around her grew muted, laughter fading into a subdued murmur of concern. It felt as if a chill swept through the crowd, replacing the warmth of camaraderie with a palpable tension.

Determined now, Kendra rallied the group. "Let's check in with the campus police," she suggested urgently, her voice rising above the stillness. Together they made their way across campus, the clamor of the party echoing behind them, but the laughter felt distant, muted by the weight of their mission.

Outside the gym, they stumbled upon another group being escorted by security. Fear pooled in Kendra's gut as she met their worried expressions. There were murmurs of "not again" and "what's going on?" Danger was drawing near, palpable in the cool air. The weight of their fear pressed down on her, and she could feel the dread rising in her throat, threatening to choke her.

Yet within the chaos ignited a defiance. Despite the looming dark, Kendra pressed forward, knowing that if they held onto each other and the spirit of the holiday, the Reaper would never extinguish their resolve. Arriving at the campus safety building, her heart raced, battling fear as she caught the determination etched on her friends' faces. They were all in this together, and together they had to face the storm.

"Let's conquer our fears," Kendra murmured as they collectively steeled themselves, stepping into the dimly lit building. Uncertainty clung to them, yet warmth radiated from their solidarity—this was their strength against the chill of fear that had tried to claim them. They found the campus police on high alert, officers discussing recent events in hushed tones, their faces grave and concerned.

"Can we help?" Kendra found herself asking, her voice steady yet filled with urgency. The officers turned to her group, their expressions shifting from surprise to understanding.

"Stay vigilant," one officer advised, his tone serious. "We are doing everything we can, but we need you all to stay safe. Please report any suspicious activity immediately." Kendra nodded, her resolve hardening. They were not just victims; they were part of a community that had the power to fight back.

As they left the safety building, Kendra felt a rush of adrenaline. The fear that had wrapped around her heart began to loosen its grip. Together, they vowed to reclaim their Halloween, to show the Reaper they were not afraid. They were a community, woven together by friendship and resilience—a force too strong to be broken.

In the days leading up to Halloween, Kendra and her friends worked tirelessly to make the Old Oak House event a success. They spent hours crafting decorations, setting up spooky props, and creating an atmosphere that would draw people in. With each task, Kendra felt her spirits lift; the weight of anxiety was replaced by the thrill of creativity. Together, they transformed the house into a haunting wonderland, filled with cobwebs, flickering lights, and eerie sound effects that echoed through the halls.

As Halloween night finally arrived, Kendra stood at the entrance of the Old Oak House, her heart pounding with anticipation. The heavy doors creaked open, revealing the lively party inside. Students bustled about in costumes, laughter and music blending into a cacophony of joy. Kendra's friends gathered around her, their costumes a vivid display of creativity and fun.

"Look at everyone!" Audrey exclaimed, her eyes sparkling with excitement. "This is amazing!"

Kendra couldn't help but smile as she took in the scene: the energy of celebration coursing through the air, washing away the shadows that had haunted them for so long. She felt a sense of belonging, a hope that perhaps they could turn the tide against the darkness.

"Let's go mingle!" Jane suggested, grabbing Kendra's hand and pulling her into the throng of students. Kendra felt the warmth of her friends surrounding her, and for the first time in weeks, she allowed herself to embrace the moment. They danced, laughed, and shared stories, and as the night progressed, Kendra felt her anxiety begin to melt away.

But as midnight approached, the mood shifted. A shrill scream pierced the air, cutting through the revelry like a knife. Kendra's heart dropped as all eyes turned to the source of the commotion. A group of students stood huddled together, panic etched across their faces.

"What happened?" Kendra asked, her voice shaking.

"Someone's been attacked!" a girl cried, her eyes wide with fear. "They found a body in the woods!"

The joy of Halloween evaporated in an instant, replaced by a thick blanket of dread. Kendra's heart raced as she exchanged horrified glances with her friends. The Reaper was not just a story; it was a living nightmare that had come to claim their Halloween.

"Stay close!" Josh shouted, his voice cutting through the chaos. "We need to stick together!"

As they huddled together, Kendra could feel the fear radiating from her friends, but she also felt a flicker of defiance. "We won't let fear control us," she said, her voice steady despite the turmoil inside. "We have to stay strong."

In that moment, Kendra realized that their unity was their greatest weapon against the darkness. They were a community, and they would face whatever came next together. As they made their way back to the safety of the campus, Kendra held onto that thought like a lifeline. They had reclaimed their Halloween for a moment, and even in the face of terror, they would continue to fight for their spirit, their joy, and their lives.

Tomorrow would bring new challenges, but for now, they had

each other. They may have been surrounded by shadows, but they were determined to face the Reaper head-on, armed with friendship and courage. Together, they would find a way to turn fear into strength, and reclaim their community from the grip of darkness. And as they walked into the night, Kendra felt a spark of hope rekindle within her—a promise that they would not let fear extinguish their light.

Chapter 9

As the vibrant energy of the party surged around her, Jane's gaze settled on Danny, who sat alone in a shadowy corner, seemingly adrift in the sea of revelry. A mischievous smile tugged at her lips, and she felt an irresistible urge to pull him into the whirlwind of laughter and music that enveloped the room. The wings of her costume fluttered with anticipation as she glided over, her heart racing with the thrill of the moment. “Hey, Dan,” she purred, her voice a playful melody against the backdrop of the festivities. The playful glint in her eyes was infectious, promising adventures that lingered just beyond the horizon. “Why don’t we head upstairs and take this party to a whole new level of fun?”

Danny looked up, his eyebrows arching in curiosity, a spark igniting in his blue eyes that mirrored her own excitement. "Upstairs?" he echoed, intrigue evident in his tone. "What's up there?" His grin widened, reflecting a mix of anticipation and the thrill of the unknown.

"Oh, you'll see," Jane replied coyly, her voice laced with mystery. The invitation hung in the air between them, charged with a sense of possibility. While the rest of the partygoers reveled in the chaos below—laughter spilling over, glasses clinking, and the rhythmic beat of music pulsating through the air—Jane and Danny stood on the precipice of an entirely different kind of adventure.

Dressed in a playful police officer's uniform that sparkled under the dim lights, complete with a twinkling badge and a cap slightly askew, Jane radiated an aura of mischief that was impossible to resist. She leaned closer to Danny, her breath whispering against his cheek, igniting a flame of anticipation within him. He was clad in a snug hockey player's uniform, its fabric accentuating his athletic build, a perfect embodiment of the party's playful spirit.

In that electric moment, unable to resist the chemistry swirling between them, Jane captured Danny's lips with her own. The kiss started softly, exploratory, but quickly deepened, passion surging between them like a tidal wave. They melted into one another, the chaos of the party fading away, swallowed by a haze of longing and desire that enveloped them.

With a subtle shift, they moved together toward the staircase, fingers intertwined, their laughter punctuating the rapid rhythm of their hearts. Each step drew them closer to the private room that promised an escape from the vibrant celebration below, a sanctuary where they could explore the connection that had ignited so unexpectedly. They reached the door, breaths quickening, anticipation hanging thick in the air like an unspoken promise.

Jane glanced back at Danny, a sly smile gracing her lips, her heart racing with excitement. "Ready?" she asked, her eyes sparkling with mischief as she pushed open the door, revealing a dimly lit sanctuary that seemed to pulse with the energy of their shared anticipation.

"More than ready," he replied, his voice low and filled with a mixture of excitement and longing. They entered the room and swiftly closed and locked the door behind them, sealing off the outside world, cocooning themselves in a space that felt charged with magic and potential.

Inside, the atmosphere was intimate, shadows flickering across the walls, creating a cocoon of warmth that invited exploration. As they locked eyes, the moment was electric; Danny felt a thrill shoot through him as Jane playfully pushed him onto the plush bed that occupied the center of the room. The fabric was soft beneath them, contrasting with the intensity of the feelings swirling in the air.

Jane joined him, her presence intoxicating, wrapping them in a warmth that blanketed the outside noise. As their lips found each other once more, the world around them blurred completely. Each kiss became a punctuation to their unspoken desires, their bodies pressing together, igniting a magnetic pull that felt undeniably powerful. The playful banter from earlier transformed into an intoxicating dance of longing, each movement resonating with a rhythm uniquely their own.

Their hands roamed eagerly, exploring the unfamiliar terrain of each other's bodies, sharing soft gasps and teasing whispers. They were creating a symphony that resonated solely for the two of them, a melody woven from the threads of their shared excitement and burgeoning desire. Gradually, they began to shed their costumes, indulging in the thrill of vulnerability. Fabric glided off, leaving behind vestiges of a themed party; Jane's uniform slipped away like whispers in the wind, and Danny's protective pads fell to the floor, the remnants of their costumes now a world away.

As they nestled against each other, skin against skin, the external music faded completely, replaced solely by the cadence of their shared heartbeat. Jane traced her fingers along Danny's jawline, exploring the contours of his face with tender reverence. He responded with a feather-light caress of her wing, enveloping her in an embrace of admiration that sent electric shivers down her spine.

"Wow, you're stunning," he breathed, holding her gaze, the innocence of their playful interactions evolving into something raw and intense. The vulnerability they shared only deepened the connection, as if they were two souls dancing in perfect harmony, unafraid to explore the depths of their desire.

"So are you," she whispered back, a teasing smile playing on her lips. Their flirtation deepened, rich with unspoken promises, as they pulled each other closer, the energy surrounding them becoming almost a living thing, alive with possibility.

With a playful shove, Jane pushed Danny onto his back, climbing over him with a laughter that rang like a sweet melody. It was a sound that intertwined seamlessly with the rhythm of their exchanged breaths as she straddled him, her eyes glinting with mischief. Danny smirked up at her, invigorated by this shift in their dynamic, feeling the rush of adrenaline coursing through him.

"Okay, officer," he chuckled, his voice teasing, "what's the charge for being too sexy?"

Leaning down, her lips brushed against his ear as she whispered conspiratorially, "Obstruction of fun." Her breath danced over his skin, igniting delightful shivers that rippled through him, setting his senses ablaze.

In response, Danny pulled her closer, hands gripping her waist with possessive urgency that sent thrilling shivers through them both. “In that case,” he murmured, his voice low with playful intensity, “I’ll have to resist arrest, won’t I?”

With that, the tension snapped, and they found themselves lost in a whirlwind of movement. Entwined, they melded together, passion sparking into an inferno that threatened to consume them. The bed creaked under the weight of their fervor, each sound echoing their electrifying connection, amplifying the energy that radiated between them.

As they moved together, breaths mingling and synchronizing in perfect harmony, nothing else mattered. Time ceased to exist within the four walls of their private sanctuary. They were enveloped in a cocoon of intimacy, delving into uncharted territory, each kiss drawing them deeper into a world of shared desire. The outside world faded into a distant memory, the laughter and music from the party below becoming a mere echo, overshadowed by the symphony of their bodies entwined.

Intervals of laughter and gasps punctuated their exploration, moments of playful teasing intertwined with fervent embraces. It was exhilarating—a sweet symphony of intimacy that brought them closer than they had imagined possible. They shared secrets in whispers, their words mingling with the soft sounds of their breaths, each syllable an invitation to explore further, deeper.

Eventually, they slowed, pursuing a more leisurely rhythm, basking in the warmth of their connection. Jane laid her head against Danny's chest, cherishing the feel of his heartbeat beneath her cheek, a steady drum that matched the cadence of their newfound intimacy. They exchanged soft smiles, laughter bubbling up as they savored the afterglow of their shared adventure, the world outside forgotten.

"Guess we really did take the party to a whole new level," Danny teased, fingers brushing gently through her hair, a contented sigh escaping him as he reveled in the intimacy of the moment.

Jane chuckled softly, peering up at him with sparkling eyes. "And there's still more fun to be had." The promise of mischief lingered in the air between them, a tantalizing invitation to continue their exploration of each other's hearts and bodies.

With renewed excitement, they curled into each other, reveling in the warmth and intimacy of the moment. Outside, the party continued thumping away, blissfully unaware of the magic blossoming just a few feet away. For Jane and Danny, this was their world—one filled with laughter, thrill, and an undeniable connection that would linger long after the festivities had faded.

As they settled into the embrace of the moment, they knew that this night, sparked by a simple invitation, would forever echo in their memories. It became a beautiful hall of whimsical musings, gaming and dancing, forming the foundation for whatever lay ahead. The possibilities were endless, their connection undeniable, and both were eager to explore where this spontaneous adventure would lead them next.

The narrative unfolded like a tapestry woven with threads of desire, playfulness, and unexpected intimacy. What began as a playful invitation transformed into a whirlwind of passion and connection, showcasing the magnetic pull between Jane and Danny. As they ventured into uncharted territory, shedding inhibitions and embracing vulnerability, they discovered a shared longing that transcended the chaos of the party below.

Their playful banter and flirtation evolved into a dance of longing and exhilaration, culminating in a moment of shared intimacy that enveloped them in a private sanctuary of desire. Each kiss, each touch, deepened their connection, creating a bond that felt both exhilarating and profound.

As they found solace in each other's arms, their laughter mingling with gasps of pleasure, they marveled at the depth of their newfound connection. In the aftermath of their passionate encounter, they reveled in the warmth of their intimacy, savoring the closeness that had blossomed unexpectedly between them.

Looking ahead to the future, Jane and Danny knew that this night would be etched in their memories as a pivotal moment—a shared adventure that laid the foundation for what lay ahead. United by a spark of excitement and a daring sense of adventure, they were eager to explore the boundless possibilities that awaited them on the horizon, ready to embrace whatever life had in store.

Chapter 9: A Night of Unforeseen Adventures (Continued)

As they found solace in each other's arms, their laughter mingling with gasps of pleasure, they marveled at the depth of their newfound connection. In the aftermath of their passionate encounter, they reveled in the warmth of their intimacy, savoring the closeness that had blossomed unexpectedly between them.

Danny's fingers continued to trail along Jane's skin, each caress igniting sparks of electricity that danced between them. The playful banter that had characterized their earlier interactions faded into a comfortable silence, punctuated only by the rhythm of their breathing. They were cocooned in this moment, a world apart from the festivities raging downstairs. Here, the outside noise was merely a distant echo, a reminder of a life that felt both thrilling and irrelevant compared to the magic they had discovered together.

"What do you think everyone is doing right now?" Danny asked softly, breaking the silence, glancing toward the door as if imagining the chaos still unfolding below. His voice was low, almost hesitant, as if he were reluctant to disrupt the fragile intimacy they had created.

Jane smiled, the corners of her lips curling upward as she met his gaze. "Probably trying to figure out where we disappeared to," she replied playfully, her tone light but laced with a deeper sincerity. "Or maybe they're just getting into even more trouble without us." The laughter that bubbled up from her felt warm and infectious, igniting a playful glint in Danny's eyes.

"Trouble has a way of finding people, doesn't it?" he remarked, a teasing smirk crossing his lips. "Especially when you're around." The spark in his gaze deepened as he leaned closer, the familiar pull of attraction swirling between them once more.

Jane's heart raced at the intimacy of the moment. "Oh, I'll take that as a compliment," she quipped, her voice teasing. "Just think of all the fun we could be missing out on if we stayed down there."

"Fun, huh?" Danny mused, his expression thoughtful. "But is all that fun worth it compared to what we have here?" He gestured around the room, encompassing the soft glow of the lamps, the plush bed beneath them, and the lingering warmth of their connection.

She bit her lip, a wave of tenderness washing over her. "You're right," she admitted, her tone softening. "There's something special about this—about us. It's like we've created our own little world up here."

Danny's gaze softened, and he brushed a strand of hair behind her ear, his fingers lingering on her cheek. "I didn't expect this night to turn into something so incredible," he confessed, sincerity radiating from him. "But I'm glad it did."

They locked eyes, sharing a moment of silent understanding, a bond forming that felt as fragile as it was powerful. The chemistry between them was palpable, a magnetic force drawing them closer, urging them to explore the depths of their desire and connection.

With a playful shove, Jane pushed Danny onto his back again, her laughter ringing out like a sweet melody. "Okay, let's not forget the fun part," she challenged, her eyes gleaming with mischief. "I believe you owe me a dance, officer."

"Is that so?" he replied, a grin spreading across his face, the playful spirit igniting once more. "Well, I'm not one to back down from a challenge."

With a swift motion, Danny pulled Jane back toward him, their lips crashing together in a fervent kiss that reignited the flames of passion between them. As they kissed, he began to sway them gently, leading an unchoreographed dance that felt both exhilarating and intimate.

Jane matched his movements, their bodies swaying in perfect harmony, the rhythm of their hearts syncing as they lost themselves in the moment. Each kiss was a step, each caress a twirl, and they danced through the warmth of their shared intimacy, laughter punctuating the air as they reveled in the joy of being together.

As they continued to sway, the laughter faded, replaced by the soft melodies of their breaths mingling. The dance transformed into something deeper—an exploration of connection that transcended the physical. They gazed into each other's eyes, the world around them fading away until it was just the two of them in a shared sanctuary of warmth and desire.

"Wow," Jane breathed, pulling back slightly to catch her breath, her cheeks flushed with a mix of exhilaration and affection. "I didn't think dancing could feel like this."

Danny chuckled softly, brushing his thumb along her jawline, his gaze unwavering. "It's not just the dancing; it's you. You make everything feel alive."

Her heart fluttered at his words, the sincerity in his eyes igniting a spark of warmth within her. "And you make me feel… seen," she replied, honesty threading through her voice. "I've never felt this way with anyone before."

"Neither have I," he admitted, his expression earnest. "I didn't know a night could change everything, but here we are."

As they shared this moment of vulnerability, the connection deepened, entwining them in a web of emotions that felt both thrilling and safe. They were explorers of each other's hearts, navigating the uncharted waters of their desires, fears, and hopes.

With a playful grin, Jane leaned in closer, her lips brushing against

Danny's ear as she whispered, “So, what’s next on our adventure?”

Danny's eyes sparkled with mischief, a playful smirk dancing on his lips. “I think we should create our own fun. Let’s make this night unforgettable.”

With that, the energy shifted once more, sparking a new wave of excitement between them. They sprang up from the bed, laughter filling the air as they began to explore the room—pushing boundaries, sharing secrets, and creating memories that would last far beyond the confines of the night.

In this private haven, they filled the space with playful antics and shared dreams, their laughter echoing against the walls, a symphony of joy that would be etched in their memories forever. As the night wore on, they were less like partygoers and more like two adventurers, united by a shared sense of daring and discovery.

"Let's see what else we can find," Jane suggested, her eyes sparkling with exhilaration. "Maybe there's something hidden in here waiting for us."

Danny raised an eyebrow, intrigued. "Like a treasure hunt?"

"Exactly! Who knows what mysteries this room holds?" she exclaimed, her excitement infectious.

With a shared sense of curiosity, they began to rummage through drawers and cabinets, unearthing forgotten trinkets and playful mementos. Each discovery was met with laughter and playful teasing, their camaraderie blossoming amidst the spontaneity of the night.

As they delved deeper into the exploration, they stumbled upon a forgotten record player tucked away in the corner. "Look at this!" Danny exclaimed, his eyes lighting up with nostalgia. "We have to see if it still works."

Jane watched with delight as he dusted off the vintage machine, his enthusiasm drawing her in. "Do you think it plays some classic tunes?"

"Only one way to find out," he replied, his fingers deftly setting it up. As the record began to spin, the warm crackle of music filled the room, enveloping them in a cozy ambiance that felt timeless.

With a laugh, Jane took Danny's hand, pulling him closer as they swayed to the rhythm of the music, the soft melodies wrapping around them like a warm embrace. The world outside faded further, leaving only the two of them, dancing in their own universe.

"This is perfect," Jane whispered, her gaze locked onto Danny's, the connection between them glowing brighter than ever.

"Just wait until we find our secret dance moves," he teased, twirling her playfully, inviting her into the dance once more.

With a burst of laughter, they embraced the music, their bodies moving in sync, a beautiful blend of spontaneity and grace. They spun and twirled, lost in each other, the night stretching out before them like a canvas waiting to be painted with memories.

As the music played on, they danced without inhibitions, their laughter echoing against the walls, creating a tapestry of joy that would linger long after the night had faded. The adventures they had embarked on together were only just beginning, and they were ready to explore every facet of this newfound connection.

"Let's make a pact," Jane declared breathlessly after a particularly exuberant spin. "No matter what happens tonight, let's promise to always embrace the unexpected."

Danny's smile widened, his heart swelling at her words. "I promise," he replied, his voice filled with sincerity. "Whatever comes our way, we'll face it together."

With a shared understanding, they solidified their pact in a gentle kiss, their lips brushing softly against each other, sealing their promise.

As the night wore on, they continued to dance and laugh, the budding romance between them growing stronger with each passing moment. They had crossed a threshold, stepping into a world of possibilities where their connection could flourish, unfettered by the chaos of the outside world.

In that room, with music painting the air and laughter echoing around them, Jane and Danny discovered more than just a fleeting romance; they uncovered a bond that would shape their lives in ways they had yet to comprehend.

This night, fueled by spontaneity and the thrill of adventure, would be the foundation of a journey that promised to be filled with laughter, love, and endless exploration—together.

Chapter 10

Detective Harris stood at the front of the dimly lit room, arms crossed tightly over his chest, his expression a mix of frustration and deep concern. The atmosphere was thick with anxiety as the group of friends—Jane, Danny, Kendra, and Josh—listened intently, hearts pounding with the weight of his words. The news of the new killer, the one who donned the infamous ghost face mask, sent icy chills racing down their spines, igniting a primal fear that they couldn't shake. Harris's warning had a stark finality to it, underscoring the chilling reality that they were not just bystanders in this story; they were potential targets.

"This killer is different," Harris reiterated, his voice low but firm, reverberating through the silence of the room. He glanced around at the anxious faces, aware of the rising tension and the way it coiled around them like a snake preparing to strike. "They know what they're doing, and they don't care about the fallout. Bloodshed, fear, panic—it's all part of the game for them. This is a methodical predator, and it's only a matter of time before they strike again."

As his words sank in, Kendra bit her lip, glancing around at her friends, her eyes reflecting the growing panic. "What do we do now? We can't just sit here and wait to be picked off, right? We need a plan." Her voice trembled slightly, underscoring the urgency of the moment.

Danny, ever the pragmatist, nodded in agreement. "We need to stay together. Strength in numbers.

If this killer is out there, we can't let our guard down. We'll keep a close eye on each other." His voice was steady, but beneath it lay an undercurrent of anxiety that mirrored the fears swirling in the room.

Josh, trying to lighten the mood despite the morbid conversation, chuckled lightly. "Yeah, because who doesn't love being a part of some old-school horror movie? If we stick together, we'll be like the characters who figure things out just in time to avoid the axe—or in this case, the knife." His attempt at humor fell flat, met with uneasy laughter and hesitant smiles, but the weight of their predicament loomed larger than any joke could dispel.

Jane remained silent, her mind racing with the implications of their situation. They had spent countless nights discussing horror movies and thrilling plots, relishing the escapism that came with the genre. But this was reality—a stark contrast to the cinematic fantasies they adored. It was hard to maintain a façade of normalcy when a killer could be lurking nearby, waiting to strike.

As the sun climbed higher in the sky, casting a warm glow that felt out of place amidst their somber conversation, the group made a collective decision to attend their psychic class. It was an unusual distraction—a way to momentarily escape the heavy dread that had settled in their chests. The class was a weekly ritual, an odd mix of spirituality and curiosity that had always provided them with a sense of community and comfort.

They filtered into the classroom, the familiar scent of incense and old books wrapping around them like a comforting embrace. But as they took their seats, a sense of unease lingered in the air. To their surprise, Audrey was missing. At first, they thought little of it; she often arrived late, lost in her own world or preoccupied with her artistic pursuits. But as the start of class approached and the instructor began to speak, concern began to creep in.

"Have any of you heard from Audrey?" Kendra asked, her voice laced with worry that echoed through the room. The others exchanged glances, shaking their heads in unison.

"No, I thought she'd be here with us," Josh replied, his brow furrowed. “Maybe she’s caught up with something?”

“Or maybe she’s just being Audrey,” Danny suggested, attempting to dismiss the worry. “You know how she can be.” His tone was light, but Jane could see the concern etched on his face.

But Jane looked unconvinced, her intuition prickling at the back of her mind. The unsettling tension that had gripped them since the announcement of the ghost face killer loomed larger than ever. “Maybe we should check on her after class. I don’t like this…” Her voice trailed off, a hint of fear creeping in.

The psychic class unfolded around them while anxiety simmered just beneath the surface. Each warm flash of conversation about old films felt unnaturally bright against the dark reality hovering over everyone. Laughter bubbled up when their instructor brought up classic horror flicks, connecting the students to a history that felt both nostalgic and haunting.

"The brilliance of these films," the instructor said, a glint of excitement in her eyes, "lies in how they tap into our primal fears. They make us confront what we cannot control or understand—like the unknown that lurks in darkened corners of our lives."

Kendra raised her hand, her gaze contemplative as she eyed her classmates. "That's why we love them, isn't it? But what about the real fear out there? The kind we're facing right now?" Her question resonated in the silence that followed, the atmosphere shifting as the reality of their situation washed over them.

The room fell silent, the weight of their circumstances palpable. The words hung heavy in the air like a fog that refused to lift. They couldn't escape the reality that they might one day become characters in a horror story—a very different narrative than the one they had always discussed with playful enthusiasm.

Once class ended, the group agreed to break away and start searching for Audrey. The lighthearted chatter faded as they navigated through shadows, feelings of dread coiling around them tighter with each passing minute.

"Danny, check her apartment," Jane suggested as they stepped out onto the sidewalk, the cold air slicing through the remnants of warmth from the classroom. “Kendra and I can go to the café she likes.”

Josh nodded, his apprehension palpable. “I’ll drive around the neighborhood. We need to find her before it’s too late.” The group dispersed, each of them burdened with an unshakeable feeling—an uninvited sense of urgency gnawing at their stomachs.

As Danny approached Audrey's building, he felt the oppressive silence that had enveloped the town. The streets, usually filled with chatter and laughter, felt eerily empty. Something was wrong.

Knocking urgently on her door, Danny’s heart raced as he called her name. “Audrey?” he ventured cautiously into the dimly lit space. The apartment was a reflection of Audrey's personality—cluttered with eclectic books, art supplies, and films stacked on every available surface. It felt like a sanctuary, but today it was heavy with an unsettling stillness.

"Audrey? Are you here?" he ventured deeper inside, anxiety tightening his chest.

The silence echoed back at him, making his skin prickle. As he examined the living room, he noticed a few scattered items on the couch—the remnants of a hurriedly abandoned project. A sketchbook lay open, pages fluttering slightly as if someone had just been there. But no sign of Audrey. Panic surged within him, and he raced back to meet up with Jane and Kendra.

Meanwhile, Jane and Kendra arrived at the café, scanning the familiar place filled with a hum of activity. Patrons chatted over coffee and pastries, the cheerful atmosphere feeling surreal given their current concerns. "Could she be sitting somewhere?" Kendra wondered aloud as they moved through the bustling crowd, the sound of laughter ringing hollow in their ears.

As they reached the back, they found an empty table—their eyes darted around in search of any sign of their friend. "Let's check the bathroom," Jane suggested, her resolve hardening. Just as they were about to leave, their phones buzzed with a message from Josh. "No sign of her. Keep looking."

Kendra felt the weight of dread press down on her. “What if she’s in trouble? What if—”

“Don’t think like that,” Jane shot back, trying to remain calm. “We need to stay focused. We’ll find her.”

Just as Kendra was about to respond, a loud crash came from beyond the café's glass doors. They rushed outside to see Josh sprinting toward them, his face pale as he struggled to catch his breath.

“Josh, what happened?” Jane exclaimed.

“It’s Audrey,” he gasped, finally managing to find his voice. “I saw her car in the alley behind that old movie theater. It's abandoned.”

Kendra felt her heart drop. "What do you mean?"

Josh gestured wildly, panic rimmed in his voice. "I don't know. Someone's—someone's been in there. I called the police, but I didn't want to wait. I thought… I thought maybe she was in trouble…"

The mention of danger triggered a primal instinct within them as the group reconvened, faces drawn and focus honed. They raced toward the old theater, each step echoing a growing realization of the terror they were tangled in.

As they approached the theater, its dilapidated façade loomed large, a haunting reminder of its once vibrant past. Flickering lights and overgrown vines told stories of abandonment, and the air felt heavy with tension. The reality of the situation pressed painfully against them as they stepped inside, the dim light revealing a cavernous space filled with shadows that seemed to writhe and shift.

Audrey, once the bold and adventurous friend, was now their missing piece, and they were determined to find her before the foretold horror unfolded. Each heartbeat was a countdown—a chilling reminder that they were not just echoes of figures from frightening films, but real people facing a nightmare.

The inside of the theater was eerily quiet, the kind of silence that amplifies every tiny sound. They stood at the entrance, eyes adjusting to the dark, taking in the rows of empty seats and the dusty stage ahead. A sense of dread settled over them, and they exchanged worried glances, each one reflecting the fear that gripped their hearts.

"Let's split up," Danny suggested, his voice steady despite the fear in his eyes. "We'll cover more ground that way. Just... keep your phones on and stay in touch."

Kendra nodded, her expression serious. "We need to find her quickly. I don't like this place."

Josh glanced around, his eyes narrowing. "If anything feels off, we regroup immediately. No heroics."

The group split up, each taking a different path through the theater. Danny felt the weight of the silence pressing down on him as he ventured toward the backstage area, his heart pounding in his chest. The corridor was dimly lit, the flickering bulbs casting unsettling shadows along the walls.

As he stepped cautiously, he could hear the faint sound of his own breathing, echoing in the stillness, amplifying his sense of unease. The backstage area was cluttered with old props, costumes hanging limply from rusty racks, and remnants of past performances littering the floor. He moved deeper, calling out, "Audrey? Are you here?"

His voice bounced off the walls, swallowed by the darkness. There was no response, just the oppressive silence that seemed to mock his efforts. A sense of dread coiled in his stomach, and he urged himself to keep moving.

Meanwhile, Jane and Kendra made their way through the main auditorium, the rows of empty seats looming like silent sentinels. The atmosphere felt thick with memories of laughter and applause, twisted now into something sinister.

"Do you think she's hiding?" Kendra asked, her voice barely above a whisper.

"Maybe," Jane replied, her eyes scanning the room. "But why would she come here? It doesn't make sense."

As they moved toward the front of the theater, they reached the stage, glancing around in search of any sign of their friend. The shadows danced around them, and Jane felt a chill run down her spine. "We need to check the dressing rooms," she suggested, her voice steady despite the fear creeping in.

Kendra nodded, swallowing hard. "Let's go."

They approached the dressing rooms, the door slightly ajar, creaking ominously as they pushed it open. The small room was cluttered with old costumes and mirrors covered in dust, but there was no sign of Audrey. "Audrey?" Jane called out, her heart racing.

Suddenly, a loud crash echoed from the back of the theater, causing both girls to jump. They exchanged terrified glances before darting back into the main hallway, their hearts pounding in unison.

"Did you hear that?" Kendra gasped, her breath coming in quick bursts.

"Yeah, we need to find Danny and Josh," Jane said, urgency lacing her voice.

As they hurried back toward the entrance, Danny emerged from the backstage area, his expression tense. "What's going on? Did you find anything?"

"No, but I heard something crash," Kendra replied, her eyes darting around, scanning for any sign of danger.

"Josh!" Danny called out, his voice echoing through the empty theater. "Where are you?"

A moment later, Josh appeared, looking disheveled and out of breath. "I checked the lobby and the bathrooms. No sign of her. We have to figure out where she could be."

Panic surged through the group as they reconvened, each face reflecting fear and determination. "What if she's in trouble?" Jane said, her voice trembling. "What if the killer got to her?"

"We can't think like that," Danny said, trying to maintain control. "We have to stay focused. We need to search the entire building."

They nodded in agreement, the weight of their situation pressing down on them. As they prepared to split up again, a loud crash echoed from the rear of the theater, sending a jolt of fear through them.

"Did you hear that?" Josh exclaimed, eyes wide.

Danny's heart raced as he nodded. "We need to check it out. Stay close."

They moved cautiously toward the sound, hearts pounding in their chests as they approached the back of the theater. The air felt electric, charged with an unseen presence, and they couldn't shake the feeling that they were being watched.

As they rounded the corner, they found the source of the noise—a heavy prop had fallen from a shelf, crashing to the ground. But as they surveyed the area, a chilling realization hit them. The prop was positioned in front of a door that led to the theater's storage area.

"Someone's been here," Jane whispered, her voice shaking.

Danny stepped forward, heart racing as he reached for the doorknob. "Let's see what's inside."

He slowly opened the door, revealing a darkened storage room filled with dust-covered props and old equipment. The air was thick with the scent of mildew, and as he stepped inside, he felt a shiver run down his spine.

"Audrey?" he called, his voice echoing in the emptiness.

But there was no response. Just the oppressive silence that seemed to press in around them.

Suddenly, Kendra gasped, pointing to the far corner of the room. "Look!"

In the dim light, they could see a faint outline—a figure slumped against the wall. Panic surged through Danny as he rushed forward, his heart racing. "Audrey!" he shouted, fear gripping him as he reached her side.

She was unconscious, her body limp against the cold floor. Her clothes were slightly torn, and there were bruises forming on her arms. Danny knelt beside her, checking for a pulse, relief flooding through him as he felt the steady beat beneath his fingers.

"Is she okay?" Kendra asked, her voice shaking.

"I think so," Danny replied, his voice tense. "But we need to get her out of here."

Josh helped Danny lift Audrey's body, and they carefully maneuvered her back toward the exit. As they made their way through the darkened theater, an unsettling feeling gnawed at Danny's gut. They had to hurry—every moment felt like a countdown, and the shadows seemed to close in around them.

Just as they reached the exit, the sound of footsteps echoed behind them, sending a wave of terror crashing over them. "Go!" Danny shouted, urgency fueling his voice as they burst through the doors and into the cool night air.

They stumbled onto the street, breathless and terrified, the weight of their ordeal crashing over them like a tidal wave. Audrey was safe, but the threat was still out there, lurking in the shadows.

"Call for help!" Kendra shouted, her voice filled with panic as they rushed to the nearest streetlight, the illumination casting long shadows behind them.

Josh pulled out his phone, his hands shaking as he dialed for help. "I'm calling the police! We need an ambulance!"

Danny glanced around, his heart racing as he scanned the darkness. "We need to get somewhere safe. We can't stay out here."

They helped carry Audrey to the side of the road, the cool air brushing against her skin, and

Danny could see the faintest hint of color returning to her cheeks.

As they waited for help to arrive, they couldn't shake the feeling that the nightmare was far from over. The shadows loomed large, and they knew that they were now intertwined in a deadly game—a fight for survival against an unseen darkness lurking in the corners of their lives.

Each heartbeat echoed like a countdown, and as the sound of sirens filled the air, they understood that this was just the beginning of their struggle against the ghost face killer. They were no longer characters in a horror story; they were the protagonists of their own terrifying tale, and the stakes had never been higher. The doctor's words brought a surge of relief mixed with anxiety. "We're doing everything we can for her," he continued, his tone professional yet compassionate. "She suffered some bruising and appears to have a mild concussion. We're monitoring her closely, but I can't provide any specific updates until she regains consciousness."

Danny felt a knot loosen in his stomach, but the lingering tension remained. "Can we see her?" he asked, hope flickering in his chest.

The doctor hesitated, glancing back toward the hallway. "Right now, I need to keep her in a quiet environment. But I assure you, as soon as she's awake and stable, I will have someone inform you."

"Thank you," Kendra said, her voice soft but filled with gratitude. As the doctor walked away, the weight of uncertainty hung heavily in the air once more.

They settled back into their chairs, eyes darting to the hallway where Audrey had been taken. "What do we do now?" Josh asked, breaking the silence that had enveloped them once again. "We can't just sit here and wait."

"Maybe we should come up with a plan," Jane suggested, her voice steady despite the anxiety coursing through her. "We need to think about how we can protect ourselves moving forward."

Kendra nodded, her brow furrowed with concern. "What if the killer knows we're here? What if they come after us next?"

Danny leaned forward, his hands clasped tightly together. "We need to get in touch with the police. They need to know that we're potential targets, and we need their protection. We can't rely solely on the hospital staff to keep us safe."

Josh pulled out his phone and began scrolling through his contacts. "I'll call the police station and see if I can get an update. Maybe they have leads on this killer." He pressed the call button and put the phone to his ear, pacing the small waiting area as he spoke.

As Josh spoke to the officer on the other end, Danny felt a surge of urgency. He glanced at Kendra and Jane, who were deep in conversation about what measures they could take to stay safe. "We should also think about self-defense," he said, his voice firm. "If we're going to be targeted, we need to know how to protect ourselves."

Jane raised an eyebrow, her expression contemplative. "What do you mean? Like taking a self-defense class?"

"Exactly," Danny replied. "We can find a local class and take it together. If we're going to face this killer, we need to be prepared for anything. Plus, it'll give us some sense of control over our situation."

Kendra nodded slowly, her anxiety beginning to shift into determination. "That sounds like a good idea. We need to empower ourselves, not just sit back and wait for something to happen."

Josh ended his call, returning to the group with a furrowed brow. "The police said they're ramping up patrols in the area but don't have any new leads on the killer. They advised us to stay alert and report any suspicious activity."

"Great," Danny said, frustration creeping into his voice. "We need more than just patrols. We need a plan to keep us safe."

Just then, the doors to the waiting area swung open, and a nurse stepped in, her expression warm but serious. "Are you all friends of Audrey?" she asked, her voice soothing.

"Yes," they replied in unison, leaning forward slightly, anticipation filling the air.

"She's awake now and asking for you," the nurse said, a small smile breaking through her professionalism. "You can see her, but please keep it brief. She needs to rest."

A rush of relief washed over them as they stood up, the anxiety that had been clutching at their hearts beginning to ease. "Thank you!" Jane exclaimed, leading the way as they followed the nurse down the hallway.

As they entered the room, Danny's heart raced. Audrey lay in the hospital bed, her face pale but her eyes alert. The machines beeped steadily beside her, and she looked up at them, a small smile breaking through her weariness.

"Hey, guys," she said softly, her voice hoarse but filled with warmth. "I'm glad you're here."

"Audrey!" Kendra rushed to her side, placing a gentle hand on her arm. "We were so worried about you. What happened?"

Audrey winced slightly, trying to sit up. "I'm okay," she reassured them, though the tremor in her voice betrayed her. "I was just… in the wrong place at the wrong time."

"What do you mean?" Danny asked, concern etched across his face. "Did someone attack you?"

She took a deep breath, her gaze dropping to the blankets covering her legs. "I went to the theater to work on a project. I thought it would be a good place to get some inspiration. But I didn't realize how dangerous it had become. I felt someone watching me, and then…"

Josh leaned closer, his expression tense. "Then what happened?"

"I turned around, and there was someone there, wearing that mask," she said, her voice trembling slightly. "I don't remember much after that. Just the fear. I must have blacked out."

The room fell silent, the weight of her words settling heavily upon them. Danny felt a chill run down his spine, and Kendra's fingers tightened around Audrey's hand. "You're safe now, that's all that matters," she said, her voice steady despite the fear that lingered.

"But we need to take this seriously," Jane interjected, her tone firm. "This killer is targeting people, and we can't let our guard down. We need to figure out how to protect ourselves."

Audrey nodded slowly, a look of determination flickering in her eyes. "You're right. We can't let fear control us. We need to stand together."

As they exchanged glances, a sense of resolve began to settle over the group. They would not allow this killer to disrupt their lives further. They would fight back, together.

"After you're discharged, we should all take a self-defense class," Danny proposed, his voice filled with conviction. "It's important that we know how to protect ourselves, especially if this killer is watching us."

"Count me in," Josh said, his expression steely. "We'll be ready for whatever comes our way."

Kendra and Jane nodded in agreement, unwavering in their resolve. "We'll also keep in touch with the police and make sure they know we're not backing down," Kendra added.

Audrey smiled weakly, pride shining in her eyes. "I'm so grateful to have you all by my side. I couldn't have made it through this without you."

As they sat together in the hospital room, the sense of unity enveloped them, a protective shield against the darkness that loomed outside. They knew the battle wasn't over, but they were determined to face whatever came next, armed with knowledge, strength, and the unbreakable bond of friendship.

Hours passed, and the mundane sounds of the hospital faded into the background as they continued to discuss their plans. The doctor returned with updates on Audrey's condition, reassuring them that she would be fine but needed to stay overnight for observation.

As the sun began to set, casting a warm glow through the window, Danny felt a surge of determination course through him. They would not be victims. They would be warriors in their own right, ready to confront the shadows that threatened their lives.

With newfound purpose, they vowed to support each other through the chaos, embracing the power of their friendship to combat the darkness that sought to engulf them. Together, they would navigate the treacherous waters of fear and uncertainty, fighting for their safety and their lives.

As the night deepened, they knew that the path ahead would be fraught with challenges, but they were ready to face them head-on. The ghost face killer might be lurking in the shadows, but they were not alone. They were a united front, prepared to confront the horror that lay ahead. The fight for survival had only just begun, and they were determined to emerge victorious, no matter the cost.

Chapter 11

In the dimly lit corner of their favorite coffee shop, Jane, Danny, Josh, and Kendra huddled together, the vibrant laughter that usually filled the air now replaced by an oppressive silence. The only sounds were the clinking of cups and the soft grind of the espresso machine, each note amplifying the tension. Their minds swirled with worry for Audrey, who had mysteriously vanished just days prior. The shock of her disappearance sent tremors through their tight-knit group, stirring a storm of anxious possibilities.

Audrey was a radiant force; her laughter had the power to light up any room. The thought of her missing felt inconceivable, like a plot twist in a horror movie that no one wanted to witness. Kendra, typically the voice of reason, stared intently at her phone, her fingers tapping an impatient rhythm against the table. The furrow in her brow revealed thoughts spiraling into darker realms. "What if something dire has happened to her?" she wondered aloud, her voice barely above a whisper, as if the weight of her words might attract unwanted attention.

"Come on," Danny said, shaking his head in disbelief. "We don't know anything yet. She could just be off on some spontaneous adventure." His tone carried a thread of optimism, a fragile hope amidst their growing despair, but Kendra found it hard to grasp.

"But that's not like her at all," Jane interjected, emotion trembling her voice. "Audrey would never leave without telling at least one of us." With each passing moment, the shadows in the room deepened, and their sense of dread expanded.

Josh sat quietly, lost in thought, his gaze fixed on the street outside as if he might miraculously spot Audrey walking by. He could almost see her, her bright smile and carefree spirit lighting up the dreary day. "There must be a logical explanation," he suggested, though his voice was thin and unsure. "Maybe she got caught up in something unexpected." Yet even he struggled to convince himself; they all knew deep down that Audrey's absence was shrouded in mystery.

Suddenly, Kendra's phone buzzed, jolting them from their anxious reverie. The screen lit up with an alarming label: "Unknown Caller."

A wave of curiosity and dread washed over the group as they turned toward Kendra. Danny's eyes narrowed, skepticism written on his face, mirroring their collective unease. "You don't have to answer that. I mean, it's probably just a telemarketer or something."

"But what if it's about Audrey?" Kendra countered, the seriousness in her expression forcing the air to grow still. Inhaled deeply, battling her fear, she picked up the phone, her heart thudding violently in her chest. "Hello?" she said, striving for a composure she didn't feel.

A chilling, mechanical voice crackled through the line, devoid of warmth or empathy. "Hello, Kendra. How does it feel to be the star of the show?"

Kendra felt cold dread gripping her insides, the color draining from her cheeks. Danny's eyes widened, shock etching his features, while Jane gasped and gripped the edge of the table as if it might anchor her. Josh leaned in closer, straining to hear the unsettling exchange.

"Where is she?" Kendra demanded, her grip tightening on the phone as it pressed against her ear. Each tick of the wall clock echoed ominously in the background, amplifying the urgency.

The voice responded with frightening detachment. "You're going to go on a little treasure hunt. Bring the cops, and she dies. Get caught by anyone, and she dies."

Kendra felt as if the ground had fallen away beneath her. Her breath quickened, but something inside ignited a fierce resolve. "I'm going to find her, and then I'm going to find you, you sick son of a bitch," she shot back, defiance bursting through the fear clawing at her throat.

The voice merely chuckled, sending chills down her spine. "Your destruction will come very soon, Kendra. You don't want to see my face just yet. I'll ensure your life crumbles into pieces." With that, the line clicked dead, leaving her staring blankly at the screen as if it might provide answers.

In that moment, the weight of their situation became starkly real, the stakes higher than any of them had imagined. "What do we do now?"

Danny asked, his earlier bravado extinguished, unease transforming into palpable fear.

"I need to go," Kendra said, determination hardening her voice. "We can't waste any more time. This is about Audrey. I'll find the clues, whatever they are."

"Wait," Josh interjected, sliding forward in his seat. "We can't just rush in without a plan. We need to think this through." He looked at all of them, his eyes pleading for logic amidst the chaos.

But Kendra shook her head. Images of Audrey, trapped and frightened, swelled in her mind. "I'm not waiting. Every second counts. If we don't act now, we may lose her forever." Fire ignited in her eyes, fueled by desperation

—a catalyst that burned through their shared anxiety.

“Okay, okay,” Jane said, her voice shaky. “Let’s at least devise a strategy. What did the voice mean by 'treasure hunt'? Maybe tracking down clues could lead us to her.”

“It’s a game to him,” Danny spat, anger simmering just beneath the surface. “He wants to toy with us. But we have to play along if it means finding Audrey.”

The group fell into a tentative rhythm, mimicking their earlier playful banter, but now threaded with urgency and unease. “We should split up,” Kendra proposed, struggling to maintain her composure. “Each of us can check different areas. We can meet back here in an hour. We need to follow any lead we have.”

"No," Josh countered, concern knitting his brow. "We can't just separate. What if something happens to one of us? This guy sounds dangerous."

"He's right," Jane chimed in, seeking common ground. "If he's watching us, we can't let him know our plans. Splitting up might give us the best chance."

Kendra hesitated, the implications of facing the unknown alone weighing heavily on her. But she knew their only chance lay in speed, in action before time slipped further away. "Okay," she conceded finally, swallowing hard. "But we need to be discreet. No calls, no attention. Just...find the clues."

With a bolstered sense of purpose, they pulled their phones from their pockets, feverishly scanning for any recent messages from Audrey or connections who might help. They exchanged determined nods before heading to the door, each carrying the fragile hope that this would lead to something more than a cruel game.

Outside, the world felt different, tinged with an unfamiliar tension. Kendra took a steadying breath, the weight of the phone lingering in her grip. The streets stood before them like a labyrinth, fraught with potential and dangers unseen. As she set off down the block, her heartbeat quickened, mingling fear with fierce determination.

She could do this. They could do this. They had to. All thoughts of how obtruded in the urgency of the moment. In her mind, she focused solely on finding Audrey and unraveling the dark web enclosing her friend.

The Search Begins

As Kendra walked briskly down the street, the cool evening air brushed against her skin, but it couldn't chill the fire of determination burning within her. She glanced over her shoulder, half-expecting to see the ghost face lurking behind her, but the street was empty, bathed in the soft glow of streetlights. She steeled herself, knowing that fear could not dictate her actions.

Danny, Jane, and Josh split off in different directions, each determined to follow any lead they could find. Kendra had decided to head toward the old movie theater where Audrey had gone before her disappearance, believing it might hold the key to understanding what had happened. The theater was shrouded in mystery, its once-vibrant facade now crumbling and overgrown with weeds, a reflection of the chaos that had enveloped their lives.

As Kendra approached the theater, her heart raced. The darkness that clung to the building felt suffocating, and she hesitated at the entrance, the weight of uncertainty pressing against her chest. Gathering her courage, she stepped inside, the door creaking loudly in the silence. The interior was dimly lit, dust motes floating in the air, illuminated by the faint light filtering through the cracked windows.

She pulled out her phone, its screen glowing softly in the dark. “If I can just find something, anything that gives me a clue,” she thought. The atmosphere felt heavy with memories, and she could almost hear the echoes of laughter and applause that had once filled this space. But now, it was just a hollow shell, a mausoleum of lost dreams.

Kendra moved cautiously through the lobby, her footsteps muffled by the thick layer of dust on the floor. She peered into the old concession stand, its counters empty and forlorn. "Audrey loved coming here," she thought, her heart aching at the thought of her friend. She opened a drawer beneath the counter, hoping to find something useful, but it was empty except for crumpled napkins and stale popcorn.

Determined, Kendra made her way toward the main auditorium, the looming darkness ahead seeming to swallow her whole. As she entered, the vastness of the room struck her. Rows of empty seats faded into shadows, and the stage at the front felt like a distant memory of better times. She took a deep breath, forcing herself to remain calm.

Suddenly, a glint caught her eye from the corner of the stage. Kendra approached cautiously, her heart racing with anticipation. As she drew closer, she saw the outline of an object half-buried in the debris. Kneeling down, she brushed away the dust and discovered a small diary—Audrey's diary.

Her hands trembled as she opened it, flipping through the pages filled with Audrey's neat handwriting. The entries chronicled her thoughts, her dreams, and her fears. Kendra's heart sank as she read the last few entries, which had grown increasingly erratic. "I feel like I'm being watched," one entry read. "Something isn't right. I can't shake this feeling..."

Kendra felt a chill run down her spine. Audrey had sensed something was wrong before she vanished. "Why didn't I notice?" Kendra thought, guilt gnawing at her. She quickly took a picture of the entries with her phone, knowing she would need to share this with the others.

Just then, a noise echoed from the back of the auditorium, a sound that sent her heart racing. It was muffled, yet it resonated through the empty space. Kendra froze, straining to listen. It was a low, rhythmic thumping, like something—or someone—was moving about.

Her instincts screamed at her to run, to escape the theater and find her friends, but the thought of leaving without Audrey propelled her forward. Taking a deep breath, she moved cautiously towards the sound, creeping along the edge of the walls to avoid being seen.

As she approached the source of the noise, she saw a flickering light coming from a doorway at the back of the theater. The thumping grew louder, and her heart raced faster. "What if it's the killer?" she thought, fear gripping her throat. Yet, she had to know. She had to find Audrey.

Pushing the door open slowly, Kendra stepped inside. The room was small and cluttered, with old props stacked haphazardly in the corners. The light flickered, casting eerie shadows that danced across the walls. As she scanned the room, her breath caught in her throat—there, in the corner, stood a figure cloaked in darkness, their back turned to her.

"Who's there?" Kendra called out, her voice steady despite the fear coursing through her veins. The figure turned slowly, revealing a face obscured by a mask—a ghost face.

Kendra's heart raced as adrenaline surged through her. "Get away from me!" she shouted, backing away instinctively, ready to flee.

The figure chuckled, a sound devoid of warmth or humanity. "You should have listened, Kendra. You're playing a dangerous game."

Kendra's mind raced. "What do you want?" she demanded, her voice trembling yet fierce. "Where's Audrey?"

"Ah, you're still searching for your friend," the figure taunted, taking a step closer. "You're not as clever as you think. The treasure hunt has just begun."

Kendra's pulse quickened as she took another step back, her instincts screaming at her to escape. "What have you done to her?"

"Find the clues, and you might just save her," the figure replied, their voice dripping with malice. "But take too long, and the clock will run out. You have until midnight."

With that, the figure turned and vanished into the shadows, leaving Kendra standing in the dim light, breathless and terrified. Panic surged through her; she had to get out of there and warn the others. She sprinted back through the auditorium, her heart racing as she pushed open the heavy doors and burst into the night.

Kendra dashed down the street toward the coffee shop, her mind racing. She had to tell Danny, Jane, and Josh what she had seen. The weight of the diary felt heavy in her bag, a reminder of the urgency of their situation.

As she reached the coffee shop, she burst through the door, her heart pounding. The familiar warmth of the café felt comforting, but she quickly scanned the room for her friends. There they were, sitting at their usual table, concern etched across their faces as they looked up at her.

"Kendra!" Danny exclaimed, standing up abruptly. "What happened? You look like you've seen a ghost."

"Where's Audrey?" Josh asked, anxiety evident in his voice.

"She's... she's in the theater," Kendra panted, her breath coming in quick bursts. "I found her diary, and I heard a noise. There was someone in there—someone wearing the jack o lantern reaper mask."

Gasps filled the air as her friends reacted to the news. "What do you mean you saw them?" Jane asked, her voice trembling.

"I confronted them," Kendra explained, her heart racing as she recounted the encounter. "They said there's a treasure hunt, and we have until midnight to find the clues to save Audrey."

Danny's expression shifted from shock to determination. "We need to figure out what that means. This is a game to him, and we can't lose."

Kendra pulled out Audrey's diary, placing it on the table. "I took a picture of the last entries. She sensed something was wrong before she disappeared. We need to analyze this for clues."

They gathered around the table, their earlier fear transforming into a sense of purpose. The café's soft lighting seemed to fade into the background as they focused on the task ahead. Kendra flipped through the pages, her fingers trembling slightly.

"What if there's a hidden message?" Josh suggested, his brow furrowing in concentration. "Maybe she wrote something that could lead us to the next clue."

As Kendra read through the entries again, she felt the weight of Audrey's words. "There's something here," she said, her voice steadying. "She wrote about feeling watched, and there's a mention of a 'hidden door' in the theater. It could be referring to something we missed."

Jane leaned in closer, scanning the words. "We have to go back there.

If there's a hidden door, it might lead us to Audrey."

Kendra nodded, her resolve hardening. "We can't waste any more time. This is our only chance."

Danny looked at each of them, determination shining in his eyes. "Let's gather what we need and head back. We stick together; we face whatever comes our way."

With that, they quickly gathered their things, making sure to keep their phones charged and ready. The urgency of the situation pushed them forward as they left the warmth of the coffee shop and stepped into the cool night air once again.

The streets seemed eerily quiet as they made their way back to the theater. The shadows danced in the glow of the streetlights, and Kendra felt her heart race with every step. The looming threat of the ghost face killer hung over them like a dark cloud, and she couldn't shake the feeling that they were being watched.

As they approached the theater, the building loomed before them, its once-vibrant exterior now a haunting reminder of the danger that lay inside. Kendra's hands trembled slightly as she pushed the door open, the creak of the hinges echoing through the hollow space.

"Stay close," Danny whispered, his voice steady yet laced with tension as they stepped inside. The air felt thick with anticipation, the darkness pressing in around them.

They moved cautiously through the lobby, Kendra leading the way toward the main auditorium. The faint sound of their footsteps echoed in the silence, amplifying the tension that coiled around them. As they reached the entrance to the auditorium, Kendra paused, taking a deep breath.

"I think the hidden door is somewhere around here," she said, scanning the room for any signs of something amiss. "Audrey mentioned it in her diary, but I don't know where to look."

"Let's check the stage first," Jane suggested, her eyes darting around the vast space. "It might be hidden behind one of the props."

They made their way to the stage, the shadows swallowing them as they moved. The remnants of past performances lay scattered about, old costumes and props creating an unsettling atmosphere. Kendra felt a chill run down her spine, but she pushed it aside, focusing on the task at hand.

As they searched, Danny knelt down to inspect a stack of old crates. "What if it's something simple?" he mused. "Like a loose board or a hidden latch?"

Kendra nodded, her mind racing with possibilities. "Let's check everything. We can't leave any stone unturned."

They examined every inch of the stage, pushing aside props and examining the walls for any signs of a hidden door. Time seemed to stretch endlessly, the weight of the clock ticking down in the back of their minds.

Suddenly, Josh's voice broke through the silence. "Hey, over here!" He had found a small trapdoor at the edge of the stage, partially hidden beneath a pile of old fabric.

"What did you find?" Kendra rushed over, her heart pounding with excitement and fear.

Josh knelt beside the trapdoor, brushing away the debris. "I think this leads down into the basement," he said, looking back at the others with a mix of excitement and trepidation. "This could be it."

"Let's open it," Kendra urged, her voice steady despite the tension in the air. "It might lead us to Audrey."

Danny and Kendra helped Josh pull the door open, revealing a dark staircase that descended into the unknown. The smell of damp earth and decay wafted up, and a shiver ran down Kendra's spine.

"Do we have any flashlights?" Danny asked, glancing around.

"I have mine," Jane replied, pulling it from her bag. She flicked it on, the beam cutting through the darkness as they prepared to descend.

"We'll go one at a time," Kendra said, her heart racing. "Keep your eyes peeled for anything unusual."

With that, they began their descent into the darkness, the air growing colder as they moved down the steps. The flashlight beam flickered across the walls, revealing damp concrete and peeling paint. Kendra felt a sense of dread wash over her, the darkness swallowing them whole.

As they reached the bottom of the staircase, they stepped into a larger room, the beam of light illuminating the space. It was filled with old props, discarded furniture, and remnants of the theater's past. The atmosphere felt heavy, almost suffocating, and Kendra could feel the tension coiling in the pit of her stomach.

"Look over there!" Jane pointed toward a corner of the room, where a stack of crates stood precariously. "It looks like something is behind them."

Kendra moved toward the crates, her heart pounding as she pushed them aside. "What if it's a trap?"

Danny cautioned, his voice low but filled with concern.

"Better to find out than to leave without knowing," Kendra replied, determination fueling her movements.

As she cleared the last crate, a small door came into view, partially hidden behind the clutter. It was old and worn, but it had a distinctive latch that caught Kendra's eye. "This has to be it," she said, her voice filled with urgency.

As she reached for the latch, she felt a surge of adrenaline. "On the count of three," she said, glancing at her friends. "One... two... three!"

With a firm pull, she opened the door, revealing a narrow

passageway that seemed to stretch into darkness. The air was stale and heavy, and a chill ran down her spine. "This must lead somewhere," Kendra said, peering into the abyss.

"Do we have any choice?" Josh replied, his voice barely above a whisper. "We have to see where it goes."

They exchanged determined glances, the gravity of their situation weighing heavily upon them. With a shared nod, they stepped into the passageway, the door creaking ominously behind them as they ventured into the unknown.

The passage was tight, forcing them to move in single file. The air felt thick and suffocating, each breath heavy with dust and uncertainty. Kendra led the way, her flashlight illuminating the walls, revealing old graffiti and faded posters that hinted at the theater's storied past.

As they moved deeper into the darkness, the sound of their footsteps echoed around them, amplifying the tension that coiled in the air. Kendra could feel her heart pounding in her chest, each beat a reminder of the stakes at play.

"Are you sure this is the right way?" Danny asked, his voice laced with concern.

"Trust me," Kendra replied, her determination unwavering. "We have to keep going. Audrey is counting on us."

Suddenly, the passage opened up into a larger room, and Kendra felt a rush of relief wash over her. The beam of her flashlight revealed a cluttered space filled with old costumes, props, and hidden treasures of the theater. But as they stepped inside, the atmosphere shifted.

The room was dimly lit, the air thick with the scent of mildew and decay. A chill ran down Kendra's spine as she scanned the room, her flashlight beam catching on something glimmering in the corner.

"What is that?" Jane asked, pointing toward the object.

Kendra moved closer, her heart racing as she approached the source of the light. It was a small, ornate box, intricately carved and covered in dust. She knelt beside it, brushing away the grime to reveal a delicate latch. "I think this might be a clue," she said, her excitement bubbling to the surface.

"Open it," Josh urged, leaning in closer to see.

Kendra hesitated for a moment, the weight of the unknown pressing down on her. "What if it's a trap?" she wondered aloud.

"Only one way to find out," Danny said, his voice steady. "We're in this together."

With a deep breath, Kendra reached for the latch and opened the box. Inside lay a collection of items—old photographs, a map, and a small note. Her hands trembled as she picked up the note, unfolding it carefully.

The handwriting was familiar, and her heart raced as she read the words aloud. "To find me, you must look where the shadows dance. Follow the path to where the light does not reach. I'll be waiting for you, but time is not on your side."

"What does it mean?" Kendra asked, her brow furrowed in confusion.

"It sounds like a riddle," Jane mused, her eyes darting over the items in the box. "Maybe the map can help us?"

Kendra unfolded the map, revealing a sketch of the theater and surrounding area. There were markings and notes, some of which seemed to indicate hidden locations within the theater. "This could be our guide," she said, excitement bubbling within her.

"Let's figure out where we need to go next," Danny said, his eyes scanning the map. "It looks like there's an X marked near the old projection room."

"Then that's where we head next," Kendra declared, determination igniting within her. "We have to hurry before it's too late."

With the map in hand, they made their way back through the passage, the urgency of the situation propelling them forward. As they emerged from the narrow hallway, they could feel the weight of the theater pressing down around them, the shadows whispering secrets they were desperate to uncover.

Navigating back through the auditorium, the weight of the moment hung heavy in the air. Each creak of the floorboards echoed like a warning, reminding them of the danger still lurking in the shadows. Kendra led the way, her flashlight illuminating the path ahead as they made their way toward the projection room.

"Do you think we're getting close?" Josh asked, glancing at the map again.

"We should be," Kendra replied, her voice steady despite the fear coursing through her veins. "It should be just around the corner."

As they approached the door to the projection room, Kendra's heart raced. The door was old and worn, the wood splintered at the edges. She reached for the handle, glancing back at her friends, who were watching her with a mix of fear and anticipation.

"Ready?" she asked, taking a deep breath.

Danny nodded, his expression resolute. "Let's do this."

With a firm push, Kendra opened the door, revealing a dark room filled with dust and cobwebs. The air felt heavy, thick with the remnants of stories long forgotten. The projector stood in the corner, its lens covered in grime, and the walls were lined with old film reels.

"Wow," Jane breathed, stepping inside. "It's like a time capsule."

Kendra scanned the room, her flashlight beam sweeping over the clutter. "Look for anything that stands out," she urged, feeling the urgency of the moment. "We need to find another clue."

As they sifted through the debris, Kendra's heart raced. The shadows danced around them, and she felt the weight of the darkness pressing in. "This place feels eerie," she muttered, glancing over her shoulder.

Suddenly, Danny shouted, "Over here!" He had found a small door tucked away in the corner, almost hidden behind a stack of old film canisters.

"Is it locked?" Kendra rushed over, her heart pounding as she reached for the handle.

Danny shook his head, excitement bubbling in his voice. "No, it's open!"

With a firm pull, they opened the door, revealing a small, darkened space beyond. "What's in there?" Josh asked, peering inside.

"Let's find out," Kendra said, her voice steady as she stepped inside. The room was cramped, and the air felt colder, sending a shiver down her spine.

As she illuminated the space with her flashlight, she gasped at the sight before her. The walls were covered with newspaper clippings, photographs, and various artifacts—all related to the theater's history. But what caught her attention the most was a large, ornate mirror hanging on the wall.

"Look at this," Kendra said, moving closer to the mirror. The surface was cracked and dusty, but it seemed to shimmer in the light, almost as if it was alive.

"What's so special about a mirror?" Danny asked, stepping beside her.

Kendra reached out to touch the glass, feeling a strange energy pulsating from it. "I don't know, but there's something here."

Suddenly, a loud crash echoed from the main auditorium, jolting them from their focus. Kendra's heart raced as fear surged through her. "What was that?"

"Stay close," Danny urged, his voice tense as they quickly exited the small room. They moved cautiously back into the auditorium, the air thick with tension as they scanned the darkness for any signs of danger.

As they stepped back into the main space, they saw shadows moving near the entrance, the flickering light casting eerie shapes that danced across the walls. "What's going on?" Kendra whispered, her heart pounding in her chest.

"I don't know," Jane replied, her voice shaking with fear. "But we need to get out of here."

Just then, a figure emerged from the shadows, their face obscured by a mask—the unmistakable ghost face. Kendra felt her blood run cold, and they all froze, fear gripping them tightly.

"Welcome to the show," the figure taunted, their voice low and mocking. "I hope you're ready for the next act."

Kendra's heart raced as the realization hit her. They were trapped, and the hunt had only just begun. "Run!" she shouted, adrenaline surging through her body.

The group sprang into action, sprinting toward the exit as the masked figure lunged at them. Kendra felt panic surge through her veins, but she pushed it aside, focusing on the urgency of the moment. They had to escape.

As they dashed through the auditorium, Kendra glanced back to see the figure closing in, their movements fluid and purposeful. "Don't look back!" Danny shouted, urging them forward.

They burst through the doors and into the cool night air, their breaths coming in quick gasps. Kendra could hear the figure's footsteps pounding behind them, and she felt a surge of fear propel her forward.

"Where do we go?" Josh yelled, glancing around for any sign of safety.

"Over there!" Kendra pointed toward a nearby alleyway, the shadows offering a brief respite from the danger. They darted into the narrow passage, pressing against the cold brick walls as they tried to catch their breath.

The alley was dark, the air thick with tension and uncertainty. Kendra's heart raced as she glanced back toward the entrance of the theater, half-expecting the ghost face to follow them. “Do you think they saw us?” she asked, her voice shaking.

“I don’t know,” Danny replied, his eyes scanning the shadows. “But we can’t stay here. We need to find somewhere safe.”

As they moved deeper into the alley, Kendra felt a sense of urgency building within her. They had to regroup and figure out their next move. “Let’s find a place where we can hide for a moment,” she suggested, her voice steadying.

They continued down the alley until they spotted an old storage shed at the far end, its door slightly ajar. “In there!” Kendra pointed, her heart racing as they rushed toward the shed.

Inside, the darkness enveloped them, but they quickly found a corner to huddle in. The air was musty and stale, filled with the scent of old wood and neglect. Kendra leaned against the wall, trying to steady her breathing as they waited for the danger to pass.

"What do we do now?" Josh asked, his voice barely above a whisper.

"We need to figure out what the voice meant by 'treasure hunt'," Kendra said, her mind racing. "There must be more clues, something we missed."

Danny pulled out the map they had found in the box, his fingers tracing the lines and markings. "We need to follow these leads. There's a chance they could take us to Audrey."

Jane nodded, her determination igniting once more. "We can't let fear dictate our actions. We need to be brave for her."

As they caught their breath, the reality of their situation settled over them like a heavy blanket. They were in this together, bound by loyalty and the unyielding desire to save their friend. The clock was ticking, and the ghost face killer was lurking in the shadows, but they refused to back down.

With a shared sense of purpose, they began plotting their next move, determined to unravel the mystery of the treasure hunt and bring Audrey home. The night was far from over, and the stakes had never been higher, but they were ready to face whatever horrors awaited them in the darkness.

Together, they would uncover the truth and fight against the terror that threatened to tear them apart.

Chapter 12

The air was thick with sorrow as Jane, Josh, Danny, and Kendra huddled together outside the charred remains of what had once been their beloved coffee shop. The flickering lights of emergency vehicles bathed the scene in an eerie glow, their bright reds and blues casting long shadows on the pavement. The police officers had just arrived, their presence offering a mix of safety and dread. They stood in clusters, exchanging hushed words, while firefighters worked tirelessly to extinguish the last remnants of the blaze that had claimed so much.

"How many more?" Danny murmured, his voice barely above a whisper. The anguish in his eyes mirrored that of the others. Each name—Sarah, David, Mary—had fallen under this tragic shadow, and now Audrey. It was as if a dark cloud loomed over them, stalking its prey, picking them off one by one. They felt helpless beneath its weight, their hearts heavy with grief and fear.

Jane clenched her hands into fists, feeling her nails bite into her palms. “We can't just wait for it to happen again. We have to do something!” Her determination rose, fueled by grief and anger. “We need to find out who is behind this. We owe it to them.” The steel in her voice resonated in the heart of their grief-drenched gathering, a rallying cry in the face of despair.

Josh shook his head, struggling to maintain his composure. “But what can we do? We can’t even be sure who we can trust. This killer could be anyone, even someone we know." The chilling thought sent shivers down their spines. Their once-close circle now brimmed with paranoia, and the air felt charged with uncertainty.

Kendra sniffed, tears pooling in her eyes as memories of happier times with Audrey flooded back. "We can't let this continue," she said softly, her voice cracking under the weight of loss. "But we can't act out of anger. We need a plan." Her practicality grounded them in this moment of chaos, a reminder that they had to channel their grief into something productive.

"I just feel so helpless," Danny added, rubbing his temples. The stress was palpable, gnawing at his insides. "What if we're next? What if we can't stop it?" The fear of losing a friend again loomed ominously over their heads, suffocating the flickers of hope that struggled to emerge.

“We can’t let fear control us,” Jane declared, a fresh defiance pushing through her grief. “We need to stick together, to look out for each other. We must be stronger than this fear!”

“Right,” Josh injected, his voice gaining resolve. “United, we stand a better chance. We need to gather as much information as we can about Audrey's last moments—what she saw or heard. Maybe there’s something we missed.”

As they exchanged somber glances, an unspoken understanding bound them together. They couldn’t afford to succumb to despair; they had to channel their heartbreak into actionable plans for justice. Audrey’s life had been stolen from them, but they could honor her memory by joining the fight against the encroaching darkness.

"Let's talk to the police," Kendra suggested, her voice steady. "They might know something that can help us."

As they began to strategize, the flickering candlelight of the emergency vehicles danced on the walls of their memories—fragile beacons of hope in the growing darkness. They would uncover the truth, confront their fears, and protect one another. The killer may have taken Audrey, but they would not take them all without a fight. Together, they were stronger, and together, they would find a way to stop the nightmare from growing.

The Aftermath of Tragedy

The fire had consumed everything in its path, leaving behind only ash and memories. Jane collapsed against a nearby tree, her sobs echoing through the chaos that had erupted in their once-quiet town. The weight of loss felt unbearable, especially knowing that Audrey was just another victim in a string of tragedies that had befallen their group.

Jane looked at Josh, whose face was blank, shock and grief etched into his features. Danny paced back and forth, his fists clenched as he tried to suppress the anger bubbling within him. Kendra stood a little way off, staring into the distance, wishing for Audrey to reappear and assure them that everything would be alright. They were each grappling with their grief, yet united in their fear—fear of what might come next.

"It's not just the fire," Josh finally managed, his voice shaking with emotion. "It's everything that's happening. Sarah, David, Mary… now Audrey. What kind of monster is doing this to us?"

Kendra turned to him, her eyes glistening with unshed tears. "I don't know how much more we can take," she said, her voice trembling. "We keep losing the people we love, and it doesn't make sense. It feels so random…"

"Random?" Danny interrupted, his voice rising with frustration. "It's not random. Someone is targeting us! We're just waiting for the next blow, and I can't stand it!" His eyes were fiery, a mix of fear and fury that reflected their collective anxiety.

The wail of sirens grew louder, the fire department and police arriving, their lights flashing in a chaotic array. This stirred a new sense of urgency, mingling with the group's grief. They approached the officers and firefighters standing amidst the smoldering ruins of their lives, seeking answers amidst the rubble.

A stocky police officer with a sympathetic demeanor stepped forward. "We need everyone to stay calm and answer some questions. We'll need to know exactly what happened tonight." He eyed their distressed faces, ready to document the unfolding tragedy.

Taking a deep breath, Jane forced herself to speak. "We were here with Audrey, and then the fire started. We... we couldn't save her." Tears streamed down her face, each word a reminder of her failure to protect her friend. "We thought it was just an accident."

"We need to tell them everything," Josh urged, stepping close to Jane, his expression resembling her own. "About Sarah, David, and Mary. They all died so suddenly. At first, we thought it was just a bad stroke of luck, but now..."

The officer nodded, his pen poised above his notepad, sensing the gravity of their words. "What do you mean? What happened to your friends?" His voice was firm but compassionate, ready to listen.

Danny stepped in, his voice a mixture of anger and fear. "It's all connected. We believe someone is picking us off one by one. And now, we're terrified that we'll be next on this twisted list." The fear hung heavy in the air, a collective heartbeat echoing their dread.

The officer exchanged a look with his partner, who was now ready to jot down notes. Kendra clutched her arms around herself, desperately wishing for reassurance, longing to hear that they were safe, that they weren't the killer's next targets. But an unsettling truth lingered beneath their skin: the nightmare was far from over.

As the investigation commenced, the four friends clung to each other, forming a protective circle around their shared grief. With an unspoken pact, they promised to uncover the truth—whatever it took. They would not let the grip of fear suffocate them or steal away their desire for justice. Each step would bring them closer to the heart of the mystery that had ensnared their lives.

In the days that followed, they sank into their mission, tirelessly sifting through their memories, trying to piece together the fragments of joy that had been shattered by the losses they endured. They questioned others in their community, sought guidance from those who had known Sarah, David, and Mary, and pored over social media, desperate for answers about Audrey's final hours.

As they unearthed scattered clues, their resolve intensified. They began to believe that they could piece together the web of terror that had raged through their hometown, determining to expose the darkness that hunted them.

Hours melted together into days, each moment tinged with an uneasy camaraderie forged in tragedy. The weight in their hearts began to lift as they transformed their grief into action; their mission threaded their souls together tighter than any friendship before.

Finally, a full moon hung overhead, casting eerie shadows against the trees where they gathered one last time. A hollow silence replaced the sounds of chaos that once consumed them. "We'll confront this," Jane declared, her eyes shining with fierce determination. "Together."

They nodded, drawing strength from one another. They would no longer be victims; they were survivors, battling against the nightmare. United, they would unveil the killer's identity and free their spirits from the chains of fear. No matter the consequences, they would protect each other—because together, they were stronger, and they would find a way to stop the darkness from encroaching further.

As they gathered in the park beneath the moonlight, the tension in the air crackled with urgency. Each of them brought their notes, scribbled thoughts, and memories of the friends they had lost. They spread everything out on a picnic table, creating a makeshift war room. Kendra took a deep breath, feeling the weight of responsibility settle on her shoulders.

"Okay," she began, her voice steady despite the turmoil inside. "We need to make sense of everything we've collected. We have to find connections between all the victims and see if there's a pattern we can discern."

Danny nodded, flipping through his notes. "Let's start with the timeline of events. Sarah was the first to go, then David, then Mary, and now Audrey. All of them were connected to us in some way."

Jane added, "We should also consider their last known locations. Where were they before their disappearances? We might find a common thread linking them."

They fell into a rhythm, each member contributing ideas and insights. As they discussed their findings, Kendra felt a sense of purpose blossom within her. They were determined to uncover the truth, and she could feel the fire of their shared resolve pushing them forward.

"Sarah was last seen at the local park, where we used to hang out," Josh recalled. "I remember she mentioned seeing someone suspicious lurking around. It always felt like a joke, something we brushed off, but what if it was more?"

"What about David?" Danny interjected. "He was at the community center for a volunteer event. He told me he felt uneasy that day. Maybe someone was watching him too."

Kendra's heart raced as they connected the dots. "And Mary was at the library when she disappeared. She had mentioned seeing a strange person hanging around the stacks."

"So we have three locations tied to three victims," Jane noted, her eyes brightening with realization. "What if we check these places to see if there are any patterns or security footage? Maybe they'll lead us to something."

Josh nodded vigorously. "And we should also talk to anyone who might have seen something unusual. If we can piece together their last moments, it could point us in the direction of the killer."

As they worked through their plan, the moonlight cast a silver glow over their gathering, illuminating their faces as they transformed their grief into action. The shadows that had once felt suffocating now seemed to shift with purpose, as if urging them onward.

"Let's split up and tackle each location," Kendra suggested, a sense of urgency pushing her forward. "We can meet back here later to share what we find. But we have to be careful—this killer is still out there."

With newfound determination, they each took on a location to investigate, their hearts pounding with a mix of fear and hope. As they departed, Kendra felt a fire ignite within her. They were no longer paralyzed by grief; they were warriors in a battle against darkness, ready to fight for their friends.

Kendra arrived at the park, her heart racing as she stepped onto the familiar path where they used to spend countless afternoons. The trees loomed overhead, their branches swaying gently in the night breeze. But tonight, the park felt different—haunted by memories of laughter now overshadowed by tragedy.

She walked through the park, her flashlight cutting through the darkness as she scanned the area for any signs of life. The swings creaked softly in the wind, and the distant sound of rustling leaves sent shivers down her spine. She couldn't shake the feeling that someone, or something, was watching her.

Taking a deep breath, Kendra focused on the task at hand. "Stay calm," she whispered to herself. "You're here for Audrey." She approached the spot where Sarah had last been seen, her heart heavy with the weight of loss.

Kendra knelt down, examining the ground for any clues—broken branches, footprints, anything that might hint at what had happened. As she brushed away fallen leaves, her fingers grazed against something cold and metallic. She dug deeper into the dirt, revealing a small pendant—a charm bracelet that had belonged to Sarah.

"Sarah..." Kendra murmured, holding the pendant up to the moonlight. It was a faint reminder of the life that had been ripped away, and emotions surged within her. This wasn't merely a piece of jewelry; it was a connection to the past, a thread linking her to the tragedy that had unfolded.

With renewed determination, Kendra slipped the pendant into her pocket and continued her search. She made her way to the community center next, her mind racing with thoughts of David. As she approached the entrance, she noticed the flickering lights inside, the remnants of an event that had once brought joy to the community.

Inside, she was greeted by the faint echo of laughter, now distant and haunting. Kendra stepped into the main hall, the walls adorned with decorations from past events. She approached the front desk, where a staff member was cleaning up after the evening's activities.

"Excuse me," Kendra said, her voice steady but filled with urgency. "I'm looking for information about David. He was here before he disappeared, and I was wondering if you had any security footage from that day."

The staff member looked up, concern etched on their face. "I'm sorry to hear about your friend. I can check the logs for you. Can you tell me the date he was here?"

Kendra provided the details, her heart racing as she waited for the staff member to pull up the footage. The seconds felt like hours, and she could feel the weight of despair pressing down on her.

"Here it is," the staff member said, pulling up the video on the computer screen. Kendra leaned in close, her breath hitching as she watched the screen.

David appeared on the footage, laughing with friends, but as the video continued, Kendra noticed a shadow lurking at the edge of the frame, a figure that seemed out of place. “Who is that?” she asked, pointing at the screen.

The staff member frowned, squinting at the image. “I’m not sure. It looks like someone was hanging around the entrance, but I can’t make out any details. I’ll save this for you.”

Kendra’s heart sank, but she felt a glimmer of hope. “Thank you. Every detail matters.” She took down the staff member’s contact information and hurried out of the community center, her mind racing with possibilities.

Next, Kendra rushed to the library, her heart pounding as she stepped inside. The familiar scent of old books filled the air, but the atmosphere felt heavy with sorrow. She approached the librarian, an older woman with kind eyes, who looked up from her desk.

"How can I help you?" the librarian asked gently.

"I'm looking for information about a friend, Mary," Kendra said, her voice steady. "She was here before she disappeared. I need to know if anyone saw her or if there's any footage from that day."

The librarian nodded solemnly. "I remember Mary. She was a bright young lady. Let me check our security logs."

As the librarian sifted through the records, Kendra felt a sense of urgency building within her. She thought of all the times they had spent in this very library, laughing and sharing stories. It was a sanctuary that now felt tainted by the tragedy that had unfolded.

After a few moments, the librarian turned back to Kendra. “I found the footage from that day. It was a quiet afternoon, but I’ll pull it up for you.”

Kendra held her breath as the librarian played the video, her eyes glued to the screen. Mary appeared, engrossed in a book, but there was something unsettling about the way she glanced around, as if sensing someone watching her.

“Can you rewind it?” Kendra asked, her heart racing. “What was that shadow in the back?”

The librarian complied, rewinding the footage. Kendra leaned in closer, her breath catching in her throat as she saw a figure lurking in the background, barely visible but unmistakably there.

"Who is that?" Kendra asked, her heart pounding.

"I'm not sure," the librarian replied, squinting at the screen. "I can check the staff logs to see if anyone reported anything unusual. But it's common for patrons to come and go."

Kendra nodded, knowing that any detail could be crucial. "Please, do whatever you can. I need to find out what happened to my friends."

As the librarian began searching through records, Kendra glanced around the library, her heart heavy with the weight of loss. The shelves seemed to loom over her, a reminder of the stories that had been silenced. She felt a sense of urgency wash over her; their time was running out.

After gathering all the information she could, Kendra left the library, her heart racing with hope and fear. She rushed back to the park where she had planned to meet her friends, her mind racing with thoughts of the connections they might uncover.

As she arrived, she found Danny, Jane, and Josh already waiting for her, their faces etched with concern. "What did you find?" Danny asked, his eyes scanning her expression for answers.

"I found things at the park, community center, and library," Kendra said breathlessly, pulling out the pendant from Sarah and showing it to them. "This was left behind. It's a sign that we need to dig deeper."

Jane took a deep breath, her eyes wide as she absorbed the weight of Kendra's findings. "And what about the footage?"

"I saw something strange," Kendra continued, her heart racing. "At the community center, there was a shadowy figure lurking near David. And at the library, Mary glanced around like she sensed someone watching her."

Josh's brow furrowed as he processed the information. "So we have two potential suspects? This could help us narrow down who we're dealing with."

"Exactly," Kendra replied, her determination solidifying. "We need to share this with the police.

They may have resources to track down these individuals and get more information."

Danny nodded, his expression resolute. "Then let's do it. We can't let fear hold us back. We have to take control of our situation."

With renewed purpose, they made their way to the police station, each step a testament to their commitment to uncovering the truth. As they entered, the atmosphere felt charged, the weight of their mission pressing down upon them.

They approached the front desk, where an officer looked up from his paperwork. "How can I help you?"

"We have information about the recent disappearances," Kendra said, her voice steady. "We think we've identified some potential suspects and have footage that could help your investigation."

The officer raised an eyebrow, intrigued. "What do you have?"

They recounted their findings, sharing every detail they had gathered. As Kendra spoke, she felt a surge of adrenaline course through her veins. This was their chance to make a difference, to contribute to the fight against the darkness that threatened their lives.

The officer nodded, taking notes as they spoke. "I appreciate you coming forward with this information. I'll make sure to pass it along to the detectives working on the case. Every lead counts."

As they finished sharing their findings, a wave of relief washed over them. They had done everything they could to bring attention to the nightmare that had unfolded. But deep down, they knew their fight was far from over.

The days turned into a blur of meetings, phone calls, and late-night discussions as they worked tirelessly to gather more information. The urgency of their mission pushed them forward, each day filled with the hope that they would find Audrey and bring an end to the terror that had gripped their community.

As they gathered in the park once more, the atmosphere felt different. The weight of their grief lingered, but it was tempered by a renewed sense of purpose. They had spent countless hours strategizing, pouring over maps, and connecting the dots between the victims.

"We need to decide our next move," Jane said, her voice firm. "We can't afford to lose sight of our goal."

Danny nodded, his expression serious. "We've gathered a lot of information, but we need to act quickly. If the killer is still out there, we can't let them slip away."

Kendra took a deep breath, feeling the weight of responsibility settle on her shoulders. "We should revisit the locations where the victims were last seen. There may be something we missed, a clue that will lead us to Audrey."

"Agreed," Josh said, determination shining in his eyes. "We can't let fear hold us back anymore. We have to confront this head-on."

As they began to outline their plan, a sense of urgency filled the air. They were no longer just a group of friends; they were a united front, bound by their shared grief and determination to uncover the truth.

With their plan in place, they set off into the night, ready to face whatever lay ahead. The shadows that had once felt suffocating now seemed to shift with purpose, urging them onward in their quest for justice.

As they moved through the darkness, Kendra felt a flicker of hope ignite within her. They would not be victims of fear; they would be warriors in their fight for the truth. Together, they would uncover the darkness that threatened to engulf them, and together, they would bring Audrey home.

The clock was ticking, and the stakes had never been higher. But they were ready to face the storm, armed with courage, determination, and the unbreakable bond of friendship. The hunt for answers had only just begun, and they would stop at nothing to find the light in the darkness.

Chapter 13

The chilling events that had unfolded in Magnolia sent shockwaves through the town, leaving residents unsettled and grief-stricken. The gruesome murders of Audrey, Sarah, David, and Mary at the hands of the notorious Reaper killer hung heavily in the air like a thick fog, suffocating any sense of normalcy. Fear coursed through the veins of every teenager, wrapping around them like barbed wire, a constant reminder of the lurking danger. For Kendra, Josh, Jane, and Danny, the specter of danger loomed large, darkening their every thought. Yet as Halloween approached, they sought refuge in the thrill of the holiday, clinging to the hope that a distraction might lift their spirits, at least temporarily.

“I can't sit around here waiting for the killer to strike again,” Kendra declared, her voice a mixture of determination and anxiety. She stood with her arms crossed, her expression resolute as she surveyed the faces of her friends. The others nodded in agreement, each of them harboring the same urge to escape the oppressive atmosphere that had settled over their lives like a lead blanket.

“We should go to Inferno Haunt,” offered Josh, a glint of mischief in his eyes. The haunt was infamous for its heart-stopping scares and grotesque decorations, a place where the thrill of terror was manufactured, and it promised an encounter with fear that was entirely artificial—a temporary reprieve from the real horrors that had gripped their community.

"Do you really think that's a good idea?" Jane asked, biting her lip, her voice laced with concern. "I mean, what if something happens? What if the killer shows up?"

Danny chimed in, trying to lighten the mood. "Come on, it's Halloween! We can't let one psycho ruin our fun. Besides, being scared is part of the deal. It'll be like facing our fears head-on." His enthusiasm, though genuine, felt like a thin veil over the anxiety that gripped them.

After some prodding, the group made plans for the night. They chose costumes that were on the lighter side—far from the brutal nature of their reality. Kendra went as a vibrant fairy, her wings shimmering in the light; Josh opted for a goofy vampire, complete with oversized fangs and a cape that seemed to swallow him whole; Jane took on the role of a witch, her black dress flowing as she twirled her broomstick; and Danny decided to be a classic ghost, donning a sheet with cut-out eyes, a playful nod to their childhood days.

As they drove toward Inferno Haunt, the sun dipped below the horizon, casting the world in shades of orange and purple. The streets were lined with carved pumpkins and decorations, a stark contrast to the darkness that hovered in their minds. Kendra felt a mix of excitement and trepidation as they approached the haunt, each passing moment heightening her awareness of the danger that still lurked in the shadows.

When they arrived at Inferno Haunt, a spine-chilling fog blanketed the entrance, the air thick with the smell of popcorn and the sounds of shrieks and laughter echoing from inside. Strange, flickering lights illuminated the twisted figures lurking throughout the grounds. Here, amidst the neon and darkness, the group could shed their worries, if only for a few hours.

As they stepped inside, a wave of excitement washed over them. They were immediately engulfed by a cacophony of screams, the air thick with dread and exhilaration. Actors in grotesque masks lunged from the shadows, and animatronics shrieked menacingly. The haunt was a jarring explosion of terror, allowing the friends to momentarily lose themselves in the chaos. Each corner they turned brought new horrors—zombies reaching out from behind walls, chainsaws roaring to life, and the smell of smoke and fright mingling in the air.

Yet, as the night wore on, flashes of fear began to creep back in. Every close encounter felt like a reminder of the murders, the line between fiction and reality blurring in the haunted halls. The sense of safety that a crowded room typically brings seemed fragile, each eerie mask evoking darker thoughts. Kendra's heart raced with adrenaline, but with each jump scare, she couldn't shake the feeling that the real danger was not far behind.

"Let's stick together," Kendra urged, glancing at her friends. The group clung to each other as they moved deeper into the haunt, navigating through the dimly lit corridors filled with chilling displays and actors eager to frighten. The laughter of other patrons echoed around them, but Kendra felt increasingly isolated, her mind racing with thoughts of what had happened to Audrey and the others.

With every jump scare, Kendra found herself glancing toward the exit, her heart pounding not just from the thrill of the haunt but also from the haunting anxiety that the real Magnolia Killer might be lurking just beyond the shadows. As they navigated the final rooms, the group clung to each other, the shared fear uniting them in a bond that felt both comforting and terrifying.

As they emerged back into the cold, moonlit night, Kendra looked at her friends and whispered, "Let's promise to stick together. No matter what happens, we face it as a team."

Their hearts were still racing from the exhilarating terror they had just experienced, but the promise offered a flicker of hope. Within the laughter and camaraderie, they sought solace, hoping that together they could stave off the nightmares that haunted them and embrace the fleeting joy of Halloween.

The Club's Dark Pulse

The night air was crisp and cool as they left Inferno Haunt, the adrenaline from their harrowing experience still coursing through their veins. They strolled through the bustling streets of Magnolia, where colorful decorations adorned houses and storefronts, and the sounds of celebration filled the air. Children darted about in their costumes, laughter ringing out like music, a stark contrast to the chilling reality that loomed over Kendra and her friends.

"I can't believe we survived that," Josh said, his voice a mix of exhilaration and disbelief. "That was intense!"

"Intense doesn't even begin to cover it," Kendra replied, her heart still racing. "I think I screamed louder than I ever have in my life."

As they continued walking, they were drawn to a nearby nightclub, pulsing with music and energy. The vibrant lights beckoned them closer, and despite their recent fears, there was an undeniable allure to the chaos within. "What do you think?" Danny asked, glancing at the entrance. "Should we check it out?"

Jane hesitated, her brow furrowing. "I don't know, guys. It might be too much right now. With everything going on…"

"But it could be fun!" Josh chimed in, trying to inject enthusiasm into the moment. "We can dance, let loose for a while. We need a break from all this darkness."

Kendra bit her lip, torn between caution and the desire for normalcy. "We can't let the fear control us," she said finally. "Let's go in. We'll stick together, right?"

With tentative nods of agreement, they stepped inside the nightclub, the atmosphere immediately enveloping them in its frenetic energy. Strobe lights flickered erratically, casting eerie shadows across the packed room while the relentless thump of hardcore music pulsed through the air like the heartbeat of some living beast. It enveloped them in its chaos, the beat synchronizing with their racing hearts as they moved toward the dance floor.

The laughter and cheers of spirited partygoers echoed around them, drowning out the rising panic lurking just below the surface of their exhilaration. It felt as if they were stepping through a portal to another world—one where reality warped into an unrecognizable thrill, seductive yet disquieting.

Kendra felt the music vibrate through her body, the bass thrumming in her chest. For a moment, it felt as if they were truly free, able to escape the shadows that haunted them. They danced together, laughter bubbling up as they moved to the rhythm, losing themselves in the music. But even as they surrendered to the moment, Kendra couldn't shake the feeling that something sinister lurked just beyond the fluorescent lights.

Without warning, the air shifted, darkening like a storm cloud over their heads. In an instant, the atmosphere transformed from festive to foreboding. The Ghostface killer struck with fluid precision, his masked visage a chilling specter of terror. The crowd roared in excitement, blissfully unaware of the horror unfolding just a few feet away.

In a heartbeat, Danny was seized from behind, a gloved hand

clamping over his mouth and muffling any cries for help. The disorienting lights and pounding rhythm of the music masked Danny's frantic struggle, making it seem as though the chaos merely provided a backdrop to the horror happening just a few steps away from the vibrant dance floor.

Kendra’s heart dropped as she turned just in time to see the glimmer of the killer’s blade flash in the strobe lights. “Danny!” she screamed, her voice piercing through the noise. Panic surged through her, galvanizing her body into motion. She lunged toward her friend, but the killer was swift, dragging Danny toward a darkened alcove, where the pulsating lights and sounds of the dance floor faded into a haunting silence.

Danny's attempts to break free were visceral—wild and desperate. Adrenaline coursed through him, igniting every fiber of his being as he fought against the cold, iron grip that held him firmly in place. His heart raced, panic constricting around him like a vice, tightening with every second he remained ensnared. The vibrant noise of the club faded to a muffled echo of his friends' laughter and cheers, blissfully unaware as they pushed toward the exit, into the cool night air. Oblivious, they continued celebrating their night, lost in the revelry, entirely naïve to the nightmare that had already begun mere feet from their escape.

Danny was thrust into a dimly lit alcove hidden behind the club, where the flickers of color and sound morphed into suffocating darkness. There, laid against the cold, unyielding floor, he was at the mercy of his tormentor, the killer looming above him like a malignant moon. Each stab inflicted was brutal, the blade sinking into his flesh with the practiced exactitude of a predator executing its prey. Blood poured from over thirty wounds, soaking the floor and splattering against the stark walls, creating a grotesque tableau that mirrored an artist's twisted vision. The vibrant red starkly contrasted with the sickly bright colors of the club's décor, illuminating the horror that unfolded, shattering the illusion of safety and revelry just beyond the walls.

A sickening silence followed once the horrific deed was done. The killer methodically stripped off the Reaper costume, shedding the last remnants of his sinister identity like a snake sloughing off skin. He stowed the mask and dark robe into a duffel bag as if discarding an old toy, leaving behind the unsettling weight of his actions, thick and suffocating. Stepping back into the neon-lit club, he blended seamlessly with the throng of oblivious patrons, their bodies undulating in rhythm to the frenetic beats and their laughter echoing like a siren song, blissfully ignorant of the atrocity that had just unfurled in the alcove.

Moments later, as if the universe conspired to continue the dance of horror and apathy, a new group of partygoers entered the venue, bubbling with excitement and anticipation. The atmosphere crackled with energy, but their exhilaration swiftly turned to horror as they stumbled upon the ghastly scene before them. Blood splattered the walls in grotesque arcs, pooling ominously on the floor. They paused, initially believing it to be part of some elaborate set design, a macabre joke crafted to enhance the club's edgy aesthetic.

"Look at this! They really went all out with the décor!" one young woman giggled, pulling out her phone to capture what she assumed was clever staging, her enthusiasm blind to the grotesque truth.

"This is wild! Is this real?" a man at the back murmured, his expression shifting from amusement to unease as he stepped closer, his shoe squelching in the pooling crimson. Laughter quickly morphed into terrified gasps, lines of anxiety etching across their faces as they examined the horrific "art," still blissfully oblivious to the truth lurking beyond the façade of liveliness.

One girl, curious and drawn to the bizarre spectacle, reached out to touch what she believed was a prop. The moment her fingers made contact, the blood warm and slick under her touch, she realized the horrifying truth of the scene. "Someone's dead here!" she screamed, her voice slicing through the artificial merriment like glass shattering. Panic erupted among the group, faces paling as they bolted from the scene, fleeing the nightmare.

Meanwhile, outside, Kendra, Jane, and Josh stood in disbelief, unsure of what had become of Danny. They speculated whether he had simply succumbed to the scares of the night, tripping over his own fears. Little did they know, he was beyond their reach—already claimed by death. The crowd outside, initially filled with laughter, now buzzed with confusion. Yet many of The Inferno Haunt Attraction's managers dismissed the commotion as a mere extension of the heightened thrill promised by their event. They believed the chaos was simply part of the night's allure.

Kendra, Jane, and Josh pressed a manager for a shortcut, urgency edging their voices. After a moment's hesitation, the manager instructed them toward the back, the area where Danny often enjoyed the frights most. With every step they took, a deeper dread settled in their stomachs. The pulsating heartbeat of the club thrummed around them, oblivious to the approaching truth.

When they finally reached the alcove, the sight that greeted them was a grotesque omen of despair. Danny lay lifeless, the vibrant spark of his life extinguished within the chaos of The Inferno Haunt Attraction. The panic of the outside crowd seemed to fade into a solemn hush as reality gripped Kendra, Jane, and Josh. The club, once a vibrant testament to freedom and festivity, loomed over them like a mausoleum of lost joy. They clung to each other, each whisper of denial suffocating under the weight of the blood-soaked memories that would haunt their every night.

In that instant, they understood—it wasn't just Danny they had lost; it was the carefree laughter and friendship they had taken for granted. They found themselves trapped in a dance of grief and horror, a macabre reminder of the fragility of life that lurked hidden beneath the revelry of a bustling nightclub Kendra fell to her knees beside Danny's lifeless body, her heart shattered into a million pieces. She could hardly comprehend the scene unfolding before her—this was her friend, her confidant, and now he lay there, a victim of a senseless act of violence. The reality of the situation washed over her like a cold wave, threatening to drown her in despair.

"No! No, no, no!" she cried, her voice raw with anguish. "Danny, please, wake up!" She shook him gently, hoping against hope that he would respond, that this was all just a cruel trick. But the warmth had left his body, and the life that once sparkled in his eyes was now extinguished. Jane stood frozen, her mind racing as she tried to process the horror in front of her. The laughter and music from the club faded into an eerie silence, replaced by the pounding of her own heartbeat in her ears. "What happened? How did this happen?" she gasped, her voice barely above a whisper.

"This can't be real," Josh murmured, his face pale as he took a step back, almost as if he were trying to distance himself from the gruesome sight. "He was just here with us. How could this happen?"

Kendra's sobs echoed through the alcove, a haunting melody of grief that pierced the stillness. The world around them blurred, and for a moment, it felt like they were trapped in a nightmare, unable to wake up. The vibrant, chaotic energy of the club felt worlds away, and the reality of their loss settled heavily on their shoulders.

"Danny..." Kendra whispered, her voice breaking. "We should have done something. We should have been here." Guilt coursed through her, mingling with her grief and transforming it into a heavy stone in her chest. She could feel the weight of their previous conversations echoing in her mind —how they had promised to stick together, to face their fears as a united front. Suddenly, the harsh sound of sirens pierced the air, cutting through the fog of despair. The realization that they needed to act quickly jolted Kendra back into focus. "We have to call the police," she said, her voice trembling but resolute. "We have to report this." Josh pulled out his phone, his hands shaking as he dialed emergency services. "This is Josh. We need help. There's been a murder at The Inferno Haunt. My friend is dead!" His words came out in a rush, urgency and panic lacing his voice. Kendra and Jane stood close, their hearts pounding as they waited for the authorities to arrive. The reality of the situation settled over them like a suffocating blanket, each second stretching into eternity. They could hear the distant sounds of chaos erupting from the club, the mingled sounds of horror and disbelief echoing through the air.

As they waited, Kendra felt a flicker of anger ignite within her. "This isn't just a random act of violence," she said, her voice steadying. "Someone is targeting us. We can't let his death be in vain. We have to find out who did this."

Jane nodded, tears still streaming down her face. "But how? We're just kids. What can we do against someone like this?"

"We're not just kids anymore," Kendra replied fiercely. "We've lost too much already. We need to fight back. We need to figure out what connects all of these murders."

Just then, the sound of police sirens grew louder, and flashing lights illuminated the alley as officers arrived on the scene. The four friends stepped aside, their expressions a mix of grief and determination as they prepared to speak to the authorities.

A tall officer approached them, his face a mask of professionalism, though the concern in his eyes betrayed the gravity of the situation. "What happened here?" he asked, scanning the scene with a practiced gaze.

Kendra took a deep breath, steeling herself. "We were at the haunt, and we came back here to check on our friend. He—he's dead. Danny is dead." The words felt heavy on her tongue, but she forced herself to continue. "He was attacked by someone. It's the Reaper killer, isn't it?"

The officer's expression shifted, a flicker of recognition crossing his face. "We're aware of the recent incidents in Magnolia. We need you to stay calm and answer some questions."

As the officer took their statements, Kendra felt a sense of urgency building within her. They needed to uncover the truth—about the

Reaper killer, about Danny's murder, and about the connection between all the victims. The police were doing their part, but she knew they couldn't rely solely on them. The killer was still out there, lurking in the shadows, and they were the only ones who truly understood the gravity of the situation.

Once the police finished taking their statements, Kendra turned to her friends, her determination palpable. "We have to gather everything we know about the victims. We need to look for patterns, connections, anything that might lead us to the killer."

Josh nodded, his eyes narrowed in focus. "We should start with the last places they were seen. Maybe there was something they noticed that we didn't."

Jane wiped her tears, her resolve strengthening. "We owe it to Danny and the others. We have to find a way to stop this."

As they made their way back to the car, the weight of their loss hung heavy in the air, but it was tempered by a fierce determination. They would not allow fear to control them any longer. They would fight back against the darkness that had taken so much from them.

The Investigation Begins

They gathered in Kendra's living room, the atmosphere thick with tension as they spread out their notes and information about the victims. Each name was a painful reminder of what they had lost, but it also fueled their determination to seek justice.

"Let's start with Audrey," Kendra said, pulling up a map of Magnolia on her laptop. "She was last seen at the coffee shop, right? What did she say before she disappeared?"

"I remember her mentioning something about feeling watched," Jane recalled, her brow furrowing as she tried to recall the details. "It might have been paranoia, but it could also be significant."

Josh leaned over the map, pointing to the coffee shop. "We should go back there and talk to the staff. Maybe they noticed someone unusual during her last visit."

Kendra nodded, her fingers flying over the keyboard as she pulled up the coffee shop's contact information. “Let’s see if we can get in touch with them. The more information we gather, the better.”

As they made phone calls and sent messages, they shared memories of their friends, weaving together the tapestry of their lives that had been so tragically cut short. Each story served as a reminder of the joy that had once filled Magnolia, a stark contrast to the fear that now permeated their lives.

Hours passed, and they finally received a response from the coffee shop. The manager agreed to meet with them, and they set a time for the following day.

“Let’s not stop there,” Kendra urged, her fire ignited. “We need to plan visits to the community center and the library as well. We can’t leave any stone unturned.”

As they continued their investigation, the sun began to set, casting long shadows across the room. The atmosphere felt charged, and Kendra could sense the urgency building within them. They were on the cusp of uncovering something significant, a thread that could lead them to the truth. The next morning, they set out early, determined to gather as much information as possible. First stop: the coffee shop. As they arrived, Kendra felt a mixture of apprehension and resolve. The familiar aroma of coffee wafted through the air, but it was tainted by the shadows of loss.

They approached the manager, a kind-faced woman with tired eyes. "Thank you for meeting with us," Kendra said, her voice steady. "We're looking for information about our friend, Audrey. She was here shortly before she disappeared."

The manager nodded, concern etching her features. "I remember Audrey. She was such a bright spirit. Please, come with me."

They followed her to a small back room, where she pulled up security footage from the day Audrey was last seen. Kendra's heart raced as they sat down to watch, hoping for a clue that could lead them closer to finding the truth.

As the footage played, Kendra watched Audrey enter the shop, her vibrant energy shining through even the grainy video. She noticed a figure lingering near the entrance, a shadowy presence that seemed to watch Audrey as she ordered her drink.

"There! Who is that?" Kendra pointed, her voice rising with urgency.

The manager squinted at the screen. "I'm not sure. They came in and left shortly after. I thought they were just a customer."

Kendra felt a knot tighten in her stomach. "Is there any way to get a clearer image? Maybe we can identify them."

The manager nodded and began to rewind the footage, focusing on the figure. After a moment, she paused the video. "This is the best angle I can get," she said, her finger hovering over the play button.

Kendra leaned in, scrutinizing the image. The figure wore a dark hoodie, their face obscured by shadows. “We need to see if the police can enhance this,” Kendra said, determination flooding her voice. “This could be crucial.”

After gathering the footage and information, they thanked the manager and headed to the community center. As they arrived, Kendra felt the weight of anticipation pressing down on her. The community center was bustling with activity, people laughing and chatting as they participated in various events.

“Let’s split up and ask around,” she suggested. “We can cover more ground that way.”

They nodded and dispersed, each approaching different groups of people. Kendra approached a group of volunteers, her heart pounding in her chest. She introduced herself and explained their search for information about David, who had volunteered there shortly before his death.

"I remember David," a middle-aged man said, his expression somber. "He was such a dedicated worker. He mentioned feeling uneasy a few days before he disappeared."

"Did he say why?" Kendra pressed, her curiosity piqued.

The man shook his head. "Just that something felt off. He didn't elaborate, but I could tell he was worried about something."

Kendra's heart raced as she connected the dots. "Thank you. That's really helpful." She exchanged contact information and promised to follow up.

Meanwhile, Jane and Josh spoke with other volunteers, gathering their own insights. After an hour of questioning, they regrouped outside the community center, each of them buzzing with information.

"Did you find anything?" Kendra asked, her eyes shining with hope.

"Some people mentioned feeling watched, just like Audrey," Jane said, her brow furrowing. "It's like they all sensed something was wrong before it happened."

Josh nodded, his expression serious. "We need to follow this lead. Let's head to the library next."

As they made their way to the library, the sun dipped lower in the sky, painting the horizon in hues of orange and pink. Kendra felt a sense of urgency building within her, the weight of their mission pressing down on her shoulders. They needed to find the truth, to uncover the connections that could lead them to the killer.

Upon arriving at the library, Kendra felt a wave of nostalgia wash over her. This had been a place of refuge for them, a sanctuary filled with stories and laughter. But now, it felt tainted by the recent tragedies.

As they entered, the familiar scent of old books enveloped them, but the atmosphere felt heavy with sadness. They approached the librarian, an elderly woman with kind eyes who had known them since childhood.

"Hello, dear," she greeted Kendra with a warm smile, though it quickly faded upon seeing the somber expressions on their faces. "What brings you here today?"

"We're looking for information about Mary," Kendra explained, her heart racing. "She was here before she disappeared, and we need to know if anyone saw anything unusual."

The librarian nodded, her brow furrowing in concern. "I remember Mary well. She was always so studious. Let me check our records."

As the librarian pulled out logs and records, Kendra felt a mix of hope and anxiety. They needed to uncover any hidden truths that could help them piece together the puzzle.

After a few moments, the librarian looked up. "I found some footage from the day Mary was last here. Would you like to see it?"

"Yes, please!" Kendra replied, her heart pounding in anticipation.

The librarian led them to a small viewing room, where they gathered around a monitor. As the footage played, Kendra felt her breath hitch in her throat. There was Mary, seated at a table, surrounded by books, but something was off. She kept glancing around, as if sensing someone watching her.

"Look!" Kendra pointed at the screen as a shadowy figure moved past the window, just outside the library. "Who is that?"

The librarian squinted at the screen. "I'm not sure. It looks like someone was lingering outside, but I can't make out any details from this angle."

"Can we enhance the footage?" Kendra asked, her mind racing.

The librarian nodded, her fingers expertly working the controls. As the image sharpened, Kendra felt a surge of adrenaline. The figure was wearing a dark hoodie, and while their face was still obscured, there was something familiar about the way they moved.

"Wait... pause it!" Kendra exclaimed, her heart racing. "I think I've seen that hoodie before."

As they continued to analyze the footage, Kendra's mind raced with possibilities. They had to find a way to connect these dots, to uncover the identity of the person who had been lurking around their friends.

"Let's gather everything we have and regroup," Kendra said, her voice steady. "We need to put this together before it's too late."

After thanking the librarian, they left the library, the weight of their discoveries heavy in their hearts. They had gathered crucial information, but the urgency was palpable. Time was not on their side, and they needed to act quickly.

Back at Kendra's house, they spread out their notes and findings, trying to piece together the tangled web that had ensnared their lives. The room was filled with tension as they shared their discoveries, each piece of information a potential breakthrough.

"Okay, let's start from the beginning," Kendra said, her voice steady as she addressed her friends. "We know that each victim sensed something was wrong before they disappeared. They all felt watched, which suggests that this killer has been observing us for a while."

Josh nodded, his brow furrowing in concentration. "And the shadowy figure we saw in the footage—it could be the same person who was lurking around the community center and the coffee shop. We need to figure out who they are."

Jane pulled out her phone, scrolling through her contacts.

"What about talking to some of the other friends we have? Maybe they've seen something or noticed someone acting strangely."

Kendra agreed, her mind racing with possibilities. "We can't leave any stone unturned. We should also consider reaching out to the police again, see if they have any updates or leads."

As they discussed their next steps, Kendra felt a renewed sense of determination. They were united in their mission, fueled by the desire to uncover the truth and bring justice to their friends. The shadows that had once felt suffocating now seemed like a challenge to overcome, a test of their strength and resolve.

"Let's make a list of everyone we should talk to and where we need to go next," Kendra suggested, her voice steady. "We have to act quickly and efficiently."

They spent the next hour compiling their list, organizing their thoughts and strategies. Each name they wrote down became a beacon of hope, a reminder that they were not alone in this fight. Together, they would confront the darkness and reclaim their lives.

The next day, they set out early, the sun barely peeking over the horizon. The chill in the air invigorated them, a reminder that they were alive and determined to make a difference. Their first stop was to meet with friends and acquaintances who might have seen something unusual.

"Let's start with people who were close to Danny," Kendra suggested as they walked through the neighborhood, her heart heavy with the weight of loss. "They might have noticed something or have information we don't."

As they approached one of Danny's friends, a boy named Ethan, Kendra felt a mix of hope and fear. They knocked on the door, and Ethan answered, his expression shifting from surprise to sorrow as he recognized them.

"Hey, guys," he said softly. "I heard about Danny. I can't believe it. I'm so sorry."

"Thanks, Ethan," Kendra replied, her voice steady despite the pain in her heart. "We're trying to gather information about what happened. We know he was with you before he disappeared. Did he mention anything unusual?"

Ethan's brow furrowed in thought. "Not really. He seemed fine, just excited about Halloween. But now that I think about it, he did mention feeling like someone was following him a few days before…"

Kendra exchanged glances with her friends, their hearts racing at the revelation. "Do you remember anything specific? A description, anything at all?"

Ethan shook his head, frustration etched across his face. "No, it was just a passing comment. I thought he was joking at first, but now…" His voice trailed off, and Kendra could see the guilt etched in his features.

"Don't blame yourself," Kendra said gently, placing a hand on his shoulder. "We need to gather all these pieces together. Anything could be important."

After spending some time with Ethan, they moved on to their next lead, a girl named Lily who had been close to Sarah. As they approached her house, Kendra felt a surge of hope. They had to uncover every detail, no matter how small, that could bring them closer to the truth.

"Lily!" Kendra called, waving as the girl stepped outside. "We're here to talk about Sarah. Can we ask you a few questions?"

Lily's expression shifted from surprise to sadness. "Of course. I can't believe everything that's happened. It's so horrible."

As they sat down with Lily, the atmosphere grew heavy with grief and fear. Kendra felt her heart race as they recounted the events leading up to Sarah's disappearance, hoping to find any clue that could lead them to the killer.

"I remember Sarah mentioning something about a guy she saw at the park," Lily said, biting her lip. "She thought he was acting strange, just sitting on a bench and watching people. She didn't think much of it at the time, but now..."

Kendra's heart pounded in her chest. "Do you know what he looked like?"

Lily shook her head, frustration evident in her eyes. "No, she didn't give a description. She just said he gave her the creeps."

"Thank you, Lily," Kendra said, her voice steady. "Every detail matters. We're going to find out who did this."

As they wrapped up their meeting, Kendra felt a sense of urgency building within her. They needed to compile what they had learned and focus on the connections between the victims. The darkness that had taken so much from them would not win. They were determined to fight back, to uncover the truth and protect each other.

As the sun set on Magnolia, Kendra and her friends gathered once more, their notes spread out before them like a map to the truth. They poured over their findings, searching for patterns, connections, anything that might lead them to the Reaper killer.

"Okay," Kendra started, her voice steady as she addressed her friends. "We've gathered a lot of information, but we need to pinpoint who this shadowy figure is. We know they were lurking at the library, the community center, and the coffee shop."

Josh nodded, his brow furrowing in concentration. "We should look into the people who were at these locations around the same time. Maybe there are connections we haven't seen yet."

Jane added, "And what about social media? We could try to see if anyone posted anything unusual during that time."

As they brainstormed, the sense of determination built within them. They would not let fear rule their lives any longer. They would confront this darkness head-on, armed with the truth.

With renewed purpose, they set to work, diving into their research and connecting the dots. They scoured social media, looking for any posts or messages that could provide insight into the killer's identity. Each piece of information felt like a stepping stone, guiding them closer to the truth.

Hours passed as they worked tirelessly, the weight of their mission fueling their determination. They stayed up late into the night, poring over their findings and piecing together the puzzle. Finally, as the clock struck midnight, Kendra leaned back in her chair, exhaustion overtaking her.

"We've done everything we can for now," she said, her voice weary but resolute. "We'll regroup tomorrow and continue the search. We're closer than ever."

As they prepared to leave, Kendra felt a sense of hope mingled with fear. They had uncovered so much, but the darkness still loomed, threatening to consume them.

"Let's stick together," Kendra reminded them, her heart pounding with determination. "No matter what happens, we face it as a team."

With that, they stepped into the night, their hearts heavy but filled with purpose. They would not be victims of fear; they would be warriors in their fight for justice. Together, they would uncover the truth and bring an end to the terror that had haunted their town.

As they walked through the quiet streets of Magnolia, Kendra could feel the weight of their mission pressing down on her. The night felt alive with possibilities, and she knew that they were on the brink of something monumental.

Together, they would face whatever darkness awaited them, armed with the strength of their friendship and the unyielding desire to protect each other. The shadows may have claimed their friends, but they would not let it take them. They were determined to find the light amidst the darkness, no matter the cost.

Chapter 14

The air was thick with the metallic scent of sirens, mingling with the acrid aroma of sweat and fear, permeating every corner of the dimly lit alley. Kendra lowered her phone, her fingers trembling slightly as the implications of the chilling message sunk in like a stone in her gut. Each heartbeat thudded in her ears, a relentless drumbeat of dread that matched the chaos swirling around them. She turned to her friends, Jane and Josh, their expressions mirroring her own sense of foreboding. In their eyes, she saw a desperate grappling with the nightmare that had just unfolded—an urgent acknowledgment that they were all in this together.

"Are you guys okay?" she croaked, her voice barely above a whisper, her throat tightening as if a noose were tightening around it.

Josh ran a shaky hand through his disheveled hair, his face pale like the first light of dawn breaking through a stormy night. "No, we're definitely not okay. Danny…" His voice trailed off, the weight of his grief palpable as he looked away, his gaze distant and unfocused. Kendra could see the glimmer of unshed tears pooling in his eyes, threatening to spill over. "I can't believe he's gone. Why did this happen?"

A heavy silence hung in the air, thick and suffocating, until Kendra interjected, forcing herself to speak with a steadiness she didn't feel. "We need to focus," she insisted, her voice steadying as she fought against the storm brewing inside her. "Did you see that message?"

She pulled out her phone once more, holding it out like a deadly weapon. "He said I could walk away, but if I do, what does that mean for you two?"

Jane stepped forward, her jaw set with fierce determination, the fire of resolve igniting within her. "That's the point," she said, her voice strong, unyielding. "He thinks he can control us with fear. We can't let him."

"But how do we fight someone like that?" Josh asked, desperation creeping under his skin, his brow furrowing with worry. "He's going after us, one by one."

Kendra swallowed hard, steeling herself against the anxiety clawing at her chest, gnawing away at her sanity. "First, we have to take this seriously," she said, her tone firm.

"We can't let him get to us. We're smarter than him. We can outsmart him, or at least we can try."

Just then, a loud commotion erupted behind them as more police arrived, pushing back the gathering crowd of onlookers, their faces a mix of horror and morbid curiosity. A reporter with a camera shouted questions, her voice slicing through the murmur of disbelief like a knife. "What's happening inside the attraction? Was there a killer? Are there more victims?"

Kendra's insides twisted at the idea of her friends being paraded for the world to speculate about, turned into mere fodder for sensationalist news. "We need to go," she said abruptly, her voice sharp with urgency. "If we stay here, we'll be just another part of this horror show. We need a plan."

Against the chaos unfolding around them, Jane nodded, her determination rekindled like a flame in the night. "Let's get back to my house. It'll be safe there. We can figure things out and find a way to stop him."

"Right," Kendra replied, her resolve solidifying. They stepped away from the scene, the blaring sirens and flashing lights fading behind them, but not the weight of the night pressing down on their shoulders. As they approached Jane's car, Kendra's heartbeat settled just slightly, a flicker of hope igniting within her.

Once inside the vehicle, Jane sped away from Inferno Haunt, leaving the cacophony of lights and noise behind. Yet even as they drove, Kendra couldn't shake the feeling that they had merely stepped from one nightmare into another. Her fingers itched to check her phone again, but she resisted, finally opting to focus on her friends, the lifelines tethering her to sanity.

As they reached Jane's house, the oppressive weight of the night pressed down, wrapping around them like a shroud woven from shadows and fear. They quickly poured into the living room, the warm light striking a stark contrast to the cold dread that hovered in their hearts like a specter.

"Let's lock the doors," Jane suggested, her voice steady as she headed to the front of the house before anyone could protest. She turned the deadbolts firmly into place, creating a fragile barricade against the unknown evils lurking outside.

Kendra followed closely, her mind racing with possibilities and plans. "What if we tried to find out who this guy is?" she proposed, her voice steadying with urgency. "Look up the email address, see if anything comes up."

"Good idea," Josh said eagerly as he slid into an armchair, logistically shifting into focus, determination flaring in his eyes. He pulled out his own phone and began typing furiously, the soft clicks of the keyboard punctuating the heavy silence that enveloped them like a thick fog. "I'll take a look at social media, see if anyone's talking about it."

Meanwhile, Jane retrieved the laptop, her movements brisk and purposeful. Kendra could feel the tension filling the space; each click of the keyboard echoed like a pulse in the stillness, a reminder of the urgency pressing down upon them. She took a moment to breathe, willing her mind to calm down, her thoughts drifting back to Danny. He had been the life of their group, his laughter lighting up even the darkest moments. Now, that light was snuffed out, leaving a void that screamed with turmoil and longing.

"Okay, I've got the laptop," Jane announced, setting it down on the coffee table with a determined thud. "Let's see what you found, Josh."

His expression was grave as he turned the screen toward them, his brows furrowed with concern. "There's not a lot of information directly related to this email address, but there are posts on forums about similar happenings around haunted attractions. People disappearing… strange occurrences… and, um, there's a connection to the name 'The Magnolia Reaper.'"

Kendra felt ice trickle down her spine, a cold wave of realization washing over her. "What do you mean 'the same name'?" she demanded, her voice rising with a mix of fear and disbelief.

"There are reports going back years about someone using that name in other hauntings! It looks like whoever it is has a pattern." He scrolled down, revealing a series of threads and posts, showcasing victims and stories that each seemed to weave into their own dark fabric of terror and despair.

"This is all connected," Kendra muttered under her breath, her heart racing again as she sifted through the grotesque information laid out before them. "And it looks like we're the latest chapter in his twisted story."

"What do we do, then?" Jane asked, anxiety threading through her voice, her hands trembling slightly. "This is bigger than us."

Kendra exhaled sharply, her mind racing ahead with a mix of fear and determination. "We can't let him dictate our decisions. We need to put together everything we have. If he's looking for a reaction, we can't give him that. We need a plan to catch him off guard—to draw him out."

Josh looked skeptical, clenching his fists in frustration. "What if it puts us in danger?"

Kendra fixed Josh with a resolute stare that was both fierce and unwavering. "Are we going to keep hiding from him? Or do we take a stand for Danny, for ourselves? We owe it to him, and we owe it to us."

Silence enveloped them as her words hung in the air, a heavy, charged moment that felt like the calm before a storm. Slowly, a flicker of determination took root in their eyes, and Jane nodded, her fear mingling with a hint of purpose. "Let's do it, then. We can't just sit here and wait for him to make the next move."

Kendra felt the knot in her chest loosen slightly, a sense of relief washing over her. “We need to set a trap. But first, we should gather what we can—anything that can help us fight back.”

They began assembling an array of materials: flashlights, a camera, duct tape, whatever they could think of that might assist in the hunt for The Reaper. Each item felt like a piece of armor, a small shred of empowerment against a foe that felt insurmountable.

As they worked, Kendra’s phone buzzed yet again, and this time she gripped it tightly as a wave of dread surged through her. She knew she had to see it. With shaky fingers, she unlocked her phone, scanning the new message that taunted her from the screen.

“Looks like sweet revenge is coming for you three. Tick tock.”

The words leaped off the screen, suffocating her with a terror that wrapped around her heart like a vice. She looked up, seeing Jane and Josh piecing together their makeshift plan, but Kendra felt panicked, the walls closing in around her. "He's coming for us," she said, her voice cracking under the weight of the revelation. "I don't know when, but he's not going to stop until we're all gone."

"Then we prepare," Jane said, a steely edge to her tone that cut through the fear. "We gather our strength, we stand our ground. We can't run away. Not now."

Kendra nodded, the fire in her heart rekindled. "All of us together, we will face him. There's no other way."

But even as she spoke the words, the icy grip of uncertainty clawed at her insides, a relentless reminder of the danger that loomed just beyond their fragile sanctuary. They were racing against time, trapped between their fear of the unknown and the undeniable fact that they had to confront a monster that had already taken too much from them.

As the night deepened outside, shadows crept through the windows, lurking just within the periphery of their vision, a constant reminder that danger was closer than they dared to hope.

"Let's finish this," Kendra said, taking a deep breath as they moved into action. With her friends by her side, they had a chance against the darkness waiting just beyond the walls. The battle was only beginning, and they were determined to emerge victorious, no matter the cost. The stakes were high, but so was their resolve. They would uncover the truth, confront the horrors of The Magnolia Reaper, and reclaim their lives from the clutches of fear.

Chapter 15

Josh and Jane stood in the dimly lit room, their breaths shallow and quick, nerves electrifying the air around them. The gravity of their decision to confront the killer pressed down like an iron weight, heavy and unyielding. "Kendra," Jane said, her steady voice barely masking the turmoil inside her, "send him a message. We want to meet."

Kendra hesitated, her heart racing as she processed the gravity of what they were about to do. Her fingers hovered above the screen of her phone, uncertainty coursing through her veins. "Where?" she finally asked, sensing the tension crackling between them like static electricity.

"The old movie theater," Josh replied, his voice low and tense. The theater had once been a vibrant hub of laughter and joy, a place where cinematic dreams came alive, but now it lay deserted, a haunting specter of its past. "It feels… appropriate."

With a trembling hand, Kendra began typing, her heart pounding against her ribcage like a trapped bird. "Tell him we want to hear his side of the story," Jane urged, her heart racing as she felt the weight of their situation press upon her. They needed answers, a way to piece together the chaos that had engulfed their town and shattered their lives.

"What if it's a trap?" Josh mused, the worry clear on his face, his brow furrowing as he contemplated the risks. "What if we walk into something we can't control?"

"But what choice do we have?" Jane shot back, her eyes fierce with determination. "We've lived with this long enough. We need to face him."

Kendra completed the message, her breath hitching as she pressed send. An oppressive silence cloaked the room, their hearts synchronized in a rhythm of fear and anticipation. The atmosphere felt charged, as if the very walls were holding their breath along with them. Then, a notification pinged—a single, chilling reply: "No cops, or someone else's blood will be on the edge of my knife."

Kendra's face drained of color as she glanced between her friends, dread pooling in her stomach.

Josh's frown deepened, and Jane inhaled sharply, her resolve momentarily faltering. "4 PM," Josh whispered, the hour looming ahead like an uninvited guest, pushing their pulse rates higher with every tick of the clock.

They gathered their composure, forming a plan as best as they could. They discussed escape routes, equipped themselves with flashlights and phones, and steeled themselves for whatever confrontation lay ahead. With each tick of the clock, their resolve grew stronger, even as unease settled deep in their bones like a heavy fog.

When the time finally came, they arrived at the theater on 152 North Brooke Ave, the parking lot devoid of life. The wind howled through the trees, a chilling melody underscoring their approach. Rain began to patter on the pavement, droplets tapping a rhythmic beat that echoed their racing hearts, while distant thunder rumbled ominously in the darkening sky.

"Remember, we're in this together," Jane whispered, seeking solace in their unity. They huddled closer, shoulders brushing, hearts hammering in their chests as they pushed forward toward the entrance.

Everything hung in the balance as they stood at the threshold of the unknown. This was their moment—for the truth to be unveiled, for the mask to be removed once and for all. Today, they would confront the darkness that had haunted them for far too long, stepping into the theater's shadows to reclaim their lives.

As Kendra, Jane, and Josh edged their way toward the back door of the theater, the dim glow from the flickering marquee illuminated their path, casting eerie shadows that danced around them like specters. A chill swept through the air, laden with anticipation and an unsettling unease. They were searching for an old connection, a clue that could piece together the mysteries surrounding Danny, who had once occupied these halls.

Suddenly, beneath a pile of discarded advertisements and candy wrappers, Kendra's fingers brushed against something cold and metallic. She pulled it from the debris—a spare key, rusted yet undeniably familiar. Their hearts raced. Danny had been a ghostly presence around the theater, a young man whose quiet demeanor kept him largely unnoticed by patrons and staff alike. In the aftermath of the Magnolia killings, he had quickly faded into memory, leaving behind only whispers of his existence.

"He always kept to himself," Jane mused, her brow furrowed in thought. "I heard he worked here part-time, but I never really knew him. Wasn't he supposed to be studying film or something?"

Josh nodded, eyes reflecting a mixture of curiosity and fear, as if the very mention of Danny's name conjured a specter from the past. "Yeah, something like that. He was always watching movies and making notes. But after everything that happened…" He trailed off, the weight of their shared grief palpable in the air, a heavy reminder of all they had lost.

Standing outside, they lifted their gazes to the front of the theater, which bustled with life. Halloween decorations draped the entrance like cobwebs, the flickers of orange and purple lights enticing moviegoers. Posters for *Halloween*, *The Nightmare Before Christmas*, *Hannibal*, and *Hocus Pocus* adorned every wall, iconic images vying for attention. Families, couples, and packs of teenagers dotted the courtyard, buzzing with excitement as they echoed their favorite lines from horror classics.

"This place used to be different after Danny..." Kendra whispered, her mind drifting to the memories of laughter and camaraderie that had once filled the theater. With the limited selection of movies each year during October, these classics held a cherished place in the hearts of the community, a nostalgic refuge from real-life horrors.

What secrets lay behind those doors now? What whispers of Danny remained hidden among the untouched relics of his life and the ghosts that roamed the aisles? The key felt heavy in Kendra's hand, as if it held stories untold, waiting for them to unlock the door to the past.

"Should we see what it opens?" Josh suggested, a mixture of excitement and apprehension threading his voice, his eyes darting toward the entrance.

"I think we should," said Jane, determination sparking in her eyes. "Danny might have left something behind—something that could help us understand what really happened."

Kendra nodded slowly, her grip tightening on the key, its cold surface a reminder that sometimes, facing the ghosts of the past was the only way to confront the fears of the present. Together, they moved closer to the door, hearts pounding, ready to uncover the secrets that lay within the darkened corners of the theater, where both the living and the dead intersected.

As Kendra, Josh, and Jane wandered through the theater, mesmerized by the stunning Halloween decorations, Kendra's phone suddenly rang, illuminating the screen with "Unknown Caller." A shiver ran down her spine; an instinctive awareness told her it was the infamous Magnolia Reaper killer on the other end. The theater, already unsettling with its creepy decor, transformed into a true nightmare as the killer's presence loomed.

Kendra hesitated, her heart racing, before answering the call. "What do you want?" she demanded, striving to maintain a calm that belied her inner turmoil. A cold, mechanical voice crackled through the receiver. "It's time to confront the mask and put an end to your destruction once and for all." Fueled by defiance, she shot back, "If you want me so badly, then come and get me!" Without a response, the line went dead.

Suddenly, the theater lights flickered and went out, plunging them into darkness. Panic surged as they fumbled for their phones, switching on the flashlights. The beams of light cut through the thick darkness, illuminating the once-familiar surroundings that now felt alien and hostile. As Josh turned around, his beam landed on the menacing mask of the Ghostface killer, a sight that sent ice coursing through Kendra's veins.

In an instant, the killer lunged, slashing Josh’s arm and stabbing him in the side. He gasped, pain radiating through him, but before he could react further, Jane bravely tackled the assailant, knocking him to the ground. The force sent them both sprawling, and Kendra felt a surge of adrenaline fuel her instincts.

Seizing the moment, Kendra drew her gun, her hands steady as she aimed at the shadowy figure. “Get away from him!” she shouted, her voice steady despite the chaos. She fired multiple shots, but the killer slipped away, disappearing into the shadows of the theater. The thunder of her heart matched the pounding of her pulse in her ears, and the fear of failure clawed at her insides.

"Josh!" Jane cried, scrambling to his side as she assessed the damage, panic etched on her face. "Are you okay? Talk to me!"

"I'll be fine," he gasped, gritting his teeth against the pain. "Just... just go after him! We have to stop him before he gets away!"

Kendra nodded, her fear transforming into fiery determination. "We can't let him escape. He knows we're here, and we're not leaving until we get answers!" With that, they plunged deeper into the theater, the darkness wrapping around them like a suffocating shroud.

As they navigated the twisted corridors, memories flooded back —echoes of laughter, the flickering glow of the screen, and the warmth of friendship. But now, the air was thick with tension and fear, and each creak of the floorboards sounded like a warning of impending danger. They reached a small room lined with posters of classic horror films, where Danny had spent countless hours. The room felt charged with his presence, a bittersweet reminder of the life once lived within these walls.

"Look!" Josh exclaimed, pointing to a tattered notebook lying on the floor, partially hidden beneath a pile of old scripts. Kendra picked it up, her heart racing as she flipped through the pages filled with Danny's neat handwriting. It was a journal, detailing his thoughts on the films he watched, but there were also sketches and notes that hinted at something darker—references to strange occurrences, sightings, and a list of names, including their own.

"This… this is everything," Kendra breathed, her voice trembling. "He was trying to uncover the truth! He knew something was happening before it all went down."

"Do you think he was trying to warn us?" Jane asked, her voice barely above a whisper, the weight of realization settling heavily on their shoulders.

"I think he was trying to protect us," Josh replied, his eyes scanning the pages frantically. "He must have felt that something was coming, something terrible."

The sound of footsteps echoed in the distance, a reminder that they were not alone. The killer was still lurking, hunting them like prey. "We need to move," Kendra urged, her pulse quickening. "We can't stay here. We need to find a way to trap him or at least get out of here alive."

They gathered what they could from the room—the journal, a few props that could serve as weapons, and their resolve. As they made their way toward the exit, the flickering lights overhead cast erratic shadows that danced along the walls, heightening their sense of dread.

"Let's split up," Kendra suggested, her voice steadying as she attempted to maintain control amidst the chaos. "If we can flank him, we might have a chance."

"Are you sure that's a good idea?" Jane asked, her eyes wide with concern.

"It's our best shot. We can't let him take any more from us," Kendra replied, determination igniting within her. "We'll meet back here in fifteen minutes. If we don't find him, we regroup and find another way out."

With a nod of understanding, they each took a flashlight and ventured into the darkness, the eerie silence amplifying their fears. Kendra moved cautiously, her heart racing as she navigated the maze of corridors, each creak of the floorboards echoing like a heartbeat in the stillness.

Suddenly, she heard a noise—a faint scuffling sound from one of the nearby rooms. Her instincts kicked into overdrive, and she approached the door cautiously, holding her breath. As she reached for the doorknob, it swung open suddenly, and she found herself face-to-face with the killer.

Time seemed to slow as she raised her flashlight, illuminating the mask that had haunted her nightmares. "You," he sneered, his voice dripping with malice. "You think you can play games with me?"

Kendra's heart raced, adrenaline flooding her veins. "What do you want?" she demanded, her voice steady, though fear coursed through her.

"Revenge," he hissed, his eyes glinting with a twisted delight. "You've taken everything from me, and now it's your turn to pay."

With a sudden burst of courage, Kendra lunged forward, swinging her flashlight at him with all her might. The impact sent him staggering back, momentarily disoriented. "Run!" she shouted, bolting down the hallway, urgency propelling her forward as she shouted for her friends. "Jane! Josh!"

They needed to regroup, to formulate a plan. The theater had become a labyrinth of horror, and the stakes had never been higher. As she dashed through the darkness, Kendra felt a renewed determination surge within her—this was their moment to reclaim their lives, to confront the monstrous figure that had cast a shadow over their existence.

With every step, she could hear the echoes of laughter from the past, the flickering memories of friendship intertwined with the grim reality of their present. They would face this darkness together, and together they would emerge victorious, no matter the cost. The time for fear was over; now was the time for action.

Chapter 16

Kendra and Jane rushed to Josh, their hands trembling with shock as they lifted him gently, trying to support his injured side. His face was pale, twisted in agony, and fear struck Kendra like a thunderbolt, electrifying her senses. "Are you alright?" they urged, the alarm evident in their voices. Blood streamed down his arm from a deep knife wound, and another torrent pooled from his side, darkening the fabric of his shirt, a horrifying testament to the brutality they had faced.

"Just… hold on," Josh gasped, his breath ragged and shallow. They could barely comprehend the depth of his injuries as they applied pressure, their hands slick with his warm blood. Desperation clawed at Kendra as she glanced around the dimly lit room, searching for a way to help. The uncertainty of their surroundings hung heavy in the air, making each second stretch like an eternity.

Suddenly, Kendra's phone buzzed violently in her pocket, breaking the grim focus of their aid. The screen displayed "Unknown Caller," which sent prickles of dread racing down her spine. Hesitating for just a second, she answered with a trembling voice, "Hello?"

"You're in over your head," a voice crackled on the other end, distorted and chilling, sending shivers coursing through her body. "HEADS UP!"

Before Kendra could respond, a deafening bang reverberated through the space—a sound far worse than thunder. It was no mere noise; it was the sickening, brutal report of a shotgun blast. In that heart-stopping moment, the lights flickered back on, illuminating a scene of unspeakable horror. Blood and brain matter splattered grotesquely across the walls, a grotesque tapestry of violence, while Josh's insides were shockingly exposed, a gruesome testament to the brutality they had been trying to escape.

"NO!!!" Kendra and Jane wailed in unison, their voices mingling in anguish as panic ricocheted in their chests. Every instinct screamed for them to flee, yet they were rooted to the spot, overwhelmed by the visceral horror of what lay before them. Time felt suspended as they prayed for a miracle, a flicker of hope amidst the devastation.

"Josh!" Jane cried, her voice thick with tears as she cradled his head in her lap, desperate to keep him grounded in the agonizing moments of reality. "Stay with us! Please!"

"I—I can't..." Josh murmured, his breath growing shallower, the light in his eyes dimming. "It hurts... I..."

Panic surged within Kendra as she desperately glanced towards the door, the shadow of the killer ominously lurking somewhere beyond their sight. There was no way to escape, no way to save him. The echo of the shotgun blast still resonated in the air, a harbinger of more violence to come.

"Help is coming," she whispered, though it felt like a feeble lie, meant only to comfort herself more than him. "Just hold on, please!"

But as Josh's eyes fluttered closed, succumbing to the pain, the reality hit them like a freight train—they were fighting against time, and it was running out fast.

As Josh lay there, lifeless, blood pooling beneath him, Kendra and Jane knelt beside their beloved friend, hearts pounding with shock and disbelief. His body, once so full of life, was now a horrifying reminder of the ruthlessness of their enemy. Kendra's shattered sob echoed through the cavernous theater, drowning out the silence. "YOU SON OF A BITCH!" she screamed, her voice a knife cutting through the suffocating air.

Tears streamed down their faces, warm against the cold reality of their surroundings. The memory of laughter and shared dreams now felt unbearably distant. Each drop of Josh's blood was a mark on their souls, punctuating the agony of his loss. They had watched as the killer had taken Sarah, David, Danny, Mary, Audrey—and now Josh. It was a growing list of casualties that haunted their nights and robbed them of peace.

Kendra pressed her trembling hands against Josh's chest, desperately willing him back to life. The warmth of his skin was fading, and panic clawed at her throat. "No, no, no…" she whispered, as if her words could somehow change the horrific reality they faced. Jane, choked with grief, clutched Kendra's arm, feeling the tremors coursing through her friend, echoing her own inner chaos.

"This isn't how it's supposed to be," Jane sobbed, her chest heaving as she glanced around the once-vibrant theater, now tainted by tragedy. The ornate decorations, once meant for celebration, felt like a mockery in the face of such monstrous loss. "We have to do something. We can't let them get away with this!"

Kendra wiped her tears with the back of her hand and met Jane's gaze. A flicker of determination ignited between them. They had mourned too long while the killer lurked in the shadows, unseen and unchallenged. "You're right. We can't let them take anyone else."

Their grief morphed into resolve, a powerful surge that pushed them toward action. "We owe it to Josh… to Sarah and everyone else,"

Kendra said, her voice steely. "This ends now."

With the images of their friends' faces blurring in her mind, a fierce anger coursed through Jane. She thought of how they had all laughed, dreamed big, and navigated the ups and downs of life together. But now, what they had shared was marred by the brutality of a faceless monster. "We need a plan," she stated, her words steadying her shivering heart.

They stood together by Josh's side, united in their grief and their rage. The air crackled with their determination. They would not let the darkness win. They would hunt down this killer, drag them out of hiding, and ensure they faced justice. "We'll find them, Kendra. We'll make them pay for what they've done," Jane vowed, her spirit ignited by righteous fury.

In that moment, the theater transformed from a place of despair into a crucible for revenge. They could feel the weight of their fallen friends resting on their shoulders, a heavy mantle urging them forward. Kendra wiped the tears from her cheeks, feeling the heat of anger rise within her. "We can't let their deaths be in vain. They deserve more than this."

Jane nodded, her resolve hardening. "We've been running, hiding, and hoping for too long. It's time to take a stand. We need to find out who this killer is and put an end to it. We need to turn the tables."

Kendra took a deep breath, her mind racing as she instinctively began to formulate a plan. "We need to gather everything we know about the killer—the patterns, the messages, anything that can give us an edge. If we can anticipate their moves, we can outsmart them."

Jane fumbled through her pockets and pulled out a small notebook. "I've been keeping track of everything since this all started. Notes about the victims, the places where things happened—everything we've heard."

"Good. We need to analyze it all," Kendra said, urgency in her voice. "We might find a connection we've missed."

As they pieced together their notes, the theater began to feel less like a tomb and more like a battleground. They sketched out a rough map of the locations where the killings had occurred, marking each incident with a symbol that represented the victims. The memories of their friends flooded back—faces, laughter, dreams for the future, now overshadowed by the tragedy that had come to define their lives.

"We need to get to the surveillance footage," Jane said, her eyes lighting up with determination. "If we can see who's been coming and going, we might catch a glimpse of the killer."

"Right. The main office should have access to it," Kendra replied, her mind racing with possibilities. "But we need to be careful. The killer could be watching us right now."

They steeled themselves, knowing that they were stepping into a dangerous game. With a shared glance filled with unspoken understanding, they moved toward the office, their hearts pounding like drums in their chests. The corridors felt alive, shadows dancing along the walls as they navigated the maze of the theater.

As they reached the office door, Kendra paused, her hand hovering over the knob. “You ready?” she asked, her voice barely above a whisper.

Jane nodded, determination etched on her face. “Let’s do this.”

Kendra turned the knob and pushed the door open, the hinges creaking ominously as they entered the darkened room. The flickering light from a computer screen cast eerie shadows, illuminating the surrounding chaos of papers strewn about—a testament to the frantic search for answers.

They wasted no time. Kendra quickly booted up the computer while Jane began rifling through the piles of papers, searching for anything that might lead them closer to the truth. "Come on, come on," Kendra muttered, her fingers flying across the keyboard as she accessed the surveillance footage.

Moments felt like hours as they scoured through the grainy video, their eyes scanning for any sign of the killer. The tension was palpable, each second stretching painfully as they replayed clips of the theater, searching for a hint, a clue, anything that might expose the monster hiding in their midst.

Then, Kendra froze, her heart racing as she spotted a figure lurking in the background of one of the tapes. "Wait! Go back!" she shouted, her voice sharp with urgency. Jane leaned over, her breath hitching as they replayed the scene.

The footage revealed a shadowy figure, their face obscured by a hood and mask, moving stealthily through the theater. Kendra's mind raced. "That's him! That's the killer!"

Jane leaned closer, eyes wide. "Can you enhance the image? We need to see more."

Kendra's fingers danced across the keyboard, pulling up the settings to enhance the video feed. As the image sharpened, they both leaned in closer, the air thick with anticipation. The figure moved with a predator's grace, stalking through the shadows, reminiscent of a ghost haunting the very place they had once found solace.

"There!" Jane pointed at a momentary glimpse of the killer's hand, revealing the glint of a knife. "We need to show this to the police!"

Kendra shook her head, her voice firm. "No. We can't risk them being tipped off. We need to handle this ourselves. We have to find out who this is before we alert anyone."

"Then what do we do?" Jane asked, desperation creeping into her tone.

Kendra's mind raced. "We set a trap. We'll lure the killer out and confront them. We can't let fear dictate our lives any longer."

Jane nodded, her resolve returning. "What do we need to do?"

"We'll use the theater to our advantage," Kendra explained, her voice steady as she laid out the plan. "We'll create a scenario that will draw them in, a bait that they can't resist. We'll make them think they have the upper hand while we're ready to catch them off guard."

As they formulated their plan, a sense of purpose washed over them. The theater, once a place of laughter and joy, would become their battleground. They would rise from the ashes of tragedy, fueled by love, rage, and a desperate need for justice. The hunt had begun, and they were ready to face the monster that had haunted their lives for far too long.

In that moment, they felt the spirits of their fallen friends guiding them, urging them forward. They would not let Josh's death be in vain. They would fight for him and for all the others who had suffered at the hands of this killer. The time for fear was over; now was the time for action. Together, they would bring the darkness into the light, and they would emerge victorious, no matter the cost.

Chapter 16

Kendra and Jane frantically searched through the remnants of what was once a vibrant theater, a place that had echoed with laughter, applause, and now, an unsettling silence that seemed to mock their desperation. The dim light from the emergency exit sign flickered sporadically, casting eerie shadows that danced along the walls, transforming the familiar into a haunting labyrinth of fear. Adrenaline surged through their veins as they rummaged through scattered props, broken stage equipment, and old costumes that lay abandoned like forgotten dreams.

Kendra's heart raced, each beat echoing in her ears, drowning out the ominous stillness that enveloped them since the lights had gone out. Panic clawed at her throat, tightening like a vice. "We need to hurry!" she whispered urgently, her voice barely more than a breath as her eyes darted around, searching for anything—anything—that could be used as a weapon against the lurking menace.

Jane, her face pale and determined, grabbed a broken chair leg, holding it tightly as if it were a lifeline. "This will have to do for now," she said, her voice trembling but resolute. The two friends huddled together, their unity a flicker of hope in the oppressive darkness, clinging to the notion that they were stronger than they appeared. The theater felt like a tomb, the air thick with memories of past performances—laughter, applause, and now, a chilling sense of impending doom.

Suddenly, the stillness shattered like glass. The Reaper killer surged forward, his black cloak a sinister blur against the backdrop of shadows. Kendra's scream pierced the air, but it was cut short as the killer lunged towards Jane, pressing a gloved hand over her mouth to muffle her protests. In one swift motion, he silenced her with duct tape across her lips, sealing her fate in an insidious grip. Kendra stood frozen, horror gripping her heart like iron fingers, her instincts screaming for her to act, but her body betrayed her, paralyzed by fear.

Before she could process the terrifying scene unfolding before her, the killer effortlessly hoisted Jane's unconscious body over his shoulder. "Help! No!" Kendra screamed, but the sound was trapped within her, the air thick with terror. She staggered backward, her mind racing with thoughts of escape, but her feet were glued to the floor, watching in horror as he dragged Jane into the upstairs room, a shadow swallowed by shadows.

With every second that passed, the silence of the theater pressed down on her like a heavy fog. Kendra's senses heightened, the adrenaline coursing through her veins like wildfire. She strained to listen as the sounds of the killer's footsteps faded into the depths of the building. The uncertainty of what was happening above filled her with frantic energy. She had to act. Summoning every ounce of courage she had left, Kendra turned toward the stairway, determination igniting a fire within her.

As she ascended the staircase, each creak of the wooden steps sounded like thunder in her ears. The dim flicker of the emergency lights barely illuminated her path, casting long shadows that seemed to taunt her. She could feel the terror of the unknown creeping back, but the urgency to save her friend surged alongside it. This was not just a battle for survival; it was a fight to prove they weren't merely victims. Kendra steeled herself for the inevitable confrontation, ready to reclaim their fate from the grip of fear.

Reaching the top of the stairs, Kendra scanned her surroundings, desperation clawing at her insides as she frantically searched for Jane. The chaos of the recent events played on repeat in her mind, a haunting loop of screams and shadows. Panic began to curl its fingers around her throat as she checked every corner, each shadowy nook seeming to mock her as it yielded no sign of her friend. Just when despair threatened to overwhelm her, her phone buzzed, illuminating the screen with Jane's name.

"Jane, are you okay?" Kendra answered, her voice trembling with fear.

To her horror, a chilling, distorted voice slithered through the line. "Oh, she's just fine. Tied up, if you catch my drift."

"Where is she, you sick psycho?" Kendra shot back, her anger igniting a flicker of determination amidst the dread that threatened to swallow her whole.

The killer's voice dripped with malice. "She's joining me for a little reunion. You'd better face the mask, or I'll use her intestines to fashion a noose around her neck." The line abruptly went dead, leaving Kendra in a whirlpool of terror and rage.

Before she could fully process the terrifying threat, the killer lunged at her from the shadows, brandishing a knife that glinted like a malevolent star in the dim light. Acting on pure instinct, she pulled out her gun, fingers shaking, and fired wildly. Panic compromised her aim; each shot went astray, ricocheting harmlessly into the walls that had witnessed countless performances. The killer let out a chilling cackle that echoed through the corridor, a sound that sent shivers down her spine. He swiftly darted up the stairs, disappearing deeper into the building.

Heart racing, Kendra found herself standing at a dimly lit hallway with two ominous doors. One stood eerily vacant, a dark abyss, while the other beckoned her with a gut-wrenching urgency. She had to choose. The weight of the decision pressed down on her, but there was no time to waste. She steeled her resolve and burst through the second door.

Inside, her worst fears materialized. Bound to a chair, Jane was unconscious, a knife wound marring her arm, crimson staining the white fabric of her shirt—a grim reminder of the peril Kendra had to face to save her friend. With trembling hands, she rushed to untie Jane from the chair, ripping the duct tape from her mouth.

“God, I thought I lost you!” Kendra whispered, her voice thick with emotion, tears threatening to spill as relief washed over her.

But just as she was freeing Jane, the masked Reaper killer entered, a sharp knife gleaming menacingly in his hand. Kendra felt a surge of adrenaline wash over her, pushing aside her fear. She stood her ground, her resolve hardening. “Okay, you finally have me. Now take off that mask and show yourself!”

The killer paused, the room thick with tension. Kendra's heart thudded painfully in her chest as she faced the looming figure, knowing that the stakes were higher than ever. “You think you can scare me?” she challenged, her voice steadier than she felt.

In that moment, Kendra knew the fight was far from over. She was ready to confront this nightmare—and to save Jane. The air crackled with danger, and as the masked figure drew closer, a fierce determination surged within her. There was no backing down now. This was a battle for survival, a fight to reclaim their lives from the abyss that threatened to consume them both.

With a final glance at Jane, Kendra prepared herself, knowing that whatever happened next would change everything. The stage was set, the players were in place, and the final act was about to begin.

Chapter 17

The atmosphere in the dimly lit upstairs room of the movie theater was suffocating, thick with the cloying scent of stale popcorn and spilled soda, a stark contrast to the dread that hung heavily in the air. The flickering light from the aging projector cast eerie shadows that danced along the walls, creating an unsettling ambiance that seemed to pulse with the tension of the moment. Kendra and Jane stood at the edge of that tension, their hearts pounding in their chests as they faced the masked killer—an entity they had never expected to confront.

The masked figure, adorned with the iconic Jack o' lantern reaper mask, loomed before them, and Kendra felt a chill creep down her spine. Tilting the mask slightly to the side, the killer fixed their gaze on Jane and Kendra, whose bodies were frozen in place, icy fear gripping their hearts. Desperation flickered in their eyes as they exchanged terrified glances, both aware that they needed to escape but paralyzed by the sight before them.

With a deliberate, almost theatrical movement, the killer lowered the dark hood that shrouded their figure. The fabric slipped down to reveal not a monstrous creature, but a face that sent shockwaves through their bodies, one that was all too familiar.

Gasps echoed in the room as the killer removed the mask, unveiling Audrey—once their friend—who had transformed into the very embodiment of terror they had witnessed in countless slasher films. The realization hit Kendra and Jane like a tidal wave, washing away any remnants of disbelief and plunging them into a sea of confusion and horror.

"Surprised to see me?" Audrey sneered, her voice dripping with icy confidence. She tossed the ghost face mask aside, allowing it to tumble to the floor with a dull thud, and stepped closer, her demeanor oscillating between menacing and almost playful. "You should have seen your faces! Priceless!"

Kendra's heart raced in her chest, caught between disbelief and horror. They had known Audrey as the girl who organized movie nights, whose laughter was infectious and whose spirit was lively. But here she stood, transformed into something unrecognizable, her eyes gleaming with a wild intensity that sent shivers down their spines.

"Why, Audrey? Why do this?" Kendra managed to stammer, her voice shaking, as she struggled to comprehend the betrayal. Innocent childhood memories flashed in her mind like a montage—sleepovers filled with laughter, sharing secrets under blankets, and late-night horror movies that had once brought them closer. It couldn't be the same girl who had shared popcorn and pillow forts, who had once been a confidante.

Audrey chuckled softly, a sound that resonated with malice. "Because this is what makes life interesting! All those horror movies? They were just practice. I needed to know what it felt like to be the one in control, the one who calls the shots." Her words dripped with a twisted sense of joy, a dissonance that left Kendra feeling nauseous.

Jane felt a surge of anger bubble to the surface. "You've crossed a line, Audrey! This isn't funny. You're scaring us!" Her voice was a blend of defiance and fear, echoing in the cavernous room, a desperate plea for reason.

"Oh, you still don't get it, do you?" Audrey's expression hardened, the playful mask slipping to reveal the darkness beneath. "This isn't about fear; it's about liberation. Life is so mundane, so boring. I just had to spice things up—start a real horror story."

The weight of their predicament settled heavily upon Kendra and Jane, the chilling reality dawning on them: they were trapped in a horror movie scripted by someone they once trusted. The once-familiar contours of the room now held a sinister edge, and they both knew they couldn't let the story end like this, not at the hands of a friend turned foe.

"You're insane!" Kendra shouted, trying to summon any shred of strength while edging backward toward the door, her mind racing with possibilities for escape.

Audrey's smile widened, but her tone turned icy, slicing through the air like a blade. "Insanity is subjective, my friend. Now, let's see how this plot unfolds." Her declaration hung in the air like a death knell, signaling the beginning of a twisted game.

With that, the night erupted into chaos, the theater morphing into a battleground where fear would fuel their fight for freedom. Kendra's heart raced, her breath hitching in her throat as she processed Audrey's revelation. The dim light from the flickering projector created ghostly shadows that accentuated the tension, making the air feel thick and electric.

"You see, Kendra," Audrey continued, her voice low yet sharp, slicing through the thick silence. "It wasn't just me. I had help. You were blind to the truth. You thought he was yours, but he was never really faithful. He strung us both along, didn't he?"

A sickening knot twisted in Kendra's stomach as Audrey's words pierced through the veil of denial. Thoughts raced through her mind—memories of Josh's warm embraces, their shared laughter, the promises whispered under the stars. The realization settled like a heavy weight in her chest, tainting every sweet memory with betrayal. "Why?" was all she could manage to choke out, desperation lacing her voice.

Audrey stepped closer, the dim light casting a haunting glow on her features, transforming her into a grotesque caricature of the friend Kendra once knew. "Because I loved him too," she explained, a trace of regret flickering in her voice, but it was overshadowed by bitterness. "But love turned into rage when I realized I was just a toy to him—a way to satisfy his cravings while he kept you, the perfect girlfriend, in the light. I wasn't just being a mistress; I was made to feel worthless."

Jane shook her head in disbelief, her anger bubbling to the surface. "This doesn't justify what you did, Audrey! You're a murderer!" she shouted, her voice echoing in the cavernous theater, drowning out the distant sounds of the film playing on the screen, a reminder of the life that had once been theirs.

With a sneer, Audrey shrugged, her confidence unwavering. "And yet, here I stand. I'm the one who survived the blast you thought would take me out. I pulled the strings; I manipulated them all, including you, even if I didn't mean to hurt you, Kendra. But honestly, how could you be such an idiot? You let love blind you!"

Kendra's heart ached—not just from the realization of Josh's betrayal but also from the pain of losing a friend in Audrey. "You played me. You both did," she murmured, tears brimming in her eyes. The walls she had built around her heart crumbled under the weight of truth and betrayal, leaving her raw and exposed.

Audrey smirked, a cruel glimmer in her eyes. "And now you see the world as it truly is—harsh and unforgiving. Welcome to reality, Kendra. You thought you knew me, thought you were special. In a way, maybe you were... but not special enough to keep his attention."

As the darkness enveloped them, Kendra felt a flicker of rage ignite within her, a deep-seated need for justice. For the first time in a long time, she felt empowered. "You'll pay for this, Audrey," she vowed, the words slipping through her clenched teeth like a deadly promise, each syllable infused with determination.

Audrey's icy smile faltered for a moment, a flicker of uncertainty crossing her features. "Perhaps, but I'll still be alive to watch it all unfold. Revenge is a dish best served with a side of survival," she replied, her voice dripping with menace.

Kendra's mind raced as she assessed her options, the adrenaline coursing through her veins sharpening her focus. She knew the road ahead would be treacherous, fraught with danger and uncertainty, but she also understood that she couldn't let this go. She would fight back, not just for herself but for the countless hearts left shattered in the wake of betrayal.

As the tension in the room reached a boiling point, Kendra felt the instinct to act surge within her. It was a primal urge, a call to survival that demanded she reclaim her strength. Turning to Jane, who stood resolute beside her, Kendra whispered urgently, "We have to stick together. We can't let her win."

Jane nodded, determination replacing the fear that had once gripped her. "What do we do?" she asked, her voice steadying as the realization of their predicament sank in.

Kendra's mind raced. "We need to find a way out of here, and we need to disarm her. If we can surprise her, maybe we can turn the tables." The flickering light from the projector continued to throw shadows across the room, each flicker igniting a spark of hope within Kendra.

Audrey's laughter cut through their whispered conversation, a chilling sound that reverberated off the walls. "How adorable! You think you can outsmart me? This is my game, and I make the rules." She stepped back, a theatrical flourish accompanying her words. "Let's see how well you play."

Kendra's blood ran cold as she realized the full extent of Audrey's madness. The shadows in the room seemed to thicken, wrapping around them like a shroud as the projector flickered ominously, casting distorted images of horror across the walls. Kendra could feel the weight of despair pressing down upon her, but she refused to succumb.

"Let's go!" Kendra urged Jane, her heart racing as she darted toward the nearest exit. They had to act swiftly, their only chance of survival hinging on their ability to escape Audrey's clutches. The two friends bolted toward the door, adrenaline surging through their veins as they pushed against the oppressive darkness.

But Audrey was quick, her laughter echoing ominously as she lunged after them, a knife gleaming in her hand. "Where do you think you're going?" she taunted, her voice dripping with malice. The sound of her footsteps echoed in the confined space, sending chills down Kendra's spine.

Kendra and Jane raced down the narrow hallway, the flickering light illuminating their path as they desperately searched for an escape. The theater felt like a labyrinth, each corridor twisting and turning, leading them deeper into the shadows. Panic clawed at Kendra's throat as she glanced back, catching a glimpse of Audrey's menacing figure hot on their heels.

"Keep running!" Kendra shouted, her voice rising above the pounding of her heart. They had to find a way out, a way to escape the nightmare that had become their reality. As they sprinted through the darkened hallways, Kendra's mind raced with possibilities, searching for anything that could give them an advantage.

With a sudden burst of determination, Kendra spotted a heavy metal door at the end of the corridor. "There! We can hide in there!" she urged, pointing toward the door that stood slightly ajar.

Jane nodded, her eyes wide with fear but resolute. Together, they dashed toward the door, pushing it open with all their strength. The room beyond was dimly lit, filled with dusty props and forgotten memories. Kendra quickly pulled Jane inside, slamming the door shut behind them.

Breathless and trembling, they leaned against the door, hearts racing as they pressed their ears against the cool wood. The sound of Audrey's footsteps grew louder, the chilling laughter echoing through the theater as she searched for them.

"What do we do now?" Jane gasped, panic seeping into her voice as they stood in the dimly lit storage room. The air was thick with dust, and the smell of mildew filled their nostrils. Shadows danced around them, creating an unsettling atmosphere that felt suffocating.

Kendra's mind raced, searching for a plan. "We need to find something we can use to defend ourselves," she whispered, scanning the room for anything that could serve as a weapon. Her eyes darted over the cluttered space, landing on a rusty crowbar resting against a stack of old crates.

"Over there!" Kendra pointed, her voice filled with urgency. They moved quietly, careful not to make any noise that could give away their position. As they reached the crowbar, Kendra grabbed it, feeling its weight in her hands. It felt reassuring, a solid object that could provide some measure of protection.

Just then, a loud bang echoed from the hallway, followed by Audrey's taunting voice. "You can't hide forever! This is my game, and I always win!" The sound sent a jolt of fear through Kendra, and she tightened her grip on the crowbar, determination flooding her veins.

"We need to make a plan," Kendra said, her voice steady despite the fear coursing through her. "If we can catch her by surprise, we might have a chance to turn the tables."

Jane nodded, her expression resolute. "We'll need to be quick.

She's unpredictable, and we can't let her catch us off guard."

As they strategized, Kendra's mind flashed back to the movies they had watched together, the countless horror films that had shaped their understanding of fear and survival. "Remember how the final girl always finds a way to fight back?" she said, her voice gaining strength. "We can be the final girls in this story."

With renewed determination, Kendra and Jane steeled themselves for what was to come. They might have been caught in a nightmare, but they weren't going to let it end in defeat. They would confront Audrey, the friend who had turned into a monster, and reclaim their lives from the horror that had ensnared them.

With the crowbar in hand, Kendra felt a surge of power. The fear that had once paralyzed her transformed into a fierce resolve. "Let's go," she whispered, leading the way as they moved toward the door, ready to face whatever awaited them on the other side.

As they cautiously opened the door, the flickering light from the projector illuminated the hallway, casting long shadows that seemed to stretch and twist like the fingers of fate. Kendra and Jane stepped into the darkness, hearts pounding, ready to confront their past and fight for their future.

The theater, once a place of joy and laughter, was now a battleground for survival. With every step they took, Kendra felt the weight of betrayal and loss, but alongside it was a fierce determination to reclaim her story. This was their moment to rewrite the ending, to take control of the narrative that had spiraled out of their hands.

As they ventured further into the heart of the theater, Kendra knew that they were not just fighting for their lives; they were fighting for the friendship that had been shattered and the trust that had been broken. They would face Audrey together, and no matter the outcome, they would emerge stronger than ever before.

As Kendra and Jane stepped into the dim hallway, the flickering light from the projector cast elongated shadows that danced eerily along the walls. The air was thick with tension, each creak of the floorboards beneath their feet echoing like a warning bell in the stillness. Kendra gripped the crowbar tightly, its cold metal reassuring against her palm, a symbol of her resolve to fight back against the nightmare that had ensnared them.

"Stay close to me," Kendra whispered, her voice barely audible, but the urgency in it was clear. Jane nodded silently, her eyes wide with a mix of fear and determination, mirroring Kendra's own resolve. Together, they ventured deeper into the heart of the theater, every instinct urging them to be cautious, to make their movements deliberate and calculated.

The hallway stretched before them, a narrow passage lit only by the flickering light of the projector, casting ghostly images on the walls. Each shadow seemed to pulse with the memories of the theater's former glory, a stark contrast to the horror that now dominated their experience. Kendra's heart raced as she thought of the countless hours spent here, laughing and enjoying films with Audrey and Jane—now all of that felt tainted by betrayal and fear.

"We need to find a way to trap her," Jane whispered, her voice shaking slightly. "If we can outsmart her, we can turn this around."

Kendra felt a rush of adrenaline at Jane's words. "Right. If we can lure her into one of the old storage rooms, we might be able to get the upper hand. She won't expect us to fight back."

As they moved cautiously down the hallway, Kendra's mind raced with ideas. They needed to create a distraction, something that would draw Audrey in and give them the chance to catch her off guard. They passed several doors, some slightly ajar, revealing darkened rooms filled with forgotten props and dusty memories. Each door was a potential hiding spot, but they needed to remain focused on their plan.

"There!" Jane pointed to a room at the end of the hallway, its door slightly open, revealing a sliver of darkness within. "That could work."

Kendra nodded, her heart pounding in her chest. "Let's do it." They made their way to the room, moving as quietly as possible, every sound amplified in the oppressive silence.

Once inside, they quickly scanned the room. Dusty costumes hung on hooks, and old props lay scattered across the floor. Kendra spotted a large wooden crate in the corner and gestured for Jane to help her move it in front of the door. Together, they pushed the crate into position, creating a makeshift barricade.

"Now we just need to wait for her," Kendra said, her voice tense with anticipation.

Jane swallowed hard, her eyes darting to the door. "What if she doesn't come? What if she figures out we're trying to trap her?"

Kendra took a deep breath, forcing herself to remain calm. "She's overconfident. She thinks she has the upper hand. That's her weakness."

As they settled into their hiding spot behind the crate, the sounds of the theater shifted. The distant echo of Audrey's laughter reverberated through the hallways, a haunting reminder of the danger they faced. Kendra could feel her heart racing, the adrenaline coursing through her veins as they waited in silence, the weight of the moment pressing down on them.

Minutes stretched into what felt like hours, the tension in the air thickening with each passing second. Kendra's mind swirled with thoughts of betrayal and revenge. She thought of the friendship she had lost, the trust that had been shattered. But alongside that pain was a fierce determination to reclaim her story, to take control of her fate.

Suddenly, the sound of footsteps echoed in the hallway, growing louder as they approached. Kendra's breath hitched in her throat as she exchanged a quick glance with Jane, both of them silently acknowledging the gravity of the moment.

"Here she comes," Kendra whispered, gripping the crowbar tightly, her knuckles turning white against the metal.

The footsteps halted outside their door, and Kendra's heart raced in her chest. They could hear Audrey's voice, taunting and playful as she called out, "Come on, girls! You think you can hide from me? This is my game!"

Kendra's stomach twisted with anxiety, but she held her ground. She could feel Jane's presence beside her, a steady reminder that they were in this together. They were not victims; they were survivors—warriors ready to fight for their lives.

With a sudden crash, Audrey threw open the door, the crate barely holding against her force. Kendra and Jane sprang into action, the element of surprise igniting their adrenaline. Kendra swung the crowbar with all her might, aiming for the masked figure standing in the doorway.

Audrey deftly sidestepped the blow, her laughter echoing in the confined space. "Is that all you've got? I expected more from you!" She lunged forward, her knife glinting menacingly in the dim light.

"Move!" Kendra shouted, shoving Jane aside as she ducked under Audrey's arm. They scrambled around the room, Kendra's mind racing as she tried to think of a way to outmaneuver her former friend. Audrey was relentless, her movements swift and calculated, a predator toying with her prey.

Jane grabbed a nearby prop—a heavy metal chair—and hurled it at Audrey, but the killer easily dodged it, her laughter ringing in Kendra's ears like a death knell. "You think you can stop me with that? Pathetic!"

Kendra and Jane exchanged frantic glances, their desperation mounting. They needed to regroup, to find a way to turn the tide in their favor. "Follow my lead!" Kendra shouted, her heart pounding as she darted toward the opposite end of the room, drawing Audrey's attention away from Jane.

Audrey chased after her, her knife gleaming in the dim light. Kendra could feel the rush of adrenaline propelling her forward as she ducked and weaved, narrowly avoiding another swipe from the blade. The thrill of the chase ignited something deep within her —a primal instinct to survive.

"Jane, now!" Kendra shouted, and Jane understood immediately. With a burst of courage, she charged at Audrey from behind, swinging the metal chair with all her strength.

The chair connected with a loud crash, sending Audrey stumbling forward, the knife flying from her grip. Kendra seized the moment, lunging toward Audrey and tackling her to the ground. They landed with a thud, Kendra's breath escaping her lungs as she fought to pin Audrey down.

"Get the knife!" Kendra shouted, urgency lacing her voice as she struggled to keep Audrey subdued.

Jane scrambled to retrieve the knife, her hands shaking as she reached for it. With trembling fingers, she grasped the hilt and yanked it away from the floor. "I've got it!" she cried, holding it up triumphantly.

Audrey writhed beneath Kendra, her eyes wide with a mixture of surprise and fury. "You think you can hold me down? You're making a big mistake!"

Kendra's heart raced, her body straining against the weight of her former friend. "You're the one who made the mistake, Audrey. You thought you could control everything, but you forgot one crucial thing: we're stronger together."

With newfound determination, Kendra pressed her weight down on Audrey, forcing her to the ground as Jane raised the knife, ready to defend herself and Kendra. "This ends now!" Jane shouted, her voice steady as she stared down at Audrey.

Audrey's expression shifted from anger to something more desperate. "You don't want to do this! You don't understand what you're getting into!"

Kendra's heart pounded in her chest, but she held firm. "No, Audrey. You don't understand.

This isn't a game anymore. You've lost control."

With a sudden burst of energy, Audrey twisted beneath Kendra, trying to break free. Kendra tightened her grip, refusing to let go. "You're not getting away this time!"

The struggle intensified, a raw battle of wills as Kendra fought to keep Audrey pinned down. Jane stood by, knife in hand, ready to strike if necessary. The realization of their strength together surged through Kendra, empowering her even in the face of danger.

"Help me hold her!" Kendra shouted as she felt Audrey's strength wane. Jane rushed forward, pressing her weight against Audrey's shoulders, helping to keep her immobilized.

In that moment, the theater felt alive with the energy of their struggle, a cacophony of fear and determination. Kendra could feel the adrenaline coursing through her veins, fueling her resolve. They would not be victims; they would reclaim their power.

With one final surge of strength, Kendra locked her arms around Audrey's wrists, pinning them to the ground. "You're done, Audrey. This ends here."

Audrey's eyes blazed with rage, but Kendra could see the flicker of desperation beneath the surface. "You think you've won? This isn't over!"

Kendra leaned in closer, her voice steady and unwavering. "It is over.

You've lost, and you'll face the consequences of your actions."

Jane held the knife firmly, ready to protect them both. "We're not afraid of you anymore," she said, her voice strong and defiant.

As the shadows of the theater loomed around them, Kendra felt a sense of clarity wash over her. This was their moment—a chance to rewrite the ending of a story that had spiraled out of control. Together, they were stronger than any fear, any betrayal, any darkness that threatened to consume them.

And as they held Audrey down, the weight of their shared history and the pain of betrayal hung heavy in the air, but so too did the promise of hope—a hope that they would emerge from this nightmare, not just as survivors, but as warriors, ready to reclaim their lives and their friendship.

The theater, once a place of laughter and joy, had transformed into a battleground of survival. And in that moment, Kendra knew they would not just escape; they would triumph. They would face the darkness together, ready to emerge into the light once more.

Chapter 18

Kendra lunged at Audrey, her heart racing as adrenaline pulsed through her veins. The dimly lit theater had morphed into a twisted battleground, each shadow a reminder of the danger that loomed. Kendra aimed to wrest the knife from Audrey's grip, desperation igniting her every movement. Yet, fate had choreographed a cruel dance, one that twisted violently in the heat of their struggle. With a sudden, brutal motion, Audrey plunged the blade into Kendra's side, sending an eruption of sharp pain sparking throughout her body like wildfire.

Kendra screamed—a raw, primal sound that echoed off the walls, filling the space with a haunting resonance. She watched, horrified, as her blood sprayed in chaotic arcs, each drop a vivid testament to her peril. The world around her began to blur, colors running like paint in the rain as shock settled over her senses. The theater, once a sanctuary of laughter and friendship, now felt like a mausoleum of nightmares.

"Come on, Kendra! You can't give up! Fight back!" she urged herself internally, the mantra swirling through her thoughts like a desperate prayer. Gathering what strength remained, she braced herself, her intentions clear: she needed to reclaim the weapon from Audrey's grasp.

But before she could muster the fortitude, Audrey seized the opportunity, shoving Kendra backward. The impact drove the air from her lungs, and she staggered, struggling to remain upright, her vision clouded and her energy waning.

"Here's the thing, bitch," Audrey taunted, her voice a venomous whisper that curled around them like smoke. "You took my love from me, and now I'm going to take yours. But first, I've got one last surprise for you before I Open you Up—in a way you'll never see coming!" The malevolence in her tone chilled Kendra to her core, wrapping around her heart like a vice.

Audrey raised the knife high, her ghostly reaper costume encasing her, rendering her a menacing silhouette against the backdrop of chaos. Kendra felt the darkness close in, but scrambled to think, to react—time became elastic in this moment of terror.

Then, as if summoned from the depths of Kendra's fear, Jane emerged. The sight was ethereal; she stood there frozen for a heartbeat, a vision of resolve in the dimness. But amidst the chaos, clarity sparked in her blue eyes as she spied the glint of metal lying nearby—the gun, almost like a beacon of hope.

A fire ignited within Jane, fierce and unwavering. With trembling hands, she reached for the cold steel, her fingers curling around it as if it were a lifeline, a promise of salvation.

"Don't you dare touch her!" Jane's voice sliced through the grim atmosphere, a powerful declaration that reverberated with unyielding determination.

Without hesitation, she aimed and pulled the trigger. The deafening blast shattered the tension like glass, reverberating through the theater as the bullet found its mark, ripping through the back of Audrey's skull. A sickening splatter followed, blood bursting forth and drenching the floor in a macabre pattern—a horrific testament to their fight for survival. Audrey's body crumpled, lifeless, marking the end of the Woodsboro killer and the tide turning in Kendra and Jane's favor.

Dazed and reeling, Kendra staggered to her feet, her gaze locking onto Jane. A surge of gratitude coursed through her, and instinctively, she rushed over to her friend, enveloping her in a fierce embrace. They clung to each other, trembling, their bodies quaking not just from the aftermath of violence but from an overwhelming wave of relief that washed over them.

As they held on tight, tears streamed down their cheeks, mingling with the blood that soaked Kendra's clothes. Each tear was a bittersweet reminder of what they had endured together—a bond forged in the crucible of horror.

Yet, amidst this moment of reprieve, a distant sound broke through the haze—the rising wail of sirens. The sound swelled, an approaching cacophony heralding the arrival of police officers and EMTs racing up the stairs of the theater. Weapons drawn, they were ready to restore order to the chaos, yet Kendra and Jane remained locked in their embrace, knowing their escape from darkness had not been in vain.

"We made it," Kendra said breathlessly between sobs, pulling back to look into Jane's eyes. "We're alive."

The weight of those words sunk in, and as the first responders burst through, the realization settled heavily around them. They were survivors. And though their bodies bore the cruel reminders of that night, their spirits had not been quelled.

"Okay, ladies," an officer said, his voice calm but firm, yet laced with urgency. "We need to get you both to safety."

They nodded, still holding onto each other as if letting go would mean unraveling the threads of courage that had stitched them together. The officers guided the two of them through the chaos, down the stairs and out the back door, where the cool night air hit them like a balm.

Stretched out on the gurneys, Kendra and Jane shared a glance one last time. Their moment of survival was marked not just by relief but by an unspoken promise —no matter what lay ahead, they would face it together.

As the EMTs loaded them into the ambulances, sirens blaring, the world outside faded into a blur. The lights twinkled above, and for the first time that night, Kendra felt a flicker of hope igniting in her chest. They had fought through darkness and despair, and now they were stepping into a new light —one where they would emerge, not as victims, but as warriors, bound by their experience and ready to reclaim their lives.

In the back of the speeding ambulance, Kendra's heart raced, but it wasn't solely from the physical trauma she had endured. The truth of their shared ordeal weighed heavily on her mind, and she couldn't shake the unsettling thoughts that swirled within. They had faced the embodiment of their worst nightmares—Audrey, the Magnolia Killer, had been the architect of their suffering, and the betrayal cut deeper than any wound.

Kendra turned to Jane, the girl who had stood by her side through thick and thin. "What happened to her? How did she become this monster?" Kendra's voice trembled, tinged with confusion and disbelief.

Jane sighed, her expression reflecting the turmoil that lay beneath the surface. "I don't know. We thought we knew her. She was our friend, Kendra. We shared everything—our fears, our dreams. How could she do this to us?"

The ambulance jolted slightly as it turned a corner, the sound of sirens blaring outside a stark reminder of the chaos that had unfolded just moments before. Kendra clenched her fists, trying to ground herself. "We have to talk to our parents. I don't want to go through this alone."

Jane nodded, her own eyes glistening with unshed tears. "I feel the same way. We promised we could handle this, but I can't be strong all the time. I need my family too."

Kendra fished her phone from her pocket, her hands shaking as she dialed her mother's number. Each ring felt like an eternity, and when her mother finally answered, Kendra's heart leapt.

"Mom, it's me," Kendra said, her voice breaking as she spoke into the phone. "We were attacked. Audrey was the killer. I'm so scared. I want to come home, but I can't leave Jane alone. I need to be with you, but you're so far away."

Her mother's voice came through the line, steady and comforting. "Kendra, I'm here for you. I'm so glad you're safe. Are you hurt?"

Kendra glanced down at the blood-soaked fabric of her shirt, the reality of her situation crashing down like a wave. "Yes, I'm hurt.

Jane is too. We're on our way to the hospital now."

"Just focus on getting better. I'll be there as soon as I can," her mother promised, her voice laced with concern. "I'll call your father. You two need support."

Kendra's heart felt heavy with the enormity of what had transpired. "Mom, we killed Audrey. She's dead. She can't hurt anyone else ever again." The confession slipped from her lips like a confession of guilt, the weight of her actions settling heavily upon her.

Her mother's silence was palpable, a moment that stretched infinitely. "I'm just glad you're okay," she finally said, her voice trembling with emotion. "You and Jane are strong. You did what you had to do."

Kendra felt a mix of relief and sorrow wash over her as she listened to her mother's words. The truth hung in the air like a specter, a reminder of the violence they had been forced to commit in order to survive. "We're still processing everything, Mom. I—I just don't know how to feel."

As the ambulance sped through the streets, Kendra and Jane exchanged glances, both of them grappling with the reality of their situation. The sirens continued to wail, a haunting soundtrack that underscored the chaos of the night.

When they arrived at the hospital, the world outside felt surreal, the blinding lights and bustling figures a stark contrast to the dark terror they had just escaped. EMTs rushed to the back of the ambulance, their faces a blur of urgency and professionalism.

"Alright, ladies, let's get you stabilized," one of the paramedics said, gently guiding them onto stretchers. Kendra felt the cool metal beneath her as she was wheeled into the emergency room, the sterile scent of antiseptic filling her nostrils.

"Stay with me, Kendra," Jane whispered, her eyes wide with fear as they were separated by the rush of medical personnel. Kendra reached for her friend's hand, squeezing it tightly.

"I'm right here," Kendra reassured her, though her own heart raced with uncertainty. They would face this together, no matter what lay ahead.

As they were treated, Kendra's mind swirled with images of Audrey, the girl they had once trusted. How could someone they knew so well become a monster? The question haunted her as the doctors worked to patch her up, stitching the wound that had nearly cost her everything.

"Just a few more stitches," the doctor said, his voice steady and calm. "You're going to be okay." Kendra nodded, though she felt the gravity of the night pressing down on her.

Once Kendra was stabilized, she was wheeled into a waiting area. Jane arrived moments later, her own injuries tended to, but the look in her eyes revealed the emotional turmoil they both shared.

"We're alive," Jane said quietly, her voice trembling. "But at what cost?"

Kendra bit her lip, the weight of their actions heavy on her heart. "We did what we had to do, Jane. She would have killed us if we hadn't fought back."

Jane looked away, her eyes glistening with unshed tears. "I know, but it doesn't make it any easier. We lost our friend tonight. I can't help but wonder how things went so wrong."

The two girls sat in silence, the enormity of their ordeal settling like a heavy fog around them. They had faced unimaginable horror, and now the reality of what they had done loomed large.

Hours passed, and the hospital began to quiet down as night turned into dawn. Kendra's body ached, but the emotional toll felt heavier than the physical pain. She longed for the comfort of her mother, for the familiarity of home.

Finally, her mother arrived, rushing into the waiting area with tears in her eyes. Kendra felt an overwhelming rush of relief as she saw her mother, the warmth of home radiating from her presence.

"Oh, Kendra!" her mother exclaimed, pulling her into a tight embrace. "I was so worried! I can't believe this happened to you."

Kendra buried her face in her mother's shoulder, letting the tears flow freely. "I'm okay, Mom. I'm okay."

Jane's mother arrived shortly after, and the two girls shared a knowing glance. They had survived, but the scars of that night would linger long after the physical wounds healed.

As the sun began to rise, casting a golden light through the hospital windows, Kendra and Jane found solace in the presence of their families. They held onto each other, drawing strength from the love and support that surrounded them.

In the days that followed, Kendra and Jane began to piece their lives back together. The road to healing would not be easy, but they faced it with newfound strength and resilience. They had fought through darkness and despair, and now they were ready to step into the light, ready to reclaim their lives and their friendship.

The experience had changed them, forged a bond that could not be broken. They would carry the memories of that night with them, but they would not let it define them. Together, they would emerge stronger, ready to face whatever challenges lay ahead. And as they held onto each other, they knew that they would always have each other's backs—warriors united, bound by their shared experiences, ready to take on the world.

The days turned into weeks as Kendra and Jane navigated the aftermath of that harrowing night. The hospital stay had been a blur of medical evaluations, emotional conversations, and overwhelming support from family and friends. While they had survived the physical ordeal, the emotional scars from their encounter with

Audrey lingered, manifesting in ways they could have never anticipated.

Kendra found herself oscillating between moments of clarity and waves of dread. The nightmares arrived uninvited, haunting her with vivid images of the theater, the knife, and Audrey's piercing gaze. Each night, she would wake in a cold sweat, her heart racing as she fought to shake off the oppressive weight of fear. The familiar sounds of her childhood home, once a source of comfort, now felt like a fragile façade, masking the chaos that lay beneath.

Jane, too, struggled with the emotional fallout. Though they had vowed to face their fears together, she wrestled with feelings of guilt and confusion. The bond they had once shared, filled with laughter and secrets, felt strained under the enormity of their shared trauma. They both felt it, the invisible barrier that loomed between them, a chasm that was difficult to cross.

One afternoon, as golden sunlight streamed through Kendra's bedroom window, she sat on her bed, her hands clutching the stuffed bear Jane had given her years ago. It had always been a symbol of comfort, a reminder of their childhood innocence. But now, it felt heavy with the weight of their experiences.

Kendra glanced at her phone, her heart racing as she contemplated reaching out to Jane. They hadn't talked much since their release from the hospital, and the silence was deafening. She knew they needed to reconnect, to confront the emotions swirling between them, but the thought of articulating her feelings felt daunting.

Finally, Kendra took a deep breath and texted Jane: *"Can we talk? I think we need to."*

Moments later, her phone buzzed in response. *"Yeah, I'd like that. Can I come over?"*

Kendra's heart leapt. *"Of course! Please come."*

The anticipation of Jane's arrival filled Kendra with a mix of excitement and anxiety. She tidied her room, pushing aside remnants of their shared childhood—the posters on the walls, the photographs capturing happier times. The echoes of their laughter felt distant now, overshadowed by the memories of that fateful night.

When Jane arrived, she appeared hesitant, her eyes reflecting the struggle they both faced. Kendra's heart ached at the sight of her friend. Jane had always been the strong one, the rock who could face any challenge with unwavering resolve. But now, she seemed fragile, as if the weight of their shared experience was too much to bear alone.

"Hey," Kendra said softly, gesturing for Jane to sit on the bed beside her. "I'm glad you came."

"Me too," Jane replied, her voice barely above a whisper. She took a deep breath, her gaze drifting to the window, where the sun cast a warm glow over the room. "I've been thinking a lot about everything that happened."

"Me too," Kendra admitted, her heart racing as she prepared to bare her soul. "I feel like I'm stuck between two worlds—the past and the present. I want to move on, but the memories keep pulling me back."

Jane nodded, her expression somber. "I've been feeling the same way. It's like we're living in a nightmare that doesn't end. I keep replaying the moments, wondering if I could have done something differently."

Kendra reached out, placing a reassuring hand on Jane's arm. "You did everything you could. We both did. We fought for our lives, and we survived."

"But at what cost?" Jane's voice trembled as she turned to face Kendra, her eyes brimming with tears. "We lost Audrey. She was our friend, and now she's gone forever. I can't help but feel like we should have seen the signs, that we could have saved her somehow."

Kendra's heart ached at the pain radiating from Jane. "It's not our fault, Jane. Audrey made her choices. We didn't push her to become that person. She was the one who chose to hurt us. We had to protect ourselves."

"But she was sick, Kendra. She needed help, and we failed her," Jane whispered, tears spilling down her cheeks. "I can't shake the feeling that we should have done something more."

Kendra felt her own tears welling up as she struggled to find the right words. "Audrey's choices were hers alone. We can't carry that burden. We have to focus on healing and moving forward."

Jane wiped her eyes with the back of her hand, her expression softening as she looked at Kendra. "You're right. I guess I just didn't expect to feel so lost after everything. I thought we would be okay after it was over."

"We will be okay," Kendra reassured her, squeezing Jane's hand tightly. "But it's going to take time. We have to lean on each other, talk about what we're feeling. We can't let this tear us apart."

A small smile broke through Jane's tears. "You're right. I don't want to lose you, Kendra. You're my best friend."

"And you're mine," Kendra replied, relief flooding through her. They both understood that the road to recovery would be long and fraught with challenges, but they were determined to navigate it together. As they talked, the afternoon sun began to set, casting a warm golden light that filled the room. They shared stories, laughter, and tears, slowly unraveling the knots of pain that bound them. Each moment of vulnerability brought them closer, reinforcing the bond they had formed through years of friendship. In the days that followed, Kendra and Jane made a conscious effort to support each other. They began attending therapy sessions together, seeking professional help to process their trauma. The sessions were difficult, filled with raw emotions that often left them exhausted, but they knew it was a necessary step toward healing. They also reconnected with their families, leaning on their parents for support. Kendra's mother flew in from Las Vegas, wrapping her daughter in a tight embrace, providing the comfort and love that Kendra desperately needed. Jane's family also rallied around her, offering reassurance and understanding as they navigated the complexities of their shared trauma. One evening, as they sat together on Kendra's porch, watching the stars twinkle in the night sky, Jane turned to Kendra and said, "You know, I've been thinking about how we can honor Audrey's memory. She may have hurt us, but there was a time when she was our friend, and I don't want to forget that."

Kendra nodded thoughtfully, her heart swelling with emotion. "Maybe we can set up a scholarship in her name or do something to help others who are struggling. It could be a way to turn a tragedy into something positive."

Jane smiled, her eyes lighting up with the idea. "I love that. We could partner with a mental health organization, raise awareness about the importance of seeking help. We can help others who might be going through what Audrey faced."

The idea sparked a sense of purpose within them, a chance to transform their pain into something meaningful. They began brainstorming ways to raise funds and create a lasting impact, determined to honor the memory of their friend while also shedding light on the importance of mental health support. As they poured their energy into this new venture, Kendra felt a sense of hope blossoming within her. The journey to healing was still ongoing, but they were no longer trapped in the shadows of their past. They were stepping into the light, reclaiming their lives, and using their experiences to make a difference in the world. With each passing day, Kendra and Jane grew stronger, and their friendship deepened. They found solace in shared laughter, in the small moments of joy that broke through the heaviness of their memories. They were determined to face whatever challenges lay ahead, knowing they had each other to rely on. As they lay under the stars that night,

Kendra whispered, "We'll get through this, Jane. Together."

"Together," Jane echoed, her voice filled with resolve. And as they gazed up at the vast expanse of the night sky, they knew that although the journey ahead would be filled with hurdles, they had the strength to overcome anything—together, as warriors bound by their shared experiences, ready to embrace life once more. A wave of relief washed over Jane as she processed the shocking revelation: the Magnolia killer was dead. Life seemed on the verge of returning to normalcy. However, the unmasking of Audrey Gunner, the figure behind the gruesome murders of six individuals—nearly eight—had not brought the clarity she had hoped for. Instead, a multitude of questions lingered in the air, heavy and suffocating. If

Audrey was indeed the killer, then who had been responsible for the attacks and harassment that had plagued them? How could she have been right there beside them all along? The horrifying thought sent a chill racing down her spine. Was this what Audrey had been trying to convey before her demise? That there was someone else involved in this twisted game? The truth remained elusive, shrouded in shadows, waiting for a confrontation. Jane understood that they would ultimately have to face the accomplice in one final showdown, only then would the full story be unveiled. While the revelation of Audrey Gunner as the Magnolia killer had provided some closure for Jane and the others, it had simultaneously opened the floodgates to more questions than answers. As Jane mulled over the information, unease settled within her. She couldn't shake the gut feeling that there was still someone out there, orchestrating the chaos from behind the scenes. The unsettling notion that Audrey might have been manipulated or used as a pawn in a larger scheme gnawed at her thoughts. Could it be that Audrey's true motive was to expose the real mastermind behind the murders? The horrifying realization that another person could be lurking, waiting to strike again, haunted her mind. It was a grim possibility that twisted in her gut, growing more sinister with each passing day. Determined to unravel the mystery, the group understood they had to act quickly. They needed to confront the accomplice and uncover the truth before it was too late. With newfound resolve, Jane devised a plan to track down the elusive figure who had been pulling the strings from the shadows, her mind racing with strategies and scenarios. As they prepared for the impending confrontation, Jane felt a mix of fear and excitement swirling within her. The unknown was both petrifying and exhilarating, and she knew they had to face it head-on. The truth was out there, waiting to be uncovered, and Jane was resolute in her determination to reveal it, no matter the cost. With a steely resolve, Jane braced herself for the inevitable confrontation. The days of living in fear and uncertainty were finally coming to an end. As they ventured into the unknown, Jane felt a sense of urgency coursing through her veins. They were on the brink of discovering the full narrative behind the Magnolia killer and the puppeteer who had orchestrated the chaos all along. The truth was tantalizingly close, a flickering beacon in the dark, and Jane was ready to embrace it, no matter how dark or twisted it might be. The final showdown awaited them, and she steeled herself to face whatever horrors lay ahead. This was not just about bringing closure to the nightmare that had haunted them; it was about reclaiming their lives and taking back the power that had been stripped from them. Jane would not let fear dictate their future; instead, she would confront it fiercely, determined to shed light on every shadow that had threatened to consume them.

That October night was nothing short of horrifying, an experience forever etched in my memory. Jane and I had narrowly escaped the bloodshed unleashed by Audrey, the girl who had become known as the killer of magnolia. October had once been my favorite time of year, a season filled with excitement and Halloween festivities. But now, everything had irrevocably changed. The ominous events at the movie theater haunted my thoughts, especially the moment Audrey's true identity was revealed. The shock and horror that engulfed me extended beyond my own fear; my heart ached for Jane as well. The betrayal from someone we had trusted with our deepest secrets shattered the foundation of our sense of security. Audrey's revelation cast a long, dark shadow over what had traditionally been a month of spooky celebrations leading up to Halloween. The joy of horror films and festive decorations was now tainted by the grim knowledge of the real evil that had lurked among us. Even now, just the thought of watching a horror film triggers memories of Audrey's deception, along with the chilling realization that we had been forced to take her life in order to survive. Our beloved tradition of visiting Spirit Halloween had been forever marred by the memories of that night. The weight of having taken another life in self-defense hung heavily on my conscience. It was a decision made in sheer terror, yet one that left an indelible mark on my soul. The guilt, coupled with the relief of having survived such an ordeal, formed a complex and haunting emotion that I struggled to navigate. Audrey's rampage claimed the lives of our friends—

David, Mary, Sarah, Josh, and Danny. Their faces haunted my dreams, their voices echoing in my ears, pleading for justice and remembrance. I could not shake the feeling of dread that clung to me like a heavy cloak. But what troubled me most was Audrey's assertion that she had an accomplice. Could it possibly be true? Was there someone else out there, lurking in the shadows, waiting to strike again? The thought sent icy chills racing down my spine. Sleep eluded me. Every time I closed my eyes, I saw the mask staring back at me, taunting me with the memories of that horrific night. As days turned into weeks, my paranoia grew. I couldn't trust anyone; every face I encountered seemed to hide a secret, and every shadow held a potential threat. I was constantly looking over my shoulder, expecting danger to leap out at me at any moment. Yet, amidst this turmoil, I made a decision. The months following that fateful October night were filled with a tumult of emotions—fear, guilt, and an unyielding determination to reclaim my life. Jane and I had survived Audrey's onslaught, but the scars left behind were deep and lasting. Each day felt like a challenge in a world that now appeared darker and more dangerous than ever. As Halloween approached, I found myself dreading the very holiday that had once brought me so much joy. The decorations that had once sparked excitement now served only as reminders of the horror we had endured. I couldn't bear the thought of watching a horror movie or visiting a haunted house, knowing that the reality we faced was far more terrifying than any fictional tale. The memory of taking Audrey's life weighed heavily on my soul. The guilt of ending another person's life, even in self-defense, was a burden I struggled to carry. I often wondered if there had been another way, if we could have found a means to stop her without resorting to such desperate measures. Yet, in the end, survival had demanded extreme action, and I had to come to terms with the choice we made.

The knowledge that Audrey had taken the lives of our friends only deepened my sorrow and guilt. Their faces and voices haunted me, a constant reminder of the lives lost that night. I couldn't shake the feeling that we had failed them—that we had let them down by not being able to protect them from Audrey's wrath. But what consumed me the most was the fear of Audrey's accomplice. The thought that someone else was out there, working alongside her, waiting to strike again, kept me on constant edge. I couldn't trust anyone; I couldn't relax, always feeling that danger lurked around every corner. Despite the fear and grief that enveloped me, I resolved not to let it control my life. I refused to let Audrey's legacy of terror define who I was. I would be strong, brave, and vigilant, always prepared for whatever might come my way. If there was another killer out there, I would face them head-on. As Halloween drew near, I forced myself to confront my fears. I visited Spirit Halloween, walked past the horror movie posters at the theater, and faced the memories that had haunted me. It wasn't easy, but I knew that I had to confront the darkness in order to move past it. On Halloween night, I lit a candle in memory of our friends, praying for their souls to find peace. I vowed to honor their memory by living my life to the fullest, embracing the joy and spirit of the holiday they loved so dearly. As I looked out at the flickering jack-o'-lanterns and absorbed the laughter of children in costumes, a sense of peace began to wash over me. The darkness that had consumed me for so long started to lift, replaced by a glimmer of hope and resilience. October would never be the same for me again, but I made a choice to not let the past define my future. I would carry the memories of that terrifying night with me, but I would not be held captive by them. I would move forward, stronger and braver than ever, ready to face whatever challenges lay ahead. As the moon rose high in the sky on that Halloween night, I realized I was not alone. I had Jane by my side, and together, we would confront whatever darkness may come, armed with courage and determination in our hearts. I would not allow fear to dictate my life. I would remain vigilant, always watching, always ready for whatever lay ahead. If another killer lurked in the shadows, I would face them head-on. October may never be the same for me again, but I refuse to let the darkness consume me. I will not allow Audrey's legacy of terror to define who I am. I will be strong, I will be brave, and I will survive. Because in the end, it is not the monsters we fear that define us, but how we choose to confront them. And I choose to face them with unwavering courage and determination. Whatever comes my way, I will be ready.

Milton Keynes UK
Ingram Content Group UK Ltd.
UKHW021934281024
450365UK00017B/1080